T0246191

Advance Praise for *Montauk to Manhattan*

"This wholly American novel follows Jack Denton, a reporter turned novelist who is simultaneously covering the Trump campaign while serving as a consultant for a TV show adaptation of his book. Denton contends with the denizens of Hollywood and the campaign trail, even as his own personal life seems to unravel in front of him. Maier's novel is one in a tidal wave of books about Trump's America and the #MeToo movement. What he adds to the discourse is to draw some intriguing historical parallels between Trump and nineteenth-century railway tycoon Austin Corbin. Maier's superimposition of a nineteenth-century plot on a modern-day one gives life to the standard 'Hollywood-is-cutthroat' tale."

—The BookLife Prize, sponsored
by *Publishers Weekly*

AN AMERICAN NOVEL

THOMAS MAIER

A POST HILL PRESS BOOK
ISBN: 979-8-88845-364-3
ISBN (eBook): 979-8-88845-365-0

Montauk to Manhattan:
An American Novel

Cover design by Cody Corcoran

Post Hill Press
New York • Nashville
posthillpress.com

Published in the United States of America
1 2 3 4 5 6 7 8 9 10

Also by Thomas Maier

Mafia Spies: The Inside Story of the CIA, Gangsters, JFK, and Castro (now a Paramount+ six-part docuseries)

Masters of Sex: The Life and Times of William Masters and Virginia Johnson, the Couple Who Taught America How to Love (adapted into an Emmy-winning Showtime drama series)

Dr. Spock: An American Life

When Lions Roar: The Churchills and the Kennedys

The Kennedys: America's Emerald Kings

The Kennedy Years: From the Pages of The New York Times (opening essay)

Newhouse: All the Glitter, Power, and Glory of America's Richest Media Empire and the Secretive Man Behind It

All That Glitters: Anna Wintour, Tina Brown, and the Rivalry Inside America's Richest Media Empire (2019 revised update to 1994's *Newhouse*)

To my wife Joyce, for all her love and wisdom.
And to my sister and her husband, Diane and Kenny Sadenwater, for all their support and for letting us stay at their place in Montauk.

"The tossing waves, the foam, the ships in distance,
The wild unrest, the snowy, curling caps—
that inbound urge and urge of waves,
Seeking the shores forever."
—Walt Whitman, "From Montauk Point" (*Leaves of Grass,* 1891–92)

"When you're a star, they let you do it. You can do anything."
—Donald Trump, heard on a secret video-
tape conversation made public in 2016

"He talked about virtue and vice as a man who is
colour-blind talks about red and green."
—Henry Adams, *Democracy: An American Novel,* 1880

CONTENTS

INTRODUCTION

"Montauk to Manhattan," as they say in Hollywood, is "inspired by" real-life headlines, though it is entirely fictional. This murder mystery in the Hamptons examines many aspects of American life, including greed, fame, race, sex, #MeToo Hollywood, the rise of Trumpism, as well as the legacy of one of the most outrageous Native American scandals in US history. The protagonist, Jack Denton, is a reporter for a New York newspaper who authors a historical novel called *The Life Line*—about the stealing of Montauk Indian lands in the 1880s by a railroad tycoon named Austin Corbin. Denton's vain attempt at the Great American Novel is given new life when it is adapted into a big-time television drama by a well-known streaming service and its controversial showrunner.

Back and forth, Denton travels between his Manhattan newsroom, covering the 2016 Trump campaign, and the on-location television set in Montauk, where *The Life Line* is being filmed and a young female "bit player" goes missing. With his personal life falling apart, Denton hopes this book-to-TV transformation might lead to some kind of redemption. Instead, he becomes a suspect in a murder.

My own interest in the Montauketts and Corbin stems from an investigative chapter that I wrote for a 1998 Newsday book about Long Island's history. It detailed the rapacious taking of tribal lands and was later cited in legal papers filed with the US Supreme Court. In a terrible miscarriage of justice, the Montauk Indian tribe was declared extinct in 1910 and has been fighting for recognition ever since. My experience with Hollywood comes mainly from the Emmy-winning television show *Masters of Sex,* based on my biography of researchers Masters and Johnson, which gave me some sense of what it's like to be on a production set. Ultimately, through the eponymous voice of reporter Denton, I combined both experiences to form *Montauk to Manhattan*—a veritable "play within a play," which uses historical fiction, both from the past and today, to look at America and ask where we are headed in the future.

—Thomas Maier, Long Island, New York, 2024

CHAPTER 1
THE VOICE OF GOD

"The SS *Louisiana* moved across the Atlantic, a mere speck on the ocean horizon, lost in the gaping greenish maw of cresting waves. Onboard the battered ship were more than a hundred passengers, including the American tycoon Austin Corbin, returning home from London.

"As the schooner neared the Long Island coast, it became stuck in a sandbar. Suddenly all aboard found themselves in mortal danger."

—*The Life Line* by Jack Denton

The first time I heard the booming voice of Max Kirkland, the Hollywood legend, I felt transfixed by his deep baritone growling into my iPhone. Nearly every rapid-fire sentence was punctuated with profanity and showbiz grandiosity. In no time, he presented an elaborate scheme to transform my small historical novel, *The Life Line,* into a big-time television drama.

Writers have been warned about the tempting lure of such pitches for more than a century, ever since novelist F. Scott Fitzgerald of *Great Gatsby* fame was enticed to move to Tinseltown, hoping in vain to transform his literary words into gold. Kirkland must have sensed my trepidation. With a sweeping theatrical tone, as if on stage in a soliloquy, he promised to make my literary dreams come true. By the time he hung up, I had agreed to sell the rights to my book without much fuss.

Now, many months later, with our contract signed and sealed, I was getting the chance to see Kirkland personally in his natural habitat—an on-location production set along the beach in Montauk. I was instructed to sit quietly behind him and watch the master at work.

Kirkland stared out at the Atlantic Ocean from his director's chair, a long-legged wooden throne in the sand. He sat perched on his seat like one of those red-tailed hawks hovering along the beach, eyeing its prey menacingly.

"How much longer are we going to have to wait, people?" he bellowed, loud enough to sound like the voice of God.

"Max," as Maximilian Betancourt Kirkland was called by friend and foe alike, was indeed almighty on the set. He was a powerful combo plate of producer, writer, and director, known in television terms as a "showrunner." Max ordered his assembled crew around the drifting sands, like an emperor crossing the desert, while they prepared the opening scene of his new creation.

Kirkland grabbed a megaphone so he could be heard above the waves. He barked out last-minute instructions to the frantic camera people, struggling to find the right angles on the rocky shoreline before shooting commenced.

The highly paid Hollywood stars, surrounded by scores of fifteen-dollar-an-hour extras, waited patiently aboard an exact replica of the sunken SS *Louisiana*, a ship carefully restored and temporarily anchored on the waterfront.

"Can't someone steady that shot?" Kirkland yelled again, upset by the jumpy images flickering on his sleek black video monitors. In disgust, he flung a copy of the script, aware that delays cost him money.

Many setbacks already beleaguered Kirkland's production. The previous week, a sperm whale's carcass washed up on shore within sight of where Max wanted to shoot. Instead of being harpooned, as in the fictional epic *Moby Dick,* this dead leviathan had been killed by a mammoth metal cargo ship cruising toward the port of New York.

Before clearing the beachfront, Kirkland was annoyed that he had to hire oceanographic experts to examine the whale's crushed head and torn gray skin. They concluded for insurance purposes that his production was not at fault. Then, to avoid environmental complaints, he paid even more to a hauling firm to take away its rotting remains.

On this day, Kirkland's petulant performance made him appear like some man-child in an outsized highchair. Only after several minutes—when he sat back in his director's seat and surrendered his electronic bullhorn to an assistant—did Kirkland seem resigned to the slow pace of the day's shoot. Eventually, an idea brightened his mood.

From a side pocket in his chair, Kirkland pulled out a worn copy of my novel, the inspiration for this production of the same name. With a flourish, he decided to read the book's opening passage to the entourage around him. Most of us sat in wooden directors' chairs like his own.

Kirkland wore his open-collared white shirts low enough to show off his hairy chest. His lively green eyes and exaggerated movements dazzled all in his thrall. Dramatically, he intoned the book's opening lines—especially "found themselves *in mortal danger*"—to emphasize the importance of the day's scene.

Ever the impresario, Kirkland made it clear that this production—a limited series by this famed, Oscar-winning movie producer, his first for Comflix, a deep-pocketed television streamer—would be as faithful to my novel as his purported $100 million budget would allow.

"What do you think, Jack? Doesn't this shipwreck scene look just as it's described in your book?" Kirkland asked. "After all, we wouldn't want to disappoint the famous writer Jack Denton, would we?"

The encampment of production assistants and other hangers-on—ensconced in the dunes behind Kirkland and the video monitors—tittered at his joke.

"It's great, Max, just great," I enthused, ignoring Kirkland's disingenuous tease. Getting off to a good start was most important to me, aware that the fate of my book was now in his hands. I knew the "famous writer" crack was a gross exaggeration at my expense. "Lucky" was more like it.

With any good fortune, my rather high-minded but poor-selling novel would now be turned into a resounding success. Originally published by an academic press, the book received virtually no attention and anemic sales. Amazon listed *The Life Line* no higher than #230,000 in "Nautical Historical Fiction." Out of desperation, I sent complimentary copies over the transom to various studios and well-known producers. Most sent back my pitch package without opening it.

Somehow, almost magically, the book came to Max's attention, and he scooped it up. News about the next Kirkland production catapulted my book onto the "TV tie-in" bestseller list. However, the cost of doing business with him, like most Faustian bargains, emerged over time.

Already, I'd learned not to contradict Max, even about my own book. As my entertainment attorney advised, only an idiot author criticizes a producer willing to pay ten times the original literary advance for the movie and television rights.

Once I'd dreamed of writing the Great American Novel, the elusive goal of so many authors who came of age in the twentieth century, a time when the public still devoured printed works. With any luck in the twenty-first century, my literary creation—which the studio lawyers called "IP" for "intellectual property"—would become Great American Binge TV, a "special television event" entertaining a new generation of cord-cutters.

The chosen alchemist for this transformation was Kirkland, a crude but critically acclaimed filmmaker now turned mega-showrunner responsible for everything in this production. He'd prove to be more of an enigma than I ever imagined—a man very much his own creation, Hollywood-style.

Piecing together Kirkland's background was hard to do. I found few clues about his views or what he was like personally. His official company bio said he had travelled decades ago to Los Angeles from the Midwest, portraying him heroically as a striver from humble beginnings who arrived without a plan. A few old news clippings said Max initially sold posters and artwork along Venice Beach. He struggled as a stand-up comedian before landing a job in a studio mailroom. He quickly learned La-La Land's lingo and talked himself into a couple of important jobs. The news clips didn't reveal much about him, only about the profits that he made.

Over the years, *Variety* and other trade publications celebrated Kirkland's motion pictures. They called them tentpole moneymakers—action-packed thrillers based on comics—that kept a studio's finances afloat. Kirkland became the darling of Hollywood studios and their Wall Street investors. Eventually, he created his own boutique production company, combining Academy Award prestige with box-office popularity. Everyone wondered, including Max, if doing television now was a step down or the crowning achievement in his career.

On that warm, late spring day along the beach, Max wore gold-rimmed aviator shades, a silver-flecked Armani jacket (size extra-large) accented by a dark scarf around his neck, and leather boots with rubber soles to navigate the sand.

"If I could, I'd dress like Lawrence of Arabia," he wisecracked when asked about his appearance on the beach.

At age fifty-seven, Max still projected himself as healthy and robust. He was living proof that men could be as vain as women, probably more so. His broad chest and arms were the byproduct of his personal trainer Gunnar—and perhaps a few testosterone supplements, too. His taut, tanned face and his plugged black scalp, weaved together like a bird's nest, suggested implants and various touch-ups along the way. Upon closer inspection, the bloodshot veins in his eyes hinted at more going on than early morning workouts in the gym.

Max liked to flatter himself into thinking he still appealed to beautiful women other than his wife. On the set, there was little reference to Max's marriage to a well-known former model who hosted her own popular reality show, *Fashions with Tatiana Kirkland*. Instead, Max tried to ingratiate himself with virtually every young actress on the set, whether invited or not, sometimes with apparent success.

"Come here, my darling, let me look at you," he commanded as Kiara Manchester, the production's female lead, walked by briskly to avoid his gaze. The acclaimed actress was headed to her position on the shipwreck, as the script called for, but she first stopped patiently for Max to gaze and take in her beauty.

In *The Life Line,* Manchester played Elizabeth Gardiner, wife of the 1880s East Hampton Town Attorney Edmund Gardiner. More significantly, she was the secret lover of railroad tycoon Austin Corbin and had travelled with him to London. On the set, the costume designer made sure Manchester's cotton chemise was faithful enough to the book's nineteenth-century character but thin enough to please Max and his sense of what today's American audience desired.

"Isn't she marvelous in this outfit, everyone?" Kirkland inquired about Manchester to the production crew, now complicit in his lust. The female assistant director looked away as if she didn't hear anything.

For many years, before the #MeToo Movement, such sexually charged comments in the entertainment industry were kept secret from the public. Men like Kirkland felt free to say and do what they wanted without consequence. Max had no idea he was standing on the precipice of change.

"When you're the showrunner, you're the king," he later explained. "You have to bend people to your will to get things done."

Manchester tried to hide her uneasiness. As a young British actress with expressive eyes, silky hair, and a proper posh accent, she possessed all the tools of a gifted performer headed for stardom. She recently appeared as Ophelia in *Hamlet* at the Young Vic and was a much-touted graduate of the Royal Academy of Dramatic Art in London. Manchester had heard tales of Kirkland's lasciviousness, including from her parents, both supporting actors from various television dramas in the 1990s. She assured them she could handle anything.

Nevertheless, Manchester seemed surprised when Max gave her a kiss—not a peck on the cheek or a glancing smooch that misses; it was an insistent smack on the lips that appeared awkward to everyone but Max. He acted as if it was another perk of being in charge.

"Americans will love you when they see you in their living rooms or bedrooms—wherever they watch TV—I'm certain of it," Kirkland declared.

Manchester wasn't amused. She allowed a polite smile before quickly leaving the director's circle and getting on with her assignment. Other lesser-known actresses in the show learned to laugh nervously among themselves about Max's toothy, unpleasant kisses, as if they were werewolf's marks, and his lingering hugs that lasted too long.

There was more to these forced encounters with the famous director than I knew, certainly more victimization than I realized at that time. The sheer magnitude of this production, however, diverted my attention. Without much thought, I watched Manchester climb into a helicopter and be whisked a few hundred yards away to the floating shipwreck scene in the ocean.

When he wasn't shouting or leering on the set, Kirkland was a nonstop talker, "a *kibitzer*," as he called himself, a key ingredient to his industry success. Max acted as if everyone was his friend, an overture that I initially accepted without question.

During one lengthy delay in filming the first scene, Kirkland motioned me aside. Once more, he reiterated his reasons for taking on this showcase project.

"It's a shame what the white man did to the Indians... er, you know, the *Native Americans*... we stole their lands, raped their women," he began as earnestly as possible. He used the same politically correct language the studio's press office advised for his interview with *The Hollywood Reporter*, when the production was "greenlit" months earlier.

"The studio wanted me to do another superhero franchise. Told them no. I wanted *this* story—to show what this country did to the Native Americans," he explained. "The time is right for a classic story of what really happened. Think of all those cowboy-and-Indian films on the TV when we were growing up as kids. What crazy shit was that, huh?"

I nodded solemnly. During our telephone negotiations for the rights, Max used the same pitch. Over time, if he kept talking, Kirkland had a way of blurting out his real feelings, a bit raw and unguarded. As his aides wandered away, Kirkland's voice lowered, so that only I could hear his confession.

"Of course, look at these Indians today—each tribe like their own separate nation. Casinos. Tax-free cigarettes. That freaking giant billboard on

Montauk Highway with the flashing lights—I could see it from my helicopter flying in from the city!"

We both laughed at his litany of grievances. At moments like this, Kirkland seemed more like a funny uncle or the savant of a barbershop than the cinematic auteur who had won the Palme d'Or at Cannes. Eventually Kirkland simmered, an old Hollywood liberal afraid of sounding like a closet reactionary. He gazed at my expressionless face, wondering what I might be thinking.

"But let's face it, Jack," he continued. "There's no doubt that the Montauk Indians had their lands stolen by this guy Austin Corbin—a goddamned thief if there ever was one. I guess every age has its hustlers. He sort of reminds you of Trump, doesn't he?"

I resisted the urge to comment. Kirkland knew that I was now covering Trump's 2016 campaign for *The New York World*, which hired me after the success of my novel and years of reporting for a local publication. The studio's contract called for me to be a consulting producer/writer, but I still drew a steady paycheck from my newspaper that paid my mounting bills at home.

Politics was my beat. I was part of *The New York World's* team coverage when Donald Trump, the former casino owner, came down his skyscraper escalator to announce his presidential candidacy. No one took him seriously. Trump's demagogic skills were on full display that day. His vulgar incitements should have been taken as a warning rather than a publicity stunt. The news desk instructed me to get reactions from New York Republicans, a vanishing breed of Nelson Rockefeller leftovers, William Buckley acolytes, and moderates derided as RINOs (Republicans In Name Only). Neither they nor I realized how consequential Trump's announcement would be.

A few moments later, Max quizzed me about Trump. Though younger reporters freely expressed themselves on Twitter, just like Trump himself, I felt an old-fashioned journalistic commandment not to voice my opinions. Certainly not reveal anything to a big mouth like Kirkland, no matter how much he was paying me.

A decade earlier, Kirkland and his wife Tatiana had attended Trump's Mar-a-Lago wedding, sitting with well-known British fashion editor Diana Trumbull and the Clintons. The former First Couple clearly had no idea back then that Trump might become a fearsome warrior in their chosen arena of presidential politics. Diana, as the Kirklands called her, was known for her pageboy hairdo, her skeletal figure, and her outsized power as the last word in the world's multibillion-dollar fashion industry. Her much-older husband was a legendary book editor with an eye for the young women in his employ. They all travelled to Trump's Florida Shangri-La as guests of The Donald.

Now, Max was beginning to sense that being friends with Trump might be out of favor with the smart set on both coasts. Kirkland wanted to test that theory on me. When I didn't take his bait, he acted dismissive.

"OK, Jack, so you're not going to tell me what you really think, like a good little reporter for the great national paper," Kirkland condemned in a jocular tone. "But tell me something—do you think Trump can win?"

Kirkland stared impatiently until I finally nodded my head.

"Yes," I admitted. "It's doubtful, but he may have more of a chance than we realize."

Max smiled, as if given a tip about a racehorse, and then shared a hoary truism he learned long ago about America:

"Sometimes you don't have to be good," he said. "Just lucky."

CHAPTER 2
TYCOONS

While waiting for the day's filming to begin, I thought of how fate had brought me to that remarkable place on the beach, like some aimless Odysseus washed up on shore. I considered myself particularly fortunate given the almost miraculous origins of my novel.

Years earlier, while struggling as a local newspaper reporter, I stumbled across the historical story of Austin Corbin, the nineteenth-century entrepreneur who would become the fictional protagonist of *The Life Line.*

Bold and ambitious, Corbin was the toast of 1880s' New York. He projected the same drive and industriousness that inspired Americans to pick up Horatio Alger's "rags-to-riches" novels. One pundit described the bald, long-bearded, and full-bellied tycoon as "part hog, part shark." But Corbin's big dreams and self-aggrandizement caught the public's fancy.

After attending Harvard Law School, Corbin became a banker, Wall Street speculator, mortgage-lending swindler, plantation owner, resort developer, and, eventually, a railroad man. His ruthless go-getter voraciousness was compared to fellow American tycoons Cornelius Vanderbilt and Jay Gould. He partnered with financier J. Pierpont Morgan in various shady enterprises. Corbin belonged to "that tribe of human monsters who prey upon poor men," observed one magazine, "who, being influenced by greed, make war upon the weak, regardless of right."

Unlike some millionaires who hide their wealth, Corbin was happy to showcase his massive mansion. He luxuriated in a gaudy lifestyle celebrated by the press. His fame grew widely, enough for him to be considered one of the leading citizens of his day. In 1882, President Chester A. Arthur paid homage to him by travelling aboard one of Corbin's Long Island Railroad express trains to visit his private summer estate. "President Arthur's Excursion: Speeding Over Long Island at the Rate of About a Mile a Minute" declared a *Brooklyn Eagle* newspaper headline touting this escapade.

Though a money man with vast interests around the country, Corbin was best known in New York for turning acres of abandoned sand dunes along Coney Island into a popular ocean resort. His stylish seaside hotels, including one called The Oriental with grand spires reaching towards the sky, catered to wealthy white Anglo-Saxon Protestants like himself. He expressly forbade so-called "undesirables" from his door, especially Blacks, Jews, and Catholic immigrants with foreign accents.

Nevertheless, thousands of other New Yorkers came to Corbin's summertime enclave. They enjoyed sunning themselves along the ocean beach, Jockey Club horse racing, and nightly fireworks concerts at an outdoor ten-thousand-seat amphitheater surrounding a man-made lagoon. Composer John Philip Sousa and his band played "Stars and Stripes Forever." Elaborate shows reenacted historical events, like Civil War naval battles, and well-known natural disasters like "The Last Days of Pompeii"—enthralling audiences with the kind of grand showmanship that movies would later provide. For five dollars, thrill seekers could go up in a hot-air balloon, as high as a quarter mile into the atmosphere. They'd be pulled back to earth with a cable after getting a bird's eye view of all Corbin had created.

Like Buffalo Bill and Houdini, Corbin realized that Americans, along with all the other necessary staples of life, needed entertainment. They wanted escape and amusement—what became the essence of Coney Island. With his high-society resort, he carved a dreamland out of the city's desert.

"To him New York owes almost all that is good at Coney Island," the *New York Times* later eulogized in his front-page 1896 obituary. Admirers like the *Times* editors took note of Corbin's Yankee ancestry and applauded the kind of entitlement behind his takeover of tribal lands during his career. "Long Island at that time was an almost unknown territory to any others than natives," said the paper of record. Corbin was the first—but certainly not the last—fast-talking New York tycoon to seek his fortune by promoting himself shamelessly in the city's newspapers.

My novel *The Life Line* revolved around Corbin's biggest boondoggle. At his zenith, he envisioned a way to make millions by short-cutting the week-long trip for steamships, square rigs, and schooners between New York City and Europe. Instead of navigating the sometimes-treacherous Long Island coastline of 120 miles, these ships could land in Montauk and travel rapidly into Manhattan aboard Corbin's private express trains. He claimed his plan would eliminate a day of travel from the Atlantic journey for international passengers and hopefully turn Montauk into another resort haven, the Miami Beach of the north.

Corbin wanted to dynamite the northern bulkhead of Montauk to create a deepwater port where the ships would land. That project alone would be a remarkable engineering feat, proof of his determination to move heaven and earth. But to connect both ends of Long Island with his railroad, Corbin would need the land rights of the remaining Montaukett Indian nation living there peacefully, a proud but diminished people in the Hamptons.

Corbin's greediness and ambition reflected all the avarice of America's Gilded Age. Up from their bootstraps, indefatigable men like Corbin seemed born to greatness. "I don't care to retire—this is my pleasure," he explained to reporters. "I like to see the machine run, to help it run, and to feel that I am steering it." As I learned from research for my novel, Corbin accomplished this shameless land grab of Native American reservations through chicanery and threats of violence. He smoothed over public opinion with full-page ads in all of New York City's newspapers and billboards, touting his multimillion dollar "Montauk to Manhattan" campaign.

More than a century later, the outrage and opulence of Corbin's story still resonated with Kirkland. By championing the Montaukett cause, he wanted to be "on the side of the angels," Max told interviewers, and he appeared convincingly sincere. He took all the proper steps, lest he be accused of "cultural appropriation"—a phrase explained to him by the studio's lawyers. After buying the rights to *The Life Line,* Max hired an elderly Montauk chief, steeped in tribal lore, as a consultant. He also vowed to film some TV scenes on what remained of an ancient Native American reservation, tucked away on Long Island's otherwise-trendy Hamptons terrain.

"This is all stolen land, Jack, and that's important to understanding our history," Max said, stating the obvious to me, as he looked up and down the beach where his cameras were now in place. "It was a brutal genocide—a war of extermination—with thousands of people erased from the map. If we are successful, this production will be the great retelling of the Native American experience. How white men like Austin Corbin ran off with the best part of America and turned the Indians into invisible people in their homeland!"

With his gravelly voice in full roar, Kirkland outlined his plans for transformational glory with our project. "Over-the-top streamers, binge-watching—they are now for us what movies were for our parents. They define our era. I want people watching at home to think about what we did to the Montauk Indians. Maybe get off of the fucking couch and march up and down the street in protest. With all this money Comflix has given us, I want to be like D. W. Griffith—only in reverse—and turn *The Birth of a Nation* on its head!"

Kirkland's eyes were aglow, with the fury of a true firebrand. How much of Max's soliloquy he truly believed was hard to figure out. He was famous for bombast about his productions, part of the marketing campaign he knew was needed in this content-rich universe of on-demand platforms and a clueless citizenry left to its own devices.

Nevertheless, Max was correct about at least one thing: the success of *The Life Line* depended all on him.

CHAPTER 3
THE SHIPWRECK SCENE

Shooting a Hollywood production, particularly at a remote location along the Atlantic Ocean, was fascinating to my untrained eyes. During the interminable wait that morning, I pulled out my iPhone to take a few photos, planning to show them later to friends. Maybe even post a few snapshots on social media to help promote the book's lagging sales.

"Excuse me, are you taking my picture?"

Max Kirkland's associate executive producer, Penelope "Penny" MacPharland, an intense, wiry woman seated in another director's chair, got up and stood facing me, as if to block the field of vision of the iPhone's lens.

"I can't have you taking my photograph," MacPharland insisted. "Are you going to post my photo online?" She didn't wait for my answer. "I once got in trouble because someone saw my photo on Facebook when I was supposed to be somewhere else. Please assure me that you weren't taking my photo. *Please don't.…*"

MacPharland's request seemed to carry an unspoken threat. I quickly put away the iPhone. MacPharland could be mercurial, at least by reputation. Any scuffle with MacPharland would be undoubtedly a losing proposition. I looked to Kirkland for relief, but he was busy speaking with others.

"Penny, don't worry—I would never take your photograph," I said in a lowered voice, the kind of soothing tone a therapist might use. Or a police psychiatrist might employ in talking a deranged sniper off a rooftop. I made sure no one else heard this bizarre exchange.

For a moment, Penny kept staring at me intently, as if she could see through me, to determine if my pledge was a lie. She walked back to her director's chair, visibly perturbed. She kept eyeing me suspiciously but said nothing more. I assumed she wouldn't give me any more trouble.

When Kirkland turned his head, I sprung up and left my chair, the one marked "Consulting Producer" on the back. I headed for a coffee at the small craft services pavilion, an impromptu cafeteria run by workers known as "crafties" on the beach parking lot.

The studio's money was evident all around. The encampment on this Hamptons beach, if not as sprawling as Normandy's D-Day invasion, certainly appeared as if the circus had come to town. In a large enclosure, the craft services food servers fed dozens throughout the day, a hungry army enlisted to the cause. Seated at these dining tables were countless key grips, prop makers, on-set dressers, painters, carpenters, stunt doubles, camerapeople, stand-ins, and extras without speaking parts.

Elsewhere along the beach parking lot, mammoth moving vans, stuffed with wires and equipment, had technicians jumping in and out of them. Dressing rooms and makeup rooms, illuminated with bright lights and mirrors, were housed in air-conditioned tents.

Discreetly to the side, security guards stood watch on two large motorhomes that seemed permanently affixed to the asphalt. Penny explained these "humongous" Winnebagos were fringe benefits mandated in the contracts of two top stars, Manchester and the Shakespearean actor Lester Wolf, who played the imposing character Austin Corbin (chosen because of his popularity as Commander Smith in a blockbuster space-fantasy movie).

As I stirred my coffee at the craft services pavilion, one of the production's lesser-known actors, a red-headed woman also in costume, approached me.

"You're the author, Jack Denton, right?" asked Vanessa Adams, as I later learned her name. "I saw you talking to Max and figured it was you. I loved your book. Especially the part I'm playing."

What an amusing lie. It was clear she hadn't read a word. Her part wasn't in my novel and had been created by Kirkland only for this pilot script. But Vanessa did exude a certain forward charm. She said everyone mistook her for a well-known star who won the Oscar for a recent musical about Los Angeles. Undeterred, she quickly got to the point of her mission.

"So, what happens to my character down the road?" she asked with the speed of a pickpocket.

Vanessa's brashness was refreshing. It reminded me of another actor who asked this same question after an early table reading when the cast rehearsed the script. He, too, wanted to know his fate.

"You're killed in an early episode," I replied to him, effectively saying he'd been written out of the show. A silent shock registered on his face until he realized I was kidding. With this eager young woman, however, I didn't have the heart to try the same joke.

"I'm helping Max with the scripts," I explained to Vanessa, "but he decides on everything—including what happens to you."

Suddenly, Kirkland himself appeared at the food pavilion. He was obviously perturbed by this young actress being out of place. MacPharland, standing by Kirkland's side, mirrored her boss's indignation.

"Shouldn't you be out on the set getting into position, Vanessa?" Max said firmly, holding back his anger.

There was a sense of possessiveness about Kirkland as he grasped this bit player's arm and steered her away from me. I was surprised he knew her name. Max looked at me with a scowl—like a jealous lover or perhaps simply a shepherd who had lost a sheep. Then he walked back to his director's chair. I followed along with my cup of coffee.

After a litany of delays, the shipwreck scene finally began around noontime. Like some cinematic maestro, Max Kirkland had orchestrated an elaborate make-believe disaster. He wanted this grand ruse to appear as close to reality as possible on screen.

First, like some divine force, Max altered the weather. Though this day was mild and overcast, Kirkland arranged for a giant set of motorized fans to simulate the gale-force winds of an actual storm. Gusts of saltwater sprayed everyone's skin and clothes.

Next, he arranged the phony shipwreck itself. Out of view of the cameras, a team of former Navy SEALs in the ocean—hired mostly for insurance reasons—released the anchor of the SS *Louisiana*. They let the ship drift forward slightly, until it became stuck on a fabricated sandbar, an underwater monstrosity made with dirt bags by the prop department. Once trapped on this underwater ridge, the SS *Louisiana* couldn't move. Everyone aboard was presumed a goner. Crushed by the swirling high waves, the vessel sank slowly into the ocean deep.

Screams from this ghost ship could be heard ashore. Cinematic close-ups on deck of actors Lester Wolf and Kiara Manchester captured this sense of panic. Television monitors next to Kirkland picked up heartfelt cries from the cast, enough to suspend disbelief by even the most hardened theatergoer.

On the beach, the middle-aged actress, Helen Thorpe, who played Corbin's long-suffering wife Margaret, jumped up and down in panic. According to the script, her character knew that her husband was due to land in New York that day. She sensed he might be on that ailing ship. She screamed for the team of lifesavers to rescue him.

Surrounding Corbin's wife were a scattering of other townspeople, all portrayed by extras and uncredited actors in nineteenth-century costumes, including Vanessa. She curled her red hair up in an elaborate bun bound to be noticed. A dozen more actors, playing rescuers from the Hamptons Life-Saving Station, rushed to the scene.

"Hurry, please *hurry*, the ship is about to break apart!" Corbin's wife moaned, just as the script demanded.

In this sequence, with plenty of action and little dialogue, the life-saving volunteers immediately embarked on their tasks. Husky men waded midway into the water with floating devices, but the shipwreck was too far away to reach it. Others jumped into rowboats meant to carry a few passengers. They hurdled over the waves towards the ship.

An elemental struggle raged between these men and nature. But the most difficult part of this life-saving ritual by the team involved a black

cast-iron carronade, which they readied to fire into the air. In the 1800s, the purpose of this short cannon was to shoot a rope-like projectile far enough across the shipwreck's bow so it could be tied to the ship's tall mast. The rope line, connected to the shore, created a last-ditch method of escape for the passengers who otherwise faced certain drowning in the wild surf.

Throughout the nineteenth century, many were killed when their ship ran aground on the last leg of their journey from the Old World to the new. During one winter's snowstorm, the crew of a schooner stuck in a sandbar tied themselves to the rigging to avoid being washed overboard—only to freeze to death before they could be saved. On her way home from Europe in 1850, author Margaret Fuller, perhaps the best-known American woman of her era, drowned in a shipwreck less than a hundred yards from the Long Island shore. Eventually, the lost lives at sea prompted enough public outcry that the government created a string of "Life-Saving Stations" along the coast.

By the 1880s, these life-saving crew members, wrapped in cork vests, were a godsend to otherwise-doomed mariners. Everything about them and their rescue procedure appeared courageous. Once fired from the cannon, a set of ropes was tautly stretched across the murky abyss—literally a "life line" between the shore and shipwreck. Large pulleys with a leg harness, known as a "breeches buoy," carried passengers to safety. Women were usually escorted along these ropes by limber young men called Lifesavers, who put themselves willingly at risk to rescue others.

On the set, in his tall director's chair, Max reacted with excitement as the makeshift cannon, known as a Lyle Gun, fired away. Its concussive blast was felt by everyone.

"Did you all see that explosion?" Kirkland erupted with glee to his inner circle. "Isn't that fantastic?!"

Max loved cinematic grandeur. Like some modern-day Francis Scott Key, he rhapsodized about the bursting red glare and the rope streaming in midair. His computer-generated shipwreck plans had been well-rehearsed with the studio's technicians and pyrotechnic experts. The Lyle Gun performed brilliantly, he told me.

"Just don't ask how much these fireworks cost," he exulted, with the confident glow of a man in the winner's circle. "Thank God, they worked."

This opening television scene was reminiscent of the memorable 1884 oil painting by Winslow Homer called "The Life Line," which portrayed an unconscious woman hanging over the waves and clutched in the arms of her rescuer. Homer's masterpiece graced the cover of my book. It also emboldened Kirkland to recreate a similar opening scene of awful peril and subtle eroticism for his new television project.

With the film crew capturing each movement, the actors' dialogue could be heard on Kirkland's television monitors. In this scene, the characters Austin Corbin and Elizabeth Gardiner were among the last passengers remaining on the sinking ship. Some characters had jumped already into rowboats, which collapsed from sheer weight. Others tried to swim for shore, only to be swept away by the sea and drowned in dramatic reenactment.

Despite their distress, Corbin and his beautiful mistress waited their turn, as if expecting a horse and carriage to whisk them away. The well-dressed couple, lashed by the winds and rain, were soaked in brine and seaweed.

From across the ropes, a muscular young man with long, shiny black hair climbed over the boat's railing and onto the ship's creaking wooden deck to rescue the couple.

"You must go now—without a moment's delay," insisted this completely drenched Lifesaver known as Stephen Pharaoh.

Corbin immediately objected.

"My God, you're an ... *Indian*," he told this Lifesaver. "I'll have none of this. How did you become part of the Life-Saving team?"

As the winds swirled violently around them, Elizabeth Gardiner pleaded with Corbin to let her leave the ship immediately. But he refused, demanding an answer. Even in this maelstrom, Corbin wouldn't allow himself to be indebted to a member of the Montauketts, the tribe whose lands he coveted to build his railway to Manhattan. With so little time left before the SS *Louisiana* collapsed, Corbin's bigotry threatened to sink them all.

According to the script, the character of Stephen Pharaoh was central to *The Life Line* plot. Aware of modern-day sensibilities, Kirkland had cast the handsome up-and-coming actor Johnny Youngblood—said to be a Native American originally from Oklahoma—in the role as Pharaoh, rather than some white actor.

Youngblood had been a rock star before discovering acting. With his good looks and charisma, Youngblood resembled Johnny Depp or a young Marlon Brando. He seemed a natural for the pivotal role of Stephen Pharaoh, a sympathetic character that Kirkland knew audiences, especially women, would respond to. As Pharaoh, Youngblood vowed to rely on stunt doubles as little as possible—an idea Max encouraged—and convinced other actors to follow his lead.

In this scene, the script demanded that Pharaoh stand up to Corbin, as few Native Americans in the 1880s would have dared. Corbin presented a formidable figure even when wet. The rain glistened off his bald pate like some marble statue, his long bristles of gray beard as inviting as nails.

"Fine, I'll take her," Pharaoh yelled over the din and chaos. He grabbed Gardiner and forcibly lifted her into the harness with him.

"No, wait..." she screamed. "Austin, save me!" Her flowered hat flew off in the violent breeze.

But the old man was too late. With Gardiner wrapped around his side, Pharaoh plunged into the open air, above the ocean waves, as the life line tugged them along together.

Kirkland's camera crew had planned this pivotal moment for months. The wide and telescopic lenses focused on the telling face of Manchester, the actress who expressed so many emotions as Gardiner within a matter of seconds. Fright, anger, surprise, and, ultimately, submission.

The cameras kept rolling as the rescuer and his reluctant passenger at first tussled in the air. Gardiner's blonde hair, now wet and darkened, dangled off her back. A red scarf around her neck flew about wildly, symbolic of the mortal danger she felt. Eventually, the scarlet fabric covered Pharaoh's face, enough so television viewers could only see his muscular physique, struggling with a rich white woman in his grasp.

Halfway across this gauntlet, an ocean breaker slammed into the couple. The forceful punch of seawater knocked out Gardiner, who suddenly stopped resisting. Her lifeless body fell backwards until halted by Pharaoh's embrace. Their bodies remained entangled, suspended from the ropes in a nearly horizontal entwine, until they were slowly pulled to safety.

"Just like Winslow Homer," Kirkland told his entourage as he watched the television monitors. No one seemed to know what the famous director was talking about. No one knew the name of Winslow Homer, the artist whose painting of this dramatic scene graced my book. So Max looked at me directly.

"I love the way she clings to him. Reminds you of 'Leda and the Swan,' doesn't it?" he continued, supremely satisfied. I nodded, without giving much heed to Kirkland's telling allusion to a rape scene from Yeats.

Several cameras recorded the characters of Pharaoh and Gardiner as they disentangled from the ropes and pulley and collapsed on the beach. Pharaoh resuscitated Gardiner with a breath-of-life maneuver—a modern life-saving technique that probably wasn't used in the 1880s but looked very much like a kiss on the screen. Slowly, Gardiner's eyes opened.

From above, Kirkland's drone cameras flew overhead with a steady buzz. They gave an almost Olympian perspective to the life-saving maneuvers on the beach. They recorded the dead bodies taken from the sea and lying on the sand, waiting to be claimed.

Kirkland's flying cameras then came closer to the doomed ship, capturing the awkward escape of Corbin. Instead of relying on the life line ropes and pulley, Corbin lowered himself into a rowboat and arrived along the shoreline.

Stomping out of the rowboat, Corbin immediately confronted Pharaoh, who was resting on the shoreline with Gardiner.

"I should have you arrested," Corbin hollered, his eyes filled with rage. "What is your name?"

The Lifesaver wasn't afraid to answer back.

"Stephen Pharaoh," replied the actor Johnny Youngblood defiantly, in a heroic way his fans would surely enjoy.

There was no further struggle between the two men. Instead, the actress playing Corbin's wife Margaret rushed up, crying with gratitude about his salvation. Mrs. Corbin feared the shipwreck, now beneath the waves, had submerged with her millionaire husband. Deliriously, she hugged and kissed Corbin and paid little mind to Gardiner's presence in this mess.

Showing no fear, Pharaoh ignored Corbin and his ungrateful threats. As the cameras followed him, Pharaoh walked down the beach, along with the other tired rescuers. He headed toward the make-believe Hamptons life-saving station, recreated from old photos by Kirkland's production crew.

Still winded from her rescue, Gardiner got up and brushed the wet sand from her dress. Instead of relying on her lover Corbin in this situation, she accepted the help of townspeople willing to bring her home to her own feckless husband, the town attorney. She looked round for Pharaoh but realized he had left without giving her the chance to thank him.

When the cameras finally stopped, all the actors heaved a sigh of relief and hastily exited the live-action set. Nearly everyone was drenched.

Kirkland said there was no need for a second take. His stuntmen had done a magnificent job of reenactment, posing as nineteenth-century Lifesavers, without anyone drowning or getting hurt. On camera, this life-saving scene looked just like *The Life Line* painting to Max, its splendor successfully replicated on film.

"This is rapturous, simply rapturous!" Kirkland said ecstatically to those in the director's circle. The tortuous planning and filming of this shipwreck scene—delayed for hours on this opening day—was finally accomplished without error.

Grabbing some blankets, Max hustled to the beachfront. He gave one blanket to his star actress Manchester, demanding another kiss from her. With a sigh, Manchester obliged, merely as a sign of her contentment with how this opening scene turned out.

But Kirkland saved most of his affection for Vanessa Adams, the same red-headed young actress I had met at the coffee van hours earlier. Her turn-of-the century clothes were barely damp because she had been part of the crowd scene on the beach. Currently, Adams had no speaking role. Perhaps she hoped to change that omission as the project progressed.

Max wrapped the last blanket around Vanessa's shoulders and hugged her. I watched silently as they walked away from the beach together.

CHAPTER 4
THE WRITERS ROOM

The next morning, I arrived late for the 10 a.m. writers room conference, full of apologies. My Friday morning car ride from the Montauk Manor hotel where I was staying took longer than expected. As warm weather neared, the one-lane highway along the south fork of Long Island tended to clog with meandering vacationers out for a spin and mirthless tractor drivers crawling along the roadside.

After driving for nearly an hour, I finally found the white-painted brick medical building in East Hampton with a second-floor office rented out to Max Kirkland and his team of professional script doctors. A small makeshift sign marked *The Life Line* was plastered on a glass door leading to the office suite.

I dashed up the stairs and entered a room full of writers far more knowledgeable about television than myself and not particularly welcoming. The only reason for my inclusion on the show's staff was that my LA-based entertainment attorney, Frank Worthington, insisted on it as part of my book rights contract. "Worthington the Warrior," he called himself, a killer with a legal codicil.

"So nice of you to join us," said Penny MacPharland, Kirkland's irksome deputy. She had short, graying black hair and a nimble figure like a dancer. She grew up the product of a Scotsman father and Creole mother, both musicians, who met in New Orleans before moving north. Prim and pompous by nature, Penny often acted like a head butler to Kirkland but was essentially his chief enabler.

In the early 2000s, before gay marriage was legalized, Penny became the partner of Kirkland's sister, Andrea, who bore a striking similarity to her boisterous brother Max in virtually all ways but their sex glands. They both possessed the distinctive Kirkland nose and chin, akin to a Roman gladiator. Andrea's union with Penny lasted less than a year. Kirkland's sister announced her love for a female grip at a competing studio and eventually moved to New Zealand. Nonetheless, Penny's working relationship with Max survived for many more years, as if they were true in-laws with familial ties.

Penny performed delicate tasks Max could not, or would not, do. Though she possessed some creative skills, Penny's main talent was internal politics, helping Kirkland navigate the treacherous waters of Hollywood. Penny also served as a go-between, a discreet intermediary, securing a steady parade of starlets, models, and other attractive women over the years as her boss desired. Kirkland's secrets were safe with Penny. Anything said within earshot of MacPharland presumably wound up being repeated to Max.

For a moment, I just stared around the writers room, ignoring MacPharland. On the long, Scandinavian wood table surrounded by five scriptwriters were scraps of paper, some blinking laptops, cell phones plugged into electric outlets, and, most surprisingly, a few marked-up copies of my novel with yellow stickies hanging out. Against one wall was a large corkboard with multicolored index cards pinned to it. Each card contained a separate scene from the pilot episode that was now being filmed. Most daunting, though, were the empty rows on the corkboard meant for other episodes in this drama yet to be written.

Early on, Kirkland explained he wanted me to help his staff visualize key portions in my book, especially what motivated a man like Austin Corbin, the acknowledged "bad guy," as history labeled him. This meeting, requiring my attendance, was called to frame out the rest of the television series.

I was surprised to find Kirkland didn't show up.

"Where's Max?" I asked. "I thought his mansion was nearby?"

The much-publicized home of Max and Tatiana Kirkland, with its twenty-seven rooms and Renaissance-style limestone walls, was one of the true architectural marvels of Sagaponack, arguably the most exclusive enclave in the Hamptons.

MacPharland explained that "Mr. Kirkland" had spent the night in Manhattan so he could attend a breakfast meeting with Steve Loomis, the streaming service's aggressive CEO. Max had signed a contract for a four-part series based on my book. But now he wanted Comflix, the parent company, to open up its vaults for more money to make an eight-part extravaganza, each two hours long, based on his expanding vision of what streaming television could be.

Hollywood critics loved that Kirkland, the famous director-producer, took risks and talked in grandiose ways. According to legend, Max was willing to change an expensive production on the fly, almost always for the better. "That's how they did *Stars Wars*—on the run," he'd explain, invoking one of his favorite classics.

Now I realized why much of the corkboard for *The Life Line* remained empty.

"Mr. Kirkland texted me to say he is on his way back from the city and should be here shortly," MacPharland informed the group. The rest of the writers appeared unimpressed with MacPharland's posturing and turned to me.

"So where did you get that sexy painting on the cover of your book?" asked Sheila Teague with her distinctive accent. She was one of only two women—and the lone woman of color—on this writing team. A veteran of television drama, Teague seemed confident enough to forge her own path in this conversation and not follow MacPharland's lead.

"It's by a painter named Homer Winslow," I explained. "I spotted it years ago in a museum. Winslow called his painting *The Life Line*—that's where I got the name for my novel."

Teague's face warmed, suggesting I might have found a friend in the writers room.

"I've always been fascinated with the life-saving stations along the Atlantic coastline a century ago," I added. "The cannon blasts and outstretched ropes. The rescue crews rushing into the waves, braving the elements—almost like the cops and firemen running into the flaming towers on 9/11."

A few more staff writers looked up from their maniacal staring at iPads and cell phones. They listened to my explanation, as Teague kept posing questions, hoping for some kind of inspiration from the nineteenth century.

"How did you come up with the idea of Austin Corbin?" inquired Teague, full of historical curiosity. She turned to the other writers. "Doesn't Corbin remind you of Donald Trump?" she asked the other staffers in what was becoming a familiar refrain.

Like some dark cloud on the ascent, Trump permeated America's political atmosphere, creeping into everyday conversation as he did the day earlier with Kirkland. I, too, was struck by the similarities between Corbin and the would-be forty-fifth president but explained to the group that I had begun writing this novel before Trump's rise from reality TV.

Teague, a middle-aged woman with a regal bearing, seemed amused. "There must be something in the American psyche that is attracted to con men like Trump and Austin Corbin," she said with her outsider's sensibility.

MacPharland's face curled up into an unbearable frown. Teague took note of her reaction and swore no offense was intended.

"So sorry, dear Penny," Teague said in her modulated tone. "I forgot that Max and Tatiana attended The Donald's wedding at Mar-a-Lago. I remember Trump married that model… what's her name, Natasha, something?"

"Melania… Melania Trump," MacPharland interjected. "And Max has never spoken to me about that trip."

The staff snickered about the Austin Corbin analogy with Trump, the presidential wannabe, assuring themselves that such a calamity could never happen to the nation.

Just then Kirkland burst into the writers room. He entered in the same overdrive way as his sports car with the personalized license plates ("MAX") exited a highway ramp. During his ride to work, Kirkland had been clearly talking to himself, a running conversation going on in his head ready to explode.

"We got the money—those bastards will pay for *more episodes*," he shouted triumphantly. "They didn't want to at first. But I convinced them. I showed them the rushes from the shipwreck scene. And they *loved* it."

Max paused to catch his breath and take in the reaction of the writers room. Naturally, the staff was excited by the prospect of more episodes, more steady paychecks at rates outlined in the Writers Guild contract. I joined in the respectful applause, which MacPharland duly noted. Max had returned like a lion with bloodied venison clenched in his teeth. He soaked in their gratitude.

MacPharland threw a sycophantic softball his way, asking about the difficulty in convincing the parent company in Manhattan to approve his budget doubling.

"These streaming companies are loaded—they have money to burn," laughed Max, who had spent a career groveling before more dubious movie financiers in Hollywood. "I said I wanted *The Life Line* to be the first big, movie-like television event. Some sprawling epic like *Titanic, Doctor Zhivago,* or something Spielberg would make. I bet these Comflix suits never picked up a Russian novel. But they're picking up our check for more episodes!"

Kirkland looked at the empty planner on the wall. "So now all you guys have to do is write these extra episodes into something memorable and fill up that corkboard!" he said, pointing to spaces for the unwritten episodes.

Max had a gift for the elevator pitch, the quick summation of a show to a group of potential backers with enough force to convince them to fork over millions. In accounting for everyday expenses, these corporate suits might niggle over nickels and dimes. But the right idea for a show from an industry mastermind like Max Kirkland could net them a fortune, lifting the company's star power on Wall Street.

As he finished recalling how his meeting ended with the streamer's executives, Kirkland's face suddenly soured.

"They did ask how it all ends—and I couldn't tell them," Max admitted. "I just said one of the characters gets murdered, Corbin steals the land, and all hell breaks loose."

Moving into a seat next to me at the table, Kirkland requested a refresher course on the novel's plot. "Jack, tell me again, what happens in your book to that Indian who Corbin tried to kill?" he asked.

Of course, we both knew "that Indian" meant Stephen Pharaoh. With the staff writers listening, I described how Pharaoh had been a leader of the Montauk tribe in the 1880s, just as the real Corbin had been the owner of the Long Island Railroad.

With the license of a novel, I turned Pharaoh into a pivotal character—a handsome, charismatic man whose family fought against Corbin and other white men aiming to take away their homelands through a crooked railroad scheme. After saving Corbin's mistress, Elizabeth Gardiner, from drowning in the shipwreck, Pharaoh later had an affair with Gardiner that, in the Hollywood lingo of forbidden romances, forever changed their lives.

My novel portrayed Gardiner as a headstrong young woman, her modern sensibility at odds with the world around her. She carried on this sexual liaison with Pharaoh behind the back of both her bookish husband and the older, money-obsessed Corbin who assumed he controlled her completely.

"Metaphorically, Pharaoh was not only a lifesaver for Gardiner from the sinking ship, but he provided a life line for her from two men who really didn't love her and treated her like a material possession," I explained like some junior college professor.

If women in the nineteenth century were second-class citizens, still without the vote, Native Americans arguably faced even more discrimination. By necessity, Pharaoh had to be careful in the white man's world. He generally avoided confrontations so as not to upset the power structure. But on a purely human level, he found himself enticed by Gardiner's suggestive advances, which my book described in rather lurid detail. She was aroused not only by Pharaoh's physical appeal but his penetrating, almost spiritual insights into her psyche, still very much at sea.

"I would imagine in the 1880s, the idea of a white woman having an affair with an Indian like Pharaoh would have caused great scandal," Teague chimed in. "That's why I think this is an ideal story for exploring race and sexual manners. Both at that time in America and, by extension, today."

When my novel was published in 2013, critics took note of the passionate love story between Pharaoh and Gardiner. Some likened Gardiner to *Madame Bovary* and the sex scenes to *Lady Chatterley's Lover*. But Kirkland was attracted to its contemporary comparisons with *The Notebook* and other steamy soap operas. It was the main reason Kirkland convinced Comflix to purchase the rights.

In putting together this television extravaganza, Kirkland faced many delicate problems beyond the adulterous *in flagrante delicto* scenes between the Pharaoh and Gardiner characters. Over the next several months, he planned to film other key moments from the book that were undoubtedly adding to the production's expense. Along with the shipwreck scene, Max wanted to recreate how Corbin's company blew up the northern side of Montauk, creating a deepwater port.

Kirkland's previous films, often dealing with human violence, were masterful in their orchestrated moments of chaos and upheaval. With a newly ramped-up budget, Max wanted his entree into this new form of cinematic television—presented in 4K high definition and none of that murky, square-box standard of old—to be no less dramatic than the grand sweep of the big screen.

With an Oscar-worthy pitch to Comflix executives, Max sold this project based on his past reputation and an impromptu pilot script still in the process of being written while being filmed. He really hadn't thought out the rest of the series. He'd depend on his band of writers to solve that problem. Max's eyes, surrounded by deep wrinkles, betrayed his anxiousness.

"I need an ending, Jack. I have plenty of sex and violence—what I don't have is an ending to the series, or even a cliffhanger for the pilot," Kirkland explained, confiding a dirty little secret to his whole group of writers as well as myself.

My prosaic response, as if talking to C-SPAN rather than a Hollywood producer, didn't help.

"Well, I imply in my novel that Corbin arranges for Pharaoh's murder, but I deliberately leave it unclear that..."

Shaking his head, Max interrupted, looking straight at me.

"Wait, *that's* the problem—I can't *imply*," Kirkland complained with his deep, crackling voice. "I need a *real* ending, not a literary one. Something that tells us what happens to our good guy Indian. I need you to come up with a mysterious, diabolical way that a person like Corbin would murder an Indian screwing his mistress."

I started to argue but Max grabbed the novel in my hand with firm determination.

"Look, Jack, he's your character—you're going to have to figure out how to kill him. You're a writer, so you must know how to murder someone, right?"

The rest of the staff laughed along with Kirkland as I nodded my acquiescence.

"Sure, I would know how to murder someone," I said facetiously.

MacPharland stared uncomfortably at me until she interrupted with a non sequitur.

"And we want more women's parts in the script, isn't that so, Max?" Penny reminded him. Kirkland paused and then realized what MacPharland meant.

"That's right," Max said, picking up Penny's cue. "I'd particularly like to see more meat put on the role played by Vanessa Adams. Give her more to say and do. I watched her in the early rushes, and she looks fabulous to me."

The implications of that last line were left on the table without comment. Max always took a special interest in at least one young female up-and-comer who he hoped would respond favorably to his encroachments. He wasn't inclined to take no for an answer. Vanessa Adams would be only the latest in a long line of women targeted on his sets.

"What about more parts for *Black* female characters, Max?" asked Teague, aware of how few African Americans like herself were in the writers union. She felt compelled to bring up this issue even if it made Max squirm. "Back in the 1880s, there were plenty of newly freed former slaves. We were called Negroes," she teased the group, drawing out the "knee" sound.

Max's face tightened into a forced grin. "I guess so... but I thought we'd have enough diversity with all these Indians," he responded.

MacPharland, who generally avoided such issues, again cleaned up Max's mess. "Let's see what we can do," she quickly urged, "and in the meantime, let's get to work."

Kirkland rose from the table. As an afterthought, he reminded us all that we were invited to a party that evening at his Sagaponack mansion called Lions Head.

Invitations from Max and his TV wife Tatiana Kirkland were a rite of summer in the Hamptons. Their lush parties were attended by the powerful and the celebrated. Gossip items about them appeared in *People* magazine, fan websites, and the city tabloids. All summer long, Max and Tatiana could be seen posing for pictures as a couple at various fundraisers and social events—from gala library benefits and invitation-only July 4th fireworks displays to sipping wine at Bridgehampton polo matches.

This year's Kirkland party promised to be exceptional, enhanced by the much-publicized expectations of a brand-new project called *The Life Line*, certain to expand Max's fame and fortune.

CHAPTER 5
MONTAUK MANOR

The writers room meeting broke up soon after Max Kirkland's departure, leaving enough time to get some sun at the place where I was staying. By 4:30 p.m. Friday afternoon, I was lying with my eyes closed in a chaise lounge, next to the heated pool at the Montauk Manor, wondering what the night would bring.

After a long, tiring week, I'd cleansed my spirits in the pool's cool clear water, like some hotel baptism for wayward visitors. After a short swim alone, I stretched out and relaxed on an empty lounge, full of carnal thoughts about the Kirkland party that evening.

As a recently divorced man, I imagined meeting some fascinating woman, a fantasy inspired by paparazzi photos of models, starlets, and beautiful friends of Max and Tatiana Kirkland dancing in my head. Plenty of these pictures were posted on Instagram and other social media, the kind of young, hip audience the stodgy *New York World* editors said they were trying to reach.

After twenty years of marriage and two kids, I was free of any domestic obligations. The husbandly yoke of Saturday lawn-mowing, Sunday church-going, midweek chores, and scheduled sex on a timetable set by my wife was gone. I tried not to think of the pain, anger, and guilt that I left behind with my broken family and old job in the suburbs.

Success with *The Life Line*—and being hired by the greatest newspaper in the world, as my editors assured me—offered the chance for a new life, ridding me of all the unhappiness and self-doubt that dwelled inside for years. Now on my own, I realized that crusty old adage—"the best reporters are born orphans and never marry"—was probably right. With the sun slowly setting, I tried to think about my future and not the past.

A strange quietude surrounded the pool. Throughout the week, much of the cast relaxed and resided at this old-fashioned, Tudor-style residence built on a hill with tennis courts and rolling lawns. Atop the Montauk Manor was a gold dome. It'd been built in the 1920s as "the most fabulous summer resort ever imagined in the western world" by Carl Fisher, another visionary millionaire with dreams similar to Austin Corbin before him. Like a castle, paramount above all else surrounding it, the Montauk Manor provided Max Kirkland's cast and crew the chance to stay in luxury at Comflix's expense.

By late Friday, most people had left for New York City or returned to their own homes for the weekend. They wouldn't come back until next week when filming resumed. A few lucky ones, including myself, were invited to the Kirklands' party.

Relaxing in the chaise with my eyes shut, I slipped momentarily into slumber until I heard a noise suddenly upon me.

"No one here, huh?" asked a chipper female voice. I opened my eyes to see Vanessa Adams gazing at me, quite matter-of-factly. "Mind if I put my stuff next to yours?"

I didn't have time to respond. She unfurled her terry cloth robe, tossed off her flip-flops, and dove into the pool like an Olympic swimmer. For the moment, I was to be her pool boy, tending to her minimal clothing left on the chair beside me. She swam a few laps at a leisurely pace, sometimes stealing a glance my way.

Vanessa's swim didn't last long. As she exited the pool, her natural beauty was on full display, like some Venus on the half shell. Wearing a bright yellow bikini, her burnt-auburn hair, blue eyes, and porcelain skin shimmered as she dried herself off slowly with a towel.

"Are you going to the party tonight?" Vanessa asked. When I said I was looking forward to it, she answered brightly, "So am I."

For a few minutes, we talked about the previous day's filming of the shipwreck scene and how closely it resembled details from my novel and from Winslow Homer's famous painting. She marveled how Lifesavers in the 1880s had come up with such an elaborate system to save so many from drowning.

"I didn't know those pulleys were called a breeches buoy until I read it in your novel," she enthused. "I read your book *twice*."

Vanessa paused hesitantly, perhaps sensing my doubt that she'd read it all. Then with a wink, she said whimsically, "Maybe you could write a few more chapters and put my character in it?"

Regardless of the truth, Vanessa Adams was clearly an accomplished performer, even if she fibbed a bit. Reciting her credits, she claimed she appeared in several small parts in movies and a bit on Broadway after studying drama at Yale. For this project, Adams said she studied the history of the Montauketts and the loss of their sacred Native American lands to Austin Corbin and visited their tribal gravesite. Her preparation seemed to match her ambitiousness.

"Did you know Stephen Pharaoh is buried near here?" she quizzed, looking out from the Montauk Manor's elevated estate to the foothills below. "I went and looked at his gravestone the other day. Supposedly the spirit of an Indian chief roams the halls of this place at night with a headdress on. Do you believe in ghosts, Jack?"

Speaking of the dead with someone so amply alive like Adams felt odd to me.

"I know the Montauketts like Stephen Pharaoh believed in spirits," I explained. "Spirits for the sea, for fire, and for their corn. And a great, good god named Cauhluntoowut who looked over everything. They believed in evil spirits but also a sense of peace with the Earth, which was their mother."

Vanessa's eyes widened as if she'd been given some special gift of knowledge.

"You're very smart," she murmured. "Did you learn that stuff researching your novel?"

I felt my face puff up in smug satisfaction. Younger women were always impressed by older men teaching them the ways of the world—or at least that was my conceit. Perhaps I had watched too many improbable rom-coms where the middle-aged actor walks off into the sunset with the perky blonde or redhead. Perhaps Vanessa viewed me as someone who could advise her, even though she undoubtedly knew more about show business than I did as a news reporter. Perhaps she viewed Kirkland as the ultimate showbiz connector for her budding career, and why Max appeared so intent on her, looking to expand Vanessa's bit part in the project.

"Yes, I learned there are spirits roaming over these lands," I replied with a wry smile. "I hope you meet only friendly ghosts, Vanessa."

She smiled without comment, as if assessing a social calculation in her mind.

Rising from my chaise lounge, I walked with Vanessa toward the hotel's side entrance, not knowing where this conversation might be headed. It turned out our rooms were not far apart, nor our intentions.

"Want to have a drink while we dry off?" she asked at her doorstep. Without reply, I followed her in.

Relaxed inside the apartment, Vanessa poured vodka and orange juice into two glasses. She mixed in a few last words of conversation. Then she rubbed her sunburnt hair in a towel, letting it fall back onto her shoulders, still damp and unkempt. We sipped our drinks on the edge of the bed until we slowly descended into an embrace.

To my surprise, Vanessa was the initiator, as if she had done her homework on me as well. I quickly overcame whatever reluctance I had with this virtual stranger, her skin moist and gleaming. The difference in our years—a divorced man of forty-four with a breathtaking woman of twenty-six—didn't seem to matter, not to her, and certainly not in my excitement. She slipped off her bathing suit and yanked my trunks off playfully.

We slid beneath the bed covers, frolicking like two dolphins in a pod, only occasionally coming up for air. The lights stayed on and the air conditioner kept humming.

For the next hour, there was no talk of show business or Max Kirkland's demands or how she wanted her acting role enhanced in the scripts. What was next for Vanessa wasn't broached until I prepared to leave.

"Give me a ride to the party, will you?" she asked, wrapping the sheets around her body. "Someone will be taking me home after the party, but I need someone to take me there."

At the time, I didn't think anything of this request, except the subtle message that I wouldn't be spending tonight with Vanessa.

"Of course, I'll stop by at seven thirty," I said cheerily. "See you then."

Closing her door, I walked away, surprised by the tone of my farewell. Instead of sounding like a suave bachelor, my voice contained the pathetic air of gratitude from a no-longer-married man, lost in unfamiliar territory. I immediately recognized the desperate friendliness of my dad-voice from an earlier life, when I solicited other parents in arranging playdates for my kids.

At the upcoming Kirkland party, full of sophisticates, I resolved to do better.

CHAPTER 6
LIONS HEAD

An hour later, we were both ready for an evening of enchantment at the Kirkland mansion. By the time I arrived at her door for pickup, Vanessa Adams had transformed from a playful ingenue in a wet bikini into a sleek, sophisticated woman, wearing a glittering evening dress with stiletto heels. I wore a black mock turtleneck underneath a light-brown jacket, more Hollywood producer than a New York writer.

When I commented on Vanessa's attire, she politely returned the compliment, with no hint of what had happened earlier between us. "Our chariot awaits," I said, escorting her into my black Lexus sports car parked nearby.

We drove off into the twilight, barely speaking at first. We listened intently to Siri, the automaton voice on my cell phone, providing directions to Lions Head. As I drove in silence, Vanessa's curiosity bubbled up to the surface.

"Nice car—how long have you owned it?" she asked.

"It's not mine—it's a rental," I said.

She seemed unimpressed, so I offered a rationale.

"I like rentals," I explained. "In my mind, renting a car is much better than owning one."

Renting cars, as I explained, was my preferred method of getting around. In a rental, you could rev up the motor a little more, play the radio a little louder, be more carefree than some owner straddled with a car loan or a lease.

During my marriage, family and friends convinced me to buy all sorts of cars planted in my driveway—especially those boxy minivans with sliding side doors for the kids—but I never liked them. A rental boosted the feeling of freedom on the road, the vicarious thrill of not having to be responsible for anything.

As a journalist flying into an unknown place (called "parachuting in"), I often relied on a rental to get around on deadline. A rental car's transient nature—constantly on the go, part of a fleet of moving vehicles around the country with no specific home—mirrored the ephemeral state of America, with its throwaway disposables and endless highways. Driving through the Hamptons in a rental seemed a natural part of this freedom.

Vanessa remained unmoved by my explanation. With her car window down, she stuck her hand out into the night, breathing in the scent of saltwater permeating the breeze.

"Don't you love it out here?" she said wistfully. "My apartment in the city is so stifling this time of year."

Despite the summertime chaos of traffic and tourists, there still existed a natural beauty to this place, about a hundred miles from Manhattan. Off the main highway, quiet roads stretched for miles without streetlights. Mansions peeked through the gates of driveways and hedgerows. The blackness of the sky allowed the moon and stars to appear larger, as a place to dream big.

"If this show is nominated for the Emmys, Max says I can sit at the table with him," Vanessa suddenly blurted out. She let the wind caress her hair. I tried hard to keep my eyes focused on the darkened road.

"I'm glad Max is counting on getting an award," I replied with a laugh. "I have a book-author friend who was nominated for an Oscar, but he wasn't invited to the ceremony. The studio gave his seat to the top star's ten-year-old daughter instead. Worst of all, they didn't win."

I turned to see Vanessa's reaction to my amusing little tale, but she seemed entranced by her own Hollywood fantasy.

"I'm hoping to get an award myself, especially if my role is developed more," she declared. "Max promised me it would be."

Her dewy earnestness, perhaps an act, nevertheless reminded me of her true age. I didn't challenge her with any world-weary cynicism. Instead, I mentioned encouragingly that Max told the writers room that afternoon that he wanted her role enlarged. She beamed at that news.

A white limousine passed us on the road, indicating we were near the Kirkland mansion. "*Your destination is on the left*," Siri affirmed.

We pulled into the long driveway and waited for an attendant to take the car. Vanessa gazed in the mirror, fixed her hair, and then turned toward me.

"I know Max's reputation is ... shall we say, as a hands-on director, even a little kinky ... but he's a *genius*," she said. "I've wanted to work with him forever." Though not explicitly, Vanessa's words made clear the nature of her relationship with Kirkland. I couldn't help frowning.

"Don't worry," she assured, "we have an understanding."

Lions Head, the Kirklands' massive oceanfront mansion, was a Hamptons legend, as resplendent as its press clippings proclaimed. Over several decades, the history of this seaside castle unfurled in a way every bit as elaborate as its design.

In the Roaring Twenties, the original home was constructed by the millionaire du Pont family, famous for their chemicals. They later sold it in the 1970s to a wealthy friend of artist Andy Warhol, known for his own kind of accelerants. By the 1980s Reagan era, a tax-dodging tycoon bought the house at auction. He rebuilt it into an oversized French chateau, calling it "Dragon's Head." This South Fork *San Simeon* came complete with outside gargoyles, an inside shark tank, a sixteenth-century Norman pub, and a bronze suit of armor standing guard. Its huge fifty-foot turret, like a giant sultan's tent, violated the local zoning codes and enraged the neighbors.

When that tacky owner's finances fell apart, a multimillionaire neighbor, well-known as a brand-name in the clothing trade, threatened to buy and tear down the annoying Dragon's Head once and for all. But Tatiana Kirkland, as a friend from the fashion world, talked this designer out of it. Instead, Tatiana and Max purchased the house themselves. They toned down its outside appearance and renamed the place "Lions Head."

As I wrangled the keys and a parking slip from the attendant, Vanessa went ahead and entered the party. A few minutes later, I walked into the grand foyer, grabbed a drink, and was met immediately by Penny MacPharland. She was annoyed, with her dark eyes glaring and face contorted. Clearly not every gargoyle had been removed from the premises.

"So, I see you came with Vanessa Adams," MacPharland said accusingly. "Does Max know about this?"

I grinned, took another sip from my cut-glass tumbler, and emerged with a considered reply.

"No, and neither does Tatiana."

That shut up MacPharland for the evening. Max might have been interested in Vanessa's whereabouts, but MacPharland knew her boss dreaded Tatiana finding out about his extramarital interests. So she melted into the crowd.

The Kirkland party at Lions Head was everything I'd imagined. Inside the mansion, I passed through several parlor rooms filled with beautiful people dressed in summery shades of egg-shell white, creamy beige, and light blue. Few guests were of color, but all appeared rich. A parade of young women—some acting in Max's production like Vanessa, but mostly models tied to Tatiana's world of fashion—floated around dreamily between the gnarly clusters of older men discussing business. In the distance, I thought I spotted Vanessa in the mingling crowd, though, as I came closer, it proved to be another red-headed actress with vaguely the same appearance. Someone mentioned seeing Vanessa with Max in another room. I had no doubt I would stumble back upon her.

Along the walls, Max's artwork, far advanced in taste from his boardwalk days in Venice Beach, was on display like its own museum. Abstract paintings in severe and slashing colors—by Pollack, Rothko, Barnett Newman, and the de Koonings—were framed and mounted. I'd read somewhere that they were worth millions, just like the shiny Jeff Koons sculpture of a balloon dog displayed in the corner. His lifetime of art collecting had yielded a fortune, another reminder that everything Max touched turned to gold.

As I moved through the house, all around me was a steady hum of conversation and laughter. Buffet tables overflowed with fruits, cheeses, salmon, lobster tails, jumbo shrimp, and briskets for the picking. To each guest's specification, waiters sliced filet mignon at carving stations with heat lamps over them and other fine meats kept in chafing dishes. They were a tribute to Max's fondness for consumption, to devour anything in sight.

In an adjoining ballroom, a DJ played a mix of rap songs from Kanye West and Lil' Kim to other crowd favorites as background music, including Jay-Z and Alicia Keys's "Empire State of Mind" and Sinatra's "New York, New York." No live band or orchestra was needed—only a spaceship-like cluster of giant speakers, sound boards, and an audio mixer. Wearing a headset, the DJ twisted knobs and dials, like an astronaut busy in space. On the dance floor, guests danced, kissed, and hugged each other slowly on the hardwood floor, circling under six dimly lit chandeliers above. Celebrities and other bold-faced names stood around, chatting with each other, while a wait staff in formalwear served hors d'oeuvres to them.

Max, in a black shirt and white jacket, tried to be witty and engaging to all his invitees, the self-appointed centerpiece for the night. But the Kirkland party wasn't a free-for-all, not the fictionalized galas of old-time Gold Coast novels. Rather, in the twenty-first century, this choreographed Hamptons event was a tightly guarded celebration, meant only for the upper reaches of American media and entertainment, not the hoi polloi. It was paid for by the corporate behemoth Comflix and protected by a phalanx of burly security guards and off-duty police, each with shaved heads, earpieces, and concealed weapons beneath their jackets. They tried to remain out of sight unless needed. They pretended not to see the dessert table of cannabis edibles, including the multicolored gummies, the THC-dipped cookies, and the waterfall of spiked chocolate fondue. They ignored pot smoking, cocaine sniffing, the casual sexual groping, and other offenses, unless done by an unfamiliar face presumably not invited.

As I moved about, another protector of the evening made herself known.

"Glad you could make it, Jack," said Tracy Hammond, Comflix's PR head, leaning towards my ear so her words could be heard above the din. "Would you like some champagne?" she asked.

When I agreed, she motioned to a waiter who poured some into a fluted crystal glass and gave it to me. Hammond clinked my glass lightly against her own, in a toast to the impending success of our show together.

As Max passed by, like a good host, he clapped his hands approvingly of our gesture. "I love everybody tonight, Jack!" he laughed, immediately headed to the next room by himself without stopping to talk.

Hammond, wearing a white chiffon dress balanced off her bare shoulders, again whispered in my ear as his publicist.

"Max likes this Pol Roger champagne because he heard Churchill used to drink it," she giggled.

A former Hollywood actress herself, Hammond was usually the most attractive woman in the room and arguably the most effective negotiator. For years as a publicity vice president at Comflix, she'd shown a remarkable ability to control the message of every corporate event, even something as inchoate as this summer party at the Kirklands. After a sip, she moved to another thought.

"Would you like to meet Steve Loomis?" she asked. Over her shoulder, I could see Loomis, the brusque CEO of Comflix, talking with other guests, including an older man who I recognized as an acclaimed director.

Hammond maneuvered through the crowd and introduced me. Without a break, Loomis kept speaking, as if giving an annual presentation to investors.

"... if our numbers continue to go up, we'll soon be the biggest streamer in the world," I heard Loomis say before he was interrupted.

"What about this man Trump?" asked the director, Sir Thaddeus Knightly, with a low, calm British accent. "Does he pose any danger to things here in the States?"

Loomis's eyes flashed with alarm. "None whatsoever," replied Comflix's chief. "My good friend Zach Preston, the television producer who worked with Trump, says Donald will be great for the entertainment industry. He says Trump's as natural on camera as Ronald Reagan was."

Hammond could tell from her boss's overly confident answer that he felt defensive towards this brilliant English director, known for winning awards on both sides of the Atlantic. She gently eased Loomis to another semicircle of less confrontational guests nearby.

For a moment, I was alone with Knightly. After introducing myself deferentially, he urged that I call him "Tad" and not "Sir." He nursed a watered-down whiskey in a small glass tumbler. His soft British voice, nearly inaudible in this crowded room, made me listen closer to his words.

From previous discussions overheard in the writers room, I knew Max wanted Knightly to help out with the directing chores for *The Life Line* if it became a large series. Showrunners often hired other well-known directors to oversee episodes they didn't direct themselves. Despite his own sizable reputation, Kirkland venerated Knightly, whom he called a "true genius" of the cinema, perhaps even greater than himself.

During his distinguished career, Knightly had directed dozens of films and television programs, including an Oscar winner and a James Bond spy flick. He had worked before with both Lester Wolf and Kiara Manchester on the London stage. But Knightly was best known for overseeing what critics called the greatest documentary ever made—the story of an extended family from his hometown in Wales that was updated with a new installment every seven years.

Before my mercantile interest in Hollywood, I'd watched the Knightly documentary with artistic admiration, as if he'd hit upon an insight, an indelible truth, that I was striving for in my own work. From this legendary filmmaker, whom I viewed as a wise man, almost a shaman, I wanted to know more.

"Why did you decide to make a documentary about a family?" I asked. "Why that one?"

Knightly explained he'd been a BBC producer when the project started in the 1980s and that it grew, as many unplanned conceptions do, as a happy accident. "It's not just about *one* family," explained the director, now well into his seventies, who was a young man when it began. "In a sense it's about *all* families."

His snow-white hair barely covered his huge head. His eyes, like apertures fully opened, seem to absorb all light in the room. He gazed directly at me, as if I was the sole representative of humanity in this cavernous place.

"I've never been much for gadgetry and special effects, even though, I must say, I did enjoy 007's car chases," he said, pausing with a wry grin. "You can make a film about love and sex, spies and mobsters, but I think inside our homes is where there is the greatest drama."

I watched him silently as he drew another sip of whiskey in contemplation.

"Family gives us a sense of place and purpose in this world but also many of its heartaches. The expectations and disappointments between parents and children. The promises and betrayals among spouses. There are the social changes about sex, class divide, and religion. All the sacramental issues of life and death are there in the flesh."

Knightly's lessons seemed borne of his own experience as well as years of observation through a camera. Though speaking in the abstract, his words came perilously close to my own reality.

"Family can be the source of our greatest joy," he said, "and our worst pain."

Before the night was over, I wandered through Lions Head with Sheila Teague and her colleagues from the writers room. We all agreed that Max had prevailed magnificently with the studio suits, garnering even more production money for *The Life Line*.

Near the back of the mansion, Sheila and I talked about another big location shoot for *The Life Line* pilot. It involved the 1882 visit of President Chester A. Arthur to Austin Corbin's Long Island seaside mansion, a place just as large as Lions Head. Sheila was writing much of the dialogue for that shoot, scheduled for several weeks ahead. I couldn't help but share a historical tidbit.

"Did you know Chester Arthur became president after James Garfield was killed by an assassin?" I offered.

Sheila nodded confidently. "Of course, I already worked that into the script," she assured. We both laughed.

A familiar-looking woman then came up to us and greeted Sheila, who made the necessary introductions.

"This is Tatiana Kirkland, our host for the evening," Sheila announced to me with aplomb. "And this is Jack Denton, the author of *The Life Line* and the inspiration for Max's latest—*and greatest*—project." Politely, we laughed again in showbiz solidarity.

I had never watched Tatiana's popular cable television fashion show, where contestants and designers competed over their best creations. But as a real-life hostess, Tatiana, a beautiful woman in her late thirties, nearly two decades younger than her equally well-known husband, couldn't be more engaging.

"Can I show you around our place?" she asked with a slight trace of an Eastern European accent. Her azure eyes flared, highlighted by mascara and her thick, luxurious eyebrows.

Tatiana wore a flowing kaftan dress with a slit in front wide enough to accentuate her embonpoint. She had been a striking, bone-thin model when Max met her, and she still appeared that way, running a multimedia fashion empire. Although her life as a successful businesswoman required many lunches, she kept fit naturally. She displayed far better results from eating goat cheese and raspberry vinaigrette salads than the personal trainer her husband employed.

As part of her introduction, Sheila mentioned the Kirklands had attended the Trump wedding a decade earlier, mainly because of Tatiana's old friendship with fellow model Melania.

"I don't talk politics," Tatiana interrupted, waving off the subject like a troublesome pest. "Too complicated for me."

This mention of politics sounded vaguely familiar to me. Somewhere in a newspaper story about Max, I remember he boasted about Tatiana's grandmother being a double agent against the Nazis during the war. Max adored tough characters he felt were like himself. He virtually bragged that Tatiana's grandmother had slit the throat of a German officer who tried to rape her. When her family moved to America, though, they all swore off politics.

The warm evening made the house a bit too stuffy. We journeyed out to the Kirklands' massive backyard, with its elaborate marble patio, smooth infinity pool, and wooden walkways leading to the ocean. The celestial view along the Atlantic, unobstructed by light pollution, was magnificent, with so many more stars visible by the naked eye.

As we walked along, Tatiana asked about the origins of my novel and the haunting painting on its cover. Gazing at the pounding waves, she said she could only imagine the terror in the hearts of those caught in a shipwreck. Tatiana admitted that she had not yet read my book but emphasized how excited Max was about converting it into "prestige" television.

"I wasn't at the last Emmy ceremony, but this time I plan to attend if Max is nominated," she said adamantly.

"Good, I'll sit right next to you," I replied, aware of another person who also wanted to be at Max's table.

She smiled gently. "It's been very nice to meet you, Mr. Denton," Tatiana said, moving back towards the house and her other party guests. "Will you be staying out here in the Hamptons for all of the series shooting?"

I explained that while I would be working with her husband's writing team on the television show, I had recently joined *The New York World* as a political reporter, assigned this Sunday to cover a Trump rally in Pennsylvania.

"In two days?" she said. "I guess you'll be seeing Melania and Donald before I do."

At that moment, I felt the vibrating buzzer of my cell phone go off in my jacket pocket, alerting me to a message. I expected it might be my new editor, checking in on the latest Trump news. But the all-caps text contained foreboding information from my ex-wife Tricia: "*JACK, YOUR COUSIN ELAINE IS IN LENOX HILL HOSPITAL. NOT LOOKING GOOD. THOUGHT YOU SHOULD KNOW.*"

For a few moments, I felt the pull of my old life as a family man, half-resentful of my ex-wife's intervention and half-grateful for it. The time on my cell phone was nearly midnight. I decided to leave the party immediately and return to the Montauk Manor so I could get a decent night's sleep and head to the hospital in the morning.

Before I entered my car, I looked around for Vanessa but couldn't find her. Instead, I drove through the darkness alone, contemplating all the personal drama that was going on in my own life.

CHAPTER 7
HOSPITAL VISIT

Propped up in bed, Elaine rallied when I walked into her hospital room the next day. She tried to appear like her old self, but too many signs of illness gave her away.

A clear bag of saline dripped into her arm. Humming, chirpy devices monitored her heart rate and breathing. She wore a light-blue hospital gown soiled with spots of blood.

"What are you doing up so early?" she quizzed. "I thought writers always slept late."

At eight o'clock on a Saturday morning, Lenox Hill Hospital—in the heart of Manhattan—seemed devoid of any visitors other than myself. I drove in from the Hamptons at dawn. In Elaine's room, a television blared above on the wall, as if it had been on all night.

"I wanted to know if you'd like to go for a run in Central Park," I deadpanned.

Elaine smiled wanly, her brave front disappearing. She let the strain of her disease show. Her sparkling blue eyes appeared drained. Her cherubic cheeks had turned pale and withdrawn. The few remaining strands of her once-bountiful brunette hair were gray and lifeless.

"Maybe not today...but I guess it's easier to run in the park now... *without breasts*," she said, imitating the comic delivery of her favorite television star. One night last summer, we binge-watched a whole season of that comedian's show in Elaine's living room while she recovered from her earlier operation. She said laughter was the best medicine.

We avoided the most obvious punchline: Elaine O'Rourke Lubinsky was a forty-three-year-old, married mother of two who had endured a double mastectomy and, despite the best efforts of modern medicine, was dying of late-stage cancer.

The banter between Elaine and myself, profane but always honest, had been flowing our entire lives. We were more like brother and sister than cousins. She was the emotional link between my old family and the new one I had tried to create. During the long drive to Lenox Hill that morning, I thought of all these connections, the many memories swimming in my brain. Like home movies from the past, these images were still in mind as I watched Elaine lying in a hospital bed, clinging to life.

Our mothers came from Ireland, part of the never-ending diaspora in search of a better life. Catherine and Siobhan Quinn were siblings born a year apart on a hilly sheep farm in County Donegal. After graduating from nursing school in Belfast, they both immigrated to the United States under the sponsorship of a cousin already in New York. They both landed jobs at Lenox Hill Hospital on the Upper East Side, where many Irish found work tending to the bodily needs and desperations of sick and elderly patients. Together they lived in Astoria, Queens, on the third floor of a walk-up apartment building, with impressive parquet floors and a window view of a children's playground outside.

While in Astoria, the two sisters both met their future husbands. Siobhan, the younger, married a medical technician named William O'Rourke, whom she first encountered on the elevated subway ride to Manhattan. Catherine was introduced to my father, Paul Denton, at a parish dance. Friends said my mother resembled an Irish Eleanor Roosevelt, with a big, toothy smile, generous heart, and a slight brogue that my ears couldn't detect. My father grew up in a Catholic orphanage, never knowing his real parents or true lineage. A handsome man with a brown pompadour and slim build, he returned from the Vietnam conflict as an Army sergeant and opened his own machine shop. A quiet, hard-working man, he happily deferred to my mother on most decisions at home.

Both Irish sisters with their American husbands eventually moved to Long Island, their golden suburb. It was a place overflowing with modern appliances and newly built split-level homes with two-car garages, far different from the sleepy nineteenth-century farmland of Austin Corbin's day. As an act of faith in the future, Elaine's parents, the O'Rourkes, lent my parents two hundred dollars so they could put a down payment on a house, built across the street from theirs on a reconverted potato farm. The O'Rourkes had already started having children, with Elaine's older brother Glenn, and hoped the Dentons would soon follow suit.

As soon as they moved in, my parents planted grass seed in the muddy front yard, a few puny trees in the back, and hoped for the best. On this "crabgrass prairie," as sociologists called it, all settlers started anew, a *tabula rasa* for young couples' innocent belief in themselves and their budding families. They seemed to realize such an opportunity, unique in the annals of America, might never happen again.

"Remember, Jack, you'll meet a lot of people in this life, but none as reliable as your own flesh and blood," my mother impressed upon me, referring to Elaine's family as well as our own. "You'll always have your family, the only ones you can truly count on."

My parents believed God's will determined everything, a divine force that provided for our needs and intervened only when necessary. After my birth in 1971, my parents, both in their late thirties, learned they couldn't have any more children, a condition known as "secondary infertility." Faulty sperm or broken fallopian tubes, whatever the cause, it really didn't matter. The doctors said their problem couldn't be solved, not even with prayer. I remained "an only child," an appellation that fit me well into adulthood.

Elaine became my surrogate sister, someone I could always trust. We were the same age and shared many experiences together. Old black-and-white Polaroid photos show us as infants, pushed in strollers by our mothers chatting merrily along the sidewalk. With Elaine's family, we celebrated an endless array of birthdays, graduations, and other happy occasions. Dinners for Thanksgiving, Christmas, and Easter rotated between our two families' homes. We thought this contentment would never end. But when we reached college, Elaine helped me through the worst moment of my young life.

On a warm summer night, my parents were killed in a car crash coming home from a movie. Police said the death of Catherine and Paul Denton was caused by a drunk driver who entered a tree-lined Long Island parkway from the wrong direction. The skid marks on the roadway showed my parents' car swerved to avoid the oncoming vehicle. It lost control and wrapped itself around an unbending maple tree. My mother died instantly; her head smashed into the windshield on the passenger's side. My father, driving without a seatbelt, flew out an open window. He was found dead, lying face down in the woods.

The drunk driver walked away from the crash without a scratch. I later heard the driver hired a well-connected lawyer who argued the roadway was slippery that night and got him off with nothing more than a traffic violation for a wrong turn. Until that moment, suburbia had been idyllic for my family, a place where awful events weren't supposed to happen. It all changed in an instant.

That night, I was out with friends at a local bar, not far from the beach. Cops and hospital officials, looking to inform me of my parents' deaths, tried to find me but without luck. Elaine told them where I could be found on a Saturday night.

While I was shooting pool, Elaine came through the tavern's door at around 2 a.m. She was accompanied by her father and two policemen who told me the awful news.

"I'm so sorry, Jack. . . ." Elaine cried, unable to say more.

Nothing was ever quite the same again. In my grief, Elaine acted as a sounding board and counselor through my darkest reveries, someone to whom I could reach out, remembering all that had been lost.

"How could this happen to my parents, especially when they believed all this holy shit about a loving God?" I asked her repeatedly. Elaine just listened, smart enough to avoid a facile answer.

I felt more like an orphan at that point than an only child. Elaine's parents helped me bury my mother and father. They didn't dwell on details surrounding my parents' deaths. Instead, they encouraged me to get on with my life. We processed insurance claims from the fatal accident so I could find enough money to finish college. Stoically, I carried on through my senior year in a cloud of depression, recriminations, and drink.

Ironically, in the darkness of that spring, Elaine altered the course of my life with an introduction to Patricia Stanton. It would mark the start of what would become my own family.

In the early 1990s, Tricia, as everyone called her, and Elaine were roommates together at a liberal arts college in New England. Their campus was a two-hour ride from Fordham University in the Bronx, where I studied to become a journalist with the aid of a scholarship. Late in my senior year, Elaine invited me to a party in her dorm. I was hesitant to go. It proved to be a setup planned by Elaine to get me out of my gloom. Just as she intended, I danced and spent much of that night talking with her attractive roommate.

Tricia was unlike any girl I had ever met, from a stratum well above my immigrant family's social class. As the daughter of Terrence F. X. Stanton, a state senator from Nassau County, she was accustomed to the money and privilege of Long Island's Gold Coast. Her father, "Big Terry," lived up to his name with a walrus-like mustache, beer belly, and catcher's-mitt hands. He was also the commodore of the Sands Point Yacht Club—a well-appointed place right out of *The Great Gatsby*—where we later married. When Elaine told her of my parents' tragedy, Tricia adopted me like a wounded pet. She pulled me out of my doldrums. Her lively humor, compassion, and death-defying sexiness could rouse any flattened spirit.

Soon after our initial meeting, Tricia extended her parents' invitation to dinner at their family home in Old Westbury. I agreed without hesitation, which pleased her. As Elaine later confided to me, Tricia's pithy manner of speaking like a future litigator, similar to her super-lawyer father, turned off many suitors not up for the challenge.

"Just be prepared," Tricia warned with a wry smile as we neared the front door. "Big Terry will try to eat you up like all my other would-be boyfriends."

"Bring it on," I said with bravado, seconds before shaking hands with her parents.

The Stanton mansion—with a soaring central hall, floating staircases up to the bedrooms, two big fireplaces, and a dining room to fit twenty—was light-years from the modest tract home where I grew up on Long Island. A particular point of pride for the Stantons was the "great room" library with Big Terry's trophies, plaques, and personal memorabilia, including a sculpture of Rough Rider Teddy Roosevelt on horseback. Along its cherrywood walls, one framed photo showed Big Terry standing beside Ronald Reagan during a presidential campaign swing through Nassau County.

"It's my father's tribute to himself," Tricia whispered on her guided tour, careful not to be heard.

Dinner proceeded along pleasantly until Big Terry quizzed me about politics. Back then, the Nassau County GOP reigned as the nation's top suburban political machine, with its most influential figure the conservative US Senator Alfonse D'Amato, often called "Senator Pothole" by his detractors. Big Terry and "Al," as he proudly called him, started together in the party's lower ranks.

Tricia's mother Audrey made a point of mentioning that D'Amato appeared regularly at the annual dinner of the "Theodore Roosevelt Republican Club" hosted at the Milleridge Inn by her husband.

"You know, Jack used to sing at the Milleridge Inn with Elaine," Tricia said to her mother. "They were a brother-sister act, going around to the tables, doing requests."

Mrs. Stanton appeared confused. "I thought you said Elaine and Jack are cousins?"

I jumped in. "We *are* cousins. I replaced Elaine's brother when he went off to college. But when the Milleridge found out we weren't a real brother-sister act, they fired us."

Tricia's mother seemed amused by this little backstory. Her father acted as though he didn't hear it.

"So, Tricia tells me you're going to be a journalist," Big Terry said, pushing back slightly from the table. "I hope you won't be like one of those liberals we see on TV."

Mrs. Stanton fidgeted, uncomfortable at the prospect of a bloody after-dinner confrontation. Tricia, with her eyes focused on me, appeared as if she were watching a matador face the bull.

"Well, with all due respect, I wouldn't label myself in such a way," I corrected in my politest voice. "I think powerful people need to be held accountable. In journalism, I write about the topics I care about, honestly and forthrightly."

"Like what topics?" asked Big Terry suspiciously.

"Protecting the environment. Investigating food and drug safety. Making sure big business doesn't abuse the little guy," I replied. "Just like my hero... *Teddy Roosevelt.*"

Mrs. Stanton chuckled at my surprise answer, relieved at the crisis averted. Big Terry, checkmated if not outwitted in this verbal match, appeared satisfied by my answer. He returned to eating his peach cobbler.

Tricia loved my firm retort to her father, almost aroused by it.

"You were so amazing tonight," she purred in my ear as we left her house. "I've never seen anyone stand up to my father like that."

During our courtship, Tricia remained enamored by my dedication to journalism with a fervent idealism thoroughly embraced. At that time, American newspapers were still at a high-water mark, with intrepid reporters Woodward and Bernstein celebrated for bringing down a corrupt president. Becoming a journalist seemed an antidote to her father's world poisoned by money and cynicism.

Soon after our initial meeting, Tricia and I went on a double date to a Bruce Springsteen concert at Madison Square Garden. Elaine brought along an NYU dental school student she'd been dating named Gary Lubinsky. At the end of the show, Tricia invited us all back to her family's house, assuring us that her parents were away on vacation.

When we reached Old Westbury, slightly high and loose, the two couples chatted by the fireplace and then slipped off into different bedrooms. Without much hesitation, Tricia steered me to her parents' king-sized mattress, shimmied down her skirt, and unbuttoned her blouse. With her willowy hair, wide green eyes, and long, supple swimmer's body, Tricia possessed a natural beauty. Wearing only a provocative smile, she presented her impressive nakedness, especially her splendid breasts, as if expecting applause.

"Let's fuck, *honestly and forthrightly*," she whispered, another teasing reminder of the phrase I'd used to impress her father.

Instead of seizing the moment, I paused momentarily like a frightened schoolboy. I wondered if the state senator might show up unexpectedly, claim I was defiling his daughter, and call the cops.

"What's the matter?" Tricia leered as she pulled at my belt. "Did those Jesuits do a number on you?" She offered sex like a gift of mercy as well as a delight. We both laughed and swiftly jumped between her parents' sheets, spending the rest of the night there.

Tricia was part of Elaine's wide circle of sorority sisters, many of whom remained incredibly loyal and enthralled by her long after college was over. Tricia shared Elaine's sense of excitement and self-assured intelligence. Their world seemed full of promise, more than it had been for earlier generations of women, with a sense of equality even on matters of sex.

When I awoke around dawn, I wandered through the Stanton mansion, searching for Tricia and Elaine. Opening a large glass sliding door, I found them in the bubbling spa next to the heated swimming pool, jumping and splashing around *au naturel*. They urged me to drop my trousers and join them like one big backyard party, skinny-dipping in the morning.

"Don't be too loud, Gary's still sleeping," Elaine advised, the waterline just under her chin. She looked at Tricia and then turned to me. I quickly slipped into the warm waters.

"Wouldn't it be wonderful if we could live somewhere close to each other someday?" Elaine said to us. "It'd be so much fun as one big family."

For the next few years, all the way to the altar, Elaine assured Tricia and myself that we were the perfect couple, a match made in heaven. I never questioned Elaine's judgment. The wedding took place after Tricia earned a law degree and I graduated with a master's degree in journalism, both at Columbia. We were determined to make our mark in the world.

During the following decade, Tricia and I lived near Elaine and her husband Gary on Long Island, just as my cousin predicted. We both started to have kids and became ensconced in careers and family life. In retrospect, we had the misbegotten notion of trying to repeat the contented times of our parents' generation in the suburbs, an idyll that became increasingly impossible for us. By the new millennium, America had changed, particularly after the 9/11 terrorist attack, and financial pressures became enormous living in a place like Nassau County.

Coming out of school, both Tricia and I had accepted low-paying jobs, staying true to our intentions, but, inexorably, the world's material demands caught up with us. Tricia didn't earn much as a legal aid criminal defense attorney for the poor and indigent. It was hardly the kind of lucrative corporate law that her father Big Terry had envisioned for her. My paycheck was even worse. I supplemented my meager wages at a nonunion local newspaper by writing books at night as a way to pay the bills.

Money remained a grinding issue between Tricia and myself, but it wasn't the only source of friction. I barely spent time at home. Even when I was there, my mind seemed elsewhere, caught up in stories and my own ambitions. By age eight, my son could mimic my lack of attention when he asked a question to his preoccupied father and waited five minutes for a delayed response. My obsession with this Hollywood project and the desire to get a new job at *The New York World* only compounded these problems.

Tricia's unhappiness with me had spilled over a few years earlier, when she took a job with a high-powered real estate firm. She fell in love with its wealthy owner—an older man near sixty, but one who would pay far more attention to her than I ever did. Tricia redid everything in her life, including her newly enhanced figure by a plastic surgeon. Irretrievably, we were headed in separate directions.

When I was busy one night covering the 2012 Republican presidential primaries, Elaine called to let me know that Tricia planned a divorce but I made no effort to change the result. Soon after, Tricia left a message on my work voicemail with the name of her family law attorney. I didn't call her back. I already knew my dream of family was over.

In her hospital room, Elaine looked at the wall clock.

"You know, Tricia is coming here soon to see me," she said, scraping out the remains of breakfast from her fruit cup. "Are you OK with that?" She combed through her sparse hair, wrecked by the ravages of chemotherapy.

Unconvincingly, I said I was fine with seeing my ex-wife and tried to act nonplussed when Tricia arrived with our two kids. They scowled and only gave a kiss to their father at Elaine's insistence. Tricia said nothing beyond hello. I couldn't blame them.

At the height of this awkwardness, Elaine's husband Gary entered the room for his morning visit. Taking the train in from Long Island, he arrived with a bag containing Starbucks and some croissants, his wife's favorite. I gravitated into conversation with him. His tired eyes looked shaken with the kind of dread that a man feels when he knows his wife is dying.

The strained politeness and deep emotions weighed heavily in the room. Finally, Elaine offered a plan, a form of relief in the same generous, intuitively kind way she'd always done.

"Why don't you guys go play some golf?" she suggested surprisingly. "Gary hasn't been out all summer because of me, stuck here in this room. I know he'd really like to join you for a round. Or just hit a bucket of balls."

Everyone reflexively said no, rejecting the idea as inappropriate under the circumstances. At this critical moment, could there be anything more insipid than playing golf, knocking a dimpled ball around a manicured meadow?

Tricia glared at me, as if I was bucking my adult responsibilities once again. Certainly, she couldn't just sail off to someplace, not with two kids in tow.

But Elaine prevailed.

"I'm serious, Jack, you'd be doing me a favor to take Gary out golfing somewhere," Elaine insisted. "This way Tricia and I can catch up, knowing that you guys are out there having some fun." She adjusted the turban that hid her nearly bald head. "This way I can get Gary out of my hair—what's left of it."

We all smiled and nodded, careful not to upset Elaine. Before long, Gary and I were driving out to Nassau County, where we would golf not far from his home with Elaine, and near the place where I used to live with Tricia and the kids. Before going out on the links, we stopped briefly at Gary's house to pick up his clubs. I'd already packed my own set in the back of my rental in the vain hope of relaxing while in the Hamptons.

By nature, Gary was gregarious like Elaine, with the same humorous outlook. A lanky man with curly brown hair, he had played on the varsity golf team throughout high school and college. He retained his athleticism in middle age with only a slight pouch to his gut. After graduating from NYU, he became a dentist, known in our neighborhood as Dr. Lubinsky, though he was still Gary to me.

As we walked along the grassy fairways and putting greens, I tried to engage Gary in conversation. He seemed terribly distracted. Gary told me his mother was minding his kids—a boy and a girl, both in junior high—and that he couldn't play for long on the 18-hole course. After nine holes, Gary and I decided to quit and go no further. He wanted to go home.

When we arrived back at the parking lot, Gary started to take off his golf shoes and heave his bag into the opened trunk of my car. I followed along with my equipment and then looked up to see him staring at me.

"You know she's dying, don't you?" Gary exclaimed. "There's nothing more the doctors can do."

I slowly shook my head in agreement, though the pain of this impending tragedy overwhelmed any attempt to comment.

Gary's eyes filled with tears. For the first time in the twenty years that we'd known each other, he began to cry.

"I watch her hug the kids in the hospital room and she's so upbeat, so full of love," he moaned. "Asking them about their homework. Promising she'll come home again soon. But they sense the truth...."

His words landed with a dizzying impact. I couldn't help but think of how much Elaine had meant to my life as well. So much of the fun and laughter of growing up had been spent with her. Elaine had been my own rock when Tricia and I divorced and my own family exploded into a hundred million pieces.

I tried to lend comfort to Gary with the best words I could conjure up, though he remained distraught.

"The cancer is everywhere now, in her lungs, her lymph nodes," he said. "They tell me there's no hope. How do I tell my kids she won't be coming home?"

We stared at each other for a moment before entering the car. I slammed the trunk closed, my own kind of fury at how cruelly fate could intervene and steal away someone so vital as Elaine. Like my own parents' death, I wondered how a loving God could let her die at the apex of life, taking her away from the husband she adored and from watching her children grow into adulthood? What could I say to Gary? In my own life, I had failed miserably at finding any meaningful answer to the messy questions I steadfastly avoided. I always hid behind my transitory work as a reporter to get away from much deeper family obligations and tangled emotions. I planned to do so once again the next day in covering the latest presidential campaign.

For the rest of our ride, Gary gazed out the passenger's side window, lost in thought, as I drove him home in silence. As he exited the car, he thanked me politely and admitted something foremost on his mind.

"I don't know what I'll do when she's gone," he uttered with a harrowing glance. Then he walked into the empty house alone.

CHAPTER 8
"GET READY FOR THIS"

Before the candidate appeared, the pounding, deafening instrumental music inside the Mohegan Sun Arena in Wilkes-Barre, Pennsylvania, throbbed against the walls. It whipped up the screaming crowd into a frenzy of presidential anticipation.

"Y'all ready for this?!"

Over the loudspeakers for nearly an hour, the campaign's playlist featured a medley of songs, including "Get Ready For This"—a techno-syncopation tune often heard at professional wrestling matches. Other familiar chants and choruses from morning-drive radio followed. I recognized the Backstreet Boys, the Beatles, Elvis Presley, the Rolling Stones, Elton John, and, as an operatic outlier, Luciano Pavarotti bellowing "Nessun Dorma."

All were over-the-top anthems to what could be called *The Greatest Hits of Donald Trump*, the soundtrack to his seemingly impossible quest for the White House.

The Donald's Wall of Sound gave me pause as I entered the arena, overflowing with Trump placards waved by locals of Wilkes-Barre. Although only two hours from Manhattan, this part of Pennsylvania was very much in Heartland territory, a region filled with dairy farms, shuttered industries, and an all-purpose hockey stadium named for a casino racetrack in the nearby Poconos. For voters there, Election Day offered a Hobson's choice between one presidential candidate who looked down her nose at them as gun-totin', God-fearing "deplorables" or the other, a completely unqualified con man, who began his campaign as a joke and would attempt to fool an entire nation.

At that moment, however, the quizzical look on my face had more to do with where to find my seat than anything else.

"Let me see your press pass," demanded an usher, part of the obstacle course of security guards, metal detectors, and campaign staffers herding the media into a roped-off area in the back.

The usher grabbed the laminated pass hanging around my neck. He peered suspiciously at its tiny photo and whether it matched the middle-aged face in front of him. Officious in his gray uniform, he took his time before coming to any judgment.

"OK, you're in," he said imperiously. As I walked past, he added, "Just tell the truth, no fake news."

Such gratuitous code words, undoubtedly echoing some Fox News announcer, left a bad taste. I was tired of the sanctimonious and the scatterbrained throwing shade on how I'd spent my lifetime career.

"Tell me, do you know what truth is?" I asked pointedly.

The usher returned an empty stare. Perhaps I appeared too dressed up, in a blue jacket and striped tie, to erupt into a hockey-like fistfight. But my question apparently contained enough threat to make this turnstile bully think twice.

"Just kidding, buddy," he replied. "Nothing but a joke."

This encounter hit a nerve. During my interminable drive to Wilkes-Barre, I thought of the tumultuousness in my own life and all the uncertainty I found as I travelled throughout America, a country searching for a leader. I kept asking myself, *Is there such a thing as truth anymore?*

Certainly truth could be elusive, hard to nail down with just facts. Often it felt like a balloon, the overinflated kind that you once held as a kid, and then, in an instant, it slipped out of your hand and floated away into the sky, forever lost in the clouds.

Historically, Americans have searched for truth in a cornucopia of ways—from the baby boomer favorites of drugs, sex, and rock-and-roll to the hidebound rituals of religion, politics, and greed. The media, as a mirror of this society, relied on a collection of empirical truths—"factoids" gleaned from government releases or "sound bites" from press conferences—rather than search for one metaphysical, uppercase Truth.

My own search was a winding, varied journey between the two. In college, the Jesuits taught that eternal verities could be found by improving the human condition, by finding Christ in each wretched soul. The sins of the institutional Church could make it hard to defend, let alone embrace. Yet without some heavenly northern star, the universe appeared evermore dark and chaotic. At Columbia, the journalism professors preached a gospel of secular truths. "If your mother says she loves you, check it out," advised my favorite teacher. The purpose of journalism was to open minds, this professor said, and "to make the agony of decision-making so intense that you can escape only by thinking."

I believed in the nobility of journalism, dedicating one's life to informing the public, even if it didn't pay very much. "Character isn't something you'll see in your paycheck but rather in the mirror," the dean told us at graduation. "Character teaches you to stand up to personal threats or legal challenges, to champion the rights of those less fortunate, without power or money, and to force your news organization to publish when cowardly editors and publishers prefer that your story go away." The dean even advised we stash away some "fuck you money" if we had to quit on principle.

My real education, though, began on the job as a workaday reporter. I discovered people in power often lied profusely. Lies were their second nature, obscuring the truth for their own purposes. As the 2016 election campaign heated up, journalism's usual equivocal approach ("but on the other hand, Mr. Hitler says...") seemed inadequate for the times. Truth and lies were beginning to mix imperceptibly, insidiously, and contagiously.

Throughout American history, the absence of truth has led always to political corruption—a pastime as familiar as baseball, shattering as the crack in the Liberty Bell, and chaotic as shooting off Fourth of July fireworks. Certainly this tradition of all-American duplicity was evident in the classic power grab by Austin Corbin against the Montauk nation.

To my eyes, the phoniness and greed of fast-talking Corbin, a tycoon from the nineteenth century, seemed very much alive in the Twitter-hyped modern candidacy of Donald Trump, as if they were related by blood as much as greed. Both were men of sizable girth, with egg-shaped physiques and perennial scowls on their faces. Each wore distinctive attire (Corbin with his wide-lapel suede coat and Trump with his red tie aglow), a look that became their calling cards. Both men wrapped their ambitious schemes in their own kind of mythmaking, aided and abetted by a complaisant press.

Watching Trump on the giant television screens above the arena, I was struck by the blind devotion his followers showed him. At his political rallies, Trump encouraged fistfights and advocated sending his likely competitor, Hillary Clinton, to jail. At its worst, these angry conclaves threatened a kind of political carnage, inciting people to commit acts that they might not have done ordinarily. As I watched the crowd stirred by the sight of their hero, I wondered whether violence might strike tonight in Wilkes-Barre.

"Who's going to vote for Trump?" asked the candidate. Surrounding him were thousands wearing hats and T-shirts bearing his name, with signs that proclaimed, "The Silent Majority Stands with Trump," in red, white, and blue.

The answer came back with a roar. Trump gave a thumbs-up sign and unctuous smile. He projected the kind of false sincerity shared by used car dealers as duped customers drive off in a jalopy.

"We're going to make that the best vote you ever cast—I promise you," said Trump, his voice echoing throughout the arena. "Make America Great, folks, remember that."

With his froggy voice and hammy gestures, Trump went through a litany of claims and counterclaims, filled with exaggerations and lies, his stock-in-trade. His message of America the Invaded—with "caravans" of unwanted immigrants approaching the Mexican border—inflamed the crowd.

"We haven't even started with Crooked Hillary yet," he said, to another wave of applause. Trump and his audience reveled in conspiracy theories about rigged elections.

Quickly, I started sending electronic notes about Trump's speech to the politics desk at *The World*, my new employer in Manhattan. During the campaign, *The World* would fact-check many Trump assertions that needed clarification—if not complete correction. As a recent hire, I was sent to Wilkes-Barre to be the eyes and ears on the scene, offering little tidbits of information with no Olympian prognostication.

My iPhone erupted with its familiar marimba tune, and I answered. Through my earbuds, I could hear Hattie Thompson's voice back in New York.

"Trump is saying there's six thousand people outside the arena waiting to get in—is that true?" she asked without a hello.

"Maybe a thousand, maybe two, I don't know for sure," I said. "But there were a lot of people on line when I came in."

I could hear Hattie typing rapidly in the background.

"You know Wilkes-Barre was won by Obama four years ago," she said. "It usually goes to the Democrats."

"I guess they found a new champ tonight," I replied.

A long silence ensued, broken only by her constant typing. "OK, thanks," Hattie finally said. She was gone in a flash.

Hattie didn't need to apologize for her rudeness. We had been friends for years, dating back to my former employer. In the early 2000s, we worked together on an investigative team that won numerous prizes. A reporting workhorse, Hattie was brilliant in exposing political corruption, environmental threats, and a wide swath of societal ills. Our crusading editor, a former foreign correspondent who covered the 1990s Gulf War, inspired us and shared our journalistic verities, until the internet and Great Recession carved the heart out of the newspaper business. The out-of-town corporate owners of our chain of newspapers fired the editor and looked to squeeze out every penny of possible profit.

Throughout America, many newspapers collapsed, leaving government ignored, ripe for abuse, and opening the door for demagogues on social media. With my idealism fading, I carried on as my paper shrunk and my paycheck dwindled. Hattie left on principle and wound up in the big-time, covering presidential politics.

Aware of my predicament at our old paper, Hattie convinced the editors of *The World* to hire me two years after she arrived. She assured them of my commitment to journalism, even though she knew vaguely of my novel-writing and television interests. *The World,* with its national and international focus, was able to add staff by building up an online audience, many of whom were galvanized by the looming possibility of a Trump presidency.

After covering New York for years, Hattie and I were well-acquainted with Trump, the real estate tycoon-turned-TV creature who craved media attention. I remembered meeting him many years earlier in Atlantic City, New Jersey, on what might have been the worst day of his life up until that point. On a chilly and damp day in the 1990s, I attended a state hearing about the expiring license for The Donald's ailing Taj Mahal casino-hotel, then drowning in debt. His future seemed over, his empire crumbling. Despite many questions about his finances, Trump's lawyer, in a virtuoso performance, overcame the regulators' serious doubts and gained another year's renewal.

After watching the near-miraculous rabbit pulled out of a hat by Trump, I never again doubted his ability to stretch the truth or avoid its repercussions.

"I feel great," Trump told me after the vote, standing out on the empty boardwalk with another reporter. "We're confident that we will be able to meet all the deadlines."

I scribbled down his response. Who knew if Trump was lying, I wondered? The only tell-tale sign seemed to be his breath. After this near-death financial inquisition about the Taj Mahal, where he and his lawyer were grilled for hours, Trump had the worst case of halitosis I ever encountered. Enough stench, as one comic used to say, to knock a buzzard off a shit wagon. Years later, I laughed to myself, remembering Trump's trench mouth as thousands cheered his image on the giant screen at the Wilkes-Barre arena.

As a presidential candidate, Trump posed a different threat to the public. No longer was he just a casino owner or the Manhattan businessman who treated friendly reporters as shills for his self-promotion. Candidate Trump had turned the media into an enemy, *the* enemy. In his rambling speech, Trump aimed his bile at the row of television cameras, network correspondents, and print reporters herded together in the back.

"I've been watching these dishonest people, some of the world's most dishonest people," Trump told the crowd, indicting the entire press corps with a single pointed finger. "They never show the crowds. We have the biggest crowds by far." More cheers came from his devoted followers. They were the same hero-worshippers that Trump claimed would still love him if he shot somebody in the middle of Fifth Avenue. "Look at that up there, at the upper deck, all those people up there," Trump stage-directed to the TV cameras. "Why don't you show it, you dishonest media?"

Eventually, I finished sending my dispatch from Wilkes-Barre. I had never seen such an angry crowd at a political rally. Trump's provocations with their sinister overtones—and the way his crowd lapped it up—left me feeling queasy and revolted. My ears were still ringing and my mind numbed. I wondered how far we were from witnessing an American *Kristallnacht.* Before the rabid festivities were fully over, I headed out a back door and started driving home to New York.

The potential for violence soon manifested itself as the crowd left the arena. I later learned one of Trump's supporters came up to a cable TV news crew, who was packing up their equipment in the back of the arena, and started shoving them. Punches were thrown. A man wearing a red MAGA hat lifted a chair high over his head threateningly and then destroyed two cameras used to record the event. Police quickly stopped the fracas, but a video snippet from it later made the national news as one of Trump's highlights for the day.

By the time I neared the George Washington Bridge, Hattie called me again on my cell to ask if I knew anything about this violent incident. I equivocated with her and avoided the truth: I was glad I'd missed it.

CHAPTER 9
ON PROBATION

Early the next morning, I returned the rental and took a subway car to the labyrinthine Times Square station. In this underground hall of noise and constant motion, musicians of every vibe performed for a few handouts, while commuters danced around each other on their way to another destination. An alphabet soup of subway-line signs led them to points all around the city.

Climbing a stairway to the street, I headed to *The World's* nearby office. A cool breeze off the Hudson River was smothered by the hot, stilted air between the Port Authority Bus Terminal and the newspaper building's looming white facade, enough to make anyone sweat. In my mind, I anticipated trouble from my Wilkes-Barre trip and resolved to face it head-on.

Though *The World* didn't enforce a dress code, expectations demanded that a reporter like myself "look professional." I wore a blue jacket, white button-down shirt, khaki pants, and muted tie. None of my previous employers cared about my appearance. But at this paper of record, an assortment of subeditors and management types all wore some kind of Brooks Brothers office uniform, one that made them indistinguishable from hedge-fund financiers and the bond sellers on Wall Street.

A few years ago, aware of my advancing age, I adopted my own modified shirt-and-tie uniform, determined to appear more like a serious adult than a college kid in a sweater. Recently, though, I added an accessory just for fun: a tan straw fedora. Wearing a hat was a touch of youthful gaiety to break up my own monotony and cover my receding hairline. The summer before, I had picked up the brimmed hat in a Banana Republic store and worn it to a *Great Gatsby*-themed party in the Hamptons for middle-aged singles. I didn't bring it to work until today. It would serve as my helmet, to shield me from any office warfare.

"What's with the hat?" asked Hattie Thompson, already hard at work.

More than any reporter I knew, Hattie worked the phones like a virtuoso. She chatted conspiratorially with sources on her headset, while two rectangular monitors above her laptop were aglow with typed sentences. *The World's* website, with its constant nonstop deadlines, left little time to think, only react.

"Hey, it's summertime," I countered, playing with the straw brim like a dandy. "I thought the hat made me look a bit younger. Closer to thirty than over forty. What do you think?"

Hattie wasn't amused.

"I think you better look out for Williams, he's pretty annoyed with you about Wilkes-Barre," she warned.

Jamal Williams, the political editor, had hired me on Hattie's recommendation. A short, squat man with a curated beard, Williams had worked in several bureaus and won a Pulitzer Prize for international reporting before ascending in the paper's hierarchy. Early in his career, Williams had been known to party heartily, supposedly sniffing cocaine once with a governor's son. But Hattie warned me that our boss was now a reformed teetotaler, hardly tolerant of any addiction except work.

At *The World*, keeping track of editors' names on the masthead was a popular occupation, both within the newsroom and especially outside, similar to Kremlin tea leaf-watching among Russian scholars. At age thirty-five, younger than much of his staff, Williams was an up-and-comer. He didn't like to be embarrassed at the morning news meeting when asked by superiors why the paper's coverage of Trump in Wilkes-Barre missed the biggest story coming out of that event.

As foretold, Williams soon appeared. He stopped at Hattie's desk and stared straight at me, looking for an explanation.

"About Wilkes-Barre last night," Williams began, in the kind of bloodless tone they teach in management training. "Hattie mentioned that you thought the Trump event was over when you left the arena. I guess, technically, it was done, before the fighting busted out. But we should have had that story. Trump's rallies have become dangerous for the press with all these threats of intimidation."

Williams motioned to his star reporter. "Hattie's doing a catch-up today," he stated. "Are you OK with that?"

There was no sense arguing. I nodded and apologized meekly, like a bad boy in day camp. My punishment was the lack of another assignment on the campaign trail, at least for now. Williams wouldn't mention anything to me for the rest of the day. Rather than push the point, I mentioned another matter on my agenda before he walked away, far more important in my eyes than his.

"Look Jamal, I'm going to be away for ten days, starting this Wednesday, and I just..."

"Something wrong?" Williams interjected. "Hattie told me that things aren't going well for you at home. If you need some time..."

"No, no, that's not it," I said, stopping him. I was a bit offended by Hattie's sharing my personal problems with the boss, and a bit amused by Jamal's attempt as staff psychologist.

"They're making a TV project based on my novel, *The Life Line*, out in the Hamptons," I explained. "And I'm supposed to be there for some of the filming."

Williams's eyes deadened. For the first time in this conversation, he appeared genuinely annoyed but didn't say a word. How could anything be more important than covering Trump for *The World*?

After an awkward pause, I reminded him that the paper's top bosses had approved this short hiatus when I was hired, along with the other time I had already spent in Montauk. Apparently they didn't tell Williams about this extra ten days or he forgot about it. He walked away in a huff.

"What's wrong with you?" Hattie remonstrated, a witness to this testy exchange. "Are you trying to get yourself fired? You're still on probation."

Hattie was undoubtedly correct about my status. She had superb journalistic instincts, which made her an ideal collaborator in the past. When we worked on investigative pieces at our old place, she threatened to quit if the bosses wavered. Once, she walked out for forty-eight hours in self-exile when a story about a favored advertiser was killed. When she asked the top editor about why it hadn't appeared, this editor replied euphemistically, "It doesn't work."

"What do you mean, '*It doesn't work*'?" Hattie demanded. She didn't let go until the editor capitulated.

At our old paper, Hattie's bravery in searching for truth was far greater than my own. I marveled at how she stuck up for her stories and never showed any signs of cowardice, a common affliction among journalists toiling in corporate newsrooms. Once when I asked Hattie if she worried about getting fired for challenging the powerful, she fobbed off any concern. "Nah, I say, 'fuck 'em if they can't take a joke,'" she laughed.

Since then, life had changed for both of us. At age forty, Hattie was married to another ex-staffer from our former paper, had moved to suburban Westchester, and was trying to balance her home life with two kids and her full-time, high-profile job. She adopted a more serious mien, speaking in a deliberative, lower tone than I remembered. At work, she now favored modern designer clothes, pearls, and tortoise-shell glasses—unlike the denim jeans and hippie granny-style eyeglasses from the past.

Although still an aggressive reporter, prolific on the presidential campaign trail, Hattie learned to become more diplomatic inside the newsroom. She paid great deference to the paper's own power figures, including Jamal Williams, who adored her in return. Her byline appeared often on the front page, and she was invited regularly on television. She earned well over $200,000 annually and wondered aloud how *The World's* new digital strategy would affect her 401K.

Backing my bid to join the paper was a calculated risk for Hattie, done out of loyalty from the past, which she probably now regretted. I couldn't conceal my doubts about staying in journalism. What Jamal Williams (and probably Hattie too) perceived as my rank fuck-up in Wilkes-Barre was my quiet refusal to go along with Trump's dishonest campaign. In its early days, print reporters and television commentators, even those who knew better, were suckered into repeating his blend of lies and half-truths. What I had witnessed in Wilkes-Barre would be repeated dozens of times during the course of his campaign—with an accelerating effectiveness. The constant tweeting, "bots" of unknown origin, and a world of internet conspiracy theories became the main news diet of the gullible and ignorant. I didn't want to be taken for a ride on his bandwagon, complicit in his blatant tomfoolery leading to the White House.

For all of his outrageousness, however, Trump was good copy for political reporters like Hattie, offering up easy and accessible quotes guaranteed to lead the top of the news. Around the country, this billionaire portrayed himself as a Middle-American Everyman, as if he served tap beer and Big Macs to his Mar-a-Lago clientele. Trump's impromptu speeches, especially when he wandered away from the teleprompter, oozed with nostalgia, faux intimacy, and underlying rancor, like some drive-time talk-radio host.

Left unexamined were darker aspects of Trump's background, like his invisible tax dodges and the many claims about his philandering. Months earlier, Hattie and I talked about writing a book together about Trump's sordid history, until she got the sense that *The World's* editors would frown on such a venture. Traditionally, high-minded political reporters at *The World*, nearly all men, felt it too distasteful to sort through claims of sexual harassment and aggression. They preferred to look the other way. Hattie realized she should do the same if she wanted to climb up the paper's masthead.

"Why isn't *The World* checking out these claims by women who say Trump grabbed and groped them?" I complained privately to her shortly after being hired. I thought Hattie would lead the charge, but I was wrong.

"We are examining them, on a case-by-case basis, as we should," Hattie replied, like a state-department spokesperson. Immediately, she realized this weak explanation wasn't good enough among old friends. She laughed and gave me a gentle push.

"C'mon Jack, *seriously*," she implored. "Do you really think people are surprised about The Donald's behavior? Especially anyone who's read the New York tabloids for the past thirty years? Besides, Jack, you're getting involved with Hollywood. Supposedly that's *way worse* than Manhattan or Washington!"

I now regretted letting Hattie know of my television tie-in book deal with Max Kirkland. She intimated that money had blinded my judgment.

But to me, Kirkland's TV adaptation of the Austin Corbin scandal was fresh and exciting, almost intoxicating, and he sold me completely. In his rendering, the deep-pocketed streamers like Comflix offered a kind of freedom that young movie makers enjoyed in the 1970s, when the old studios collapsed and a new generation made memorable films that broke the traditional mold. In the same way, Max wanted to take my book and turn it into a contemporary work of cinematic art, appealing to the binge-watching audience at home.

This was heady stuff compared to print. I realized shrinking American newspapers, even the best, had a diminishing impact on the public, their reputation for truth-telling compromised by online outlets that emphasized clicks over facts. At this point, I wanted to be my own boss as a writer, not a hack beholden to some corporation. Much of my career had been spent working for newspapers owned by billionaires oblivious to the vast disparities in the country. Like *The Wizard of Oz*, some owners were good witches, but most were bad. They cheated their workers with diminishing wages and the public with fewer news pages. Once-thriving papers were now called "zombie" publications, with most of their readers dead and gone.

In this new reality, many journalists buried their heads or made excuses, either for the paycheck or to curry favor. I felt I could no longer be part of this deception. I counted on the upcoming release of *The Life Line* to provide my escape.

For the remainder of that afternoon, I sat at my office desk in solitude, temporarily banished from covering the campaign. I kept reading the paper's coverage on its website, pretending to be busy. Unexpectedly, at the end of the workday, another colleague stopped by.

"I heard from Hattie that they're making a television series from your novel—congratulations, that's *awesome*," said Anna Melendez, a multimedia producer for the paper. "You probably don't know me—I'm Anna," she added, extending her hand.

Melendez was one of several young podcast programmers, code writers, and "multiplatform" news producers hired to slowly replace the dying breed of older print reporters. To show off her abilities, she decided to write a piece for the Sunday feature section about books turned into programming for the emerging television streamers. She wanted to ask me about *The Life Line* project.

With the hour nearing six, I invited her to join me for a drink at a nearby bar and grill, often frequented by the paper's staff. She agreed and my dour mood brightened, ready for a change in my disposition. Early in my career, an older editor offered two pieces of archaic but seemingly sage advice: "Never write a headline longer than a newspaper boy can shout in one breath" and "Don't get involved with the women in the office." At that time, I was already married to Tricia and laughed off this unsolicited advice the same way that I, as a nonsmoker, brushed cigarette ashes off a seat along the rewrite desk.

But now, as a divorced, middle-aged man, the prospect of getting involved with a younger female colleague seemed appealing, a challenging voyage into unknown territory. As we walked together, I focused on encouraging her to talk about herself.

"Tell me, Anna, where did you grow up?" I asked, sounding more like Mister Rogers than a candidate for a one-night stand.

By the time we sat down for a drink, inside a booth facing each other, Anna had turned the conversation back to business. She asked some perfunctory questions about me and writing my novel, but it became evident her main interest was Max Kirkland.

"Last summer, we produced a video for *The World* at his Lions Head mansion, and Max and Tatiana showed us all around," she said. "It's quite a place."

With fangirl devotion, Melendez described filming one of the Kirklands' lavish summer parties in the Hamptons attended by many celebrities, politicians, and well-known personalities. "I felt like I was in a Gatsby novel," she mentioned. "Do you know much about where Kirkland came from? What's he like?"

I shared how Kirkland had orchestrated the filming of the big shipwreck scene in *The Life Line* and how the upcoming television series was derived from my book. But, in reality, I didn't know much about Kirkland, only his apocryphal Horatio Alger story about being a poor kid who came to Hollywood and made good.

"Max is a bit of a mystery to me," I admitted, "but the fate of *The Life Line* is in his hands." I often described my relation to Kirkland this way.

In the dim light of the bar, as she stroked the stem of her wineglass with her fingers, Anna looked increasingly attractive. I watched her glossy, rounded lips as she posed questions and parsed every word of my replies. Her fulsome, honey-colored hair shined and her eyes glimmered. Though we were twenty years apart in age, my mind fantasized for a moment that she might find me attractive.

"I wondered if we might..." I began.

Her mind was somewhere else. "Do you think this television project will further victimize the Montaukett tribe, which has been long seeking government recognition as a tribe?" she interjected.

The question caught me by surprise. Defensively, I rejected her premise.

"I don't know what you're talking about. It was my investigative work, a series of stories years ago for my old paper, that showed how Austin Corbin stole the Native American lands for his railroad. The Montauketts have cited my stories in the legal papers to get tribal recognition."

Anna wasn't impressed.

"Do you think your novel expropriates the story of an indigenous people for your own purposes?" she asked, continuing her line of questioning.

"Look, I don't know what you're talking about," I replied. "All I know is that *The Life Line* was bought by a big streamer and now it's Max Kirkland's problem."

The conversation quickly ended and we both went our separate ways after leaving the bar. I walked back to my pied-à-terre apartment in the Flatiron District—established in the waning days of my marriage to Tricia—and grumbled how I had been sandbagged by a reporter from my own newspaper, more concerned with politics than art. I wondered if I should call someone at Comflix and let them know about this hit job being prepared at my own paper.

By the time I reached my building and climbed up two flights of stairs, I had simmered down and thought better of any extreme measures. There was no need to alert Comflix's PR people to a critical attack that might never materialize. Besides, the memory of Anna's good looks at the bar, her insinuating manner, and the lingering lust of a middle-aged man without a mate got the better of me. Impulsively, I pulled out the cell phone number Anna had given me at the start of our conversation. I texted her with an apology in my own fashion: *"Sorry, I wanted to talk more about hanging out than work. Maybe we can get together soon and try it again?"*

I pressed the green "send" button and heard the phone's whooshing sound as the message went expressly on its way. Despite my friendly overture, I would soon forget about this text and Anna herself.

Getting home late, I looked inside my empty refrigerator for something to eat and instead poured myself another drink. I turned on the television, hoping to catch up with the news, and heard an arriving new text, blinking on my cell phone. This message, from my frustrated divorce attorney, caught me by surprise once again: *"Your child support hearing is next week. Your ass needs to be there!"*

CHAPTER 10
CHANGING FASHIONS

Rather than face my workplace reality in Manhattan, I drove out the next morning to Montauk, where Max Kirkland's television troupe was making steady progress with my fiction. The schedule called for a shoot at the Montauk railroad station, a flashpoint in Austin Corbin's eighteenth-century scheme, though the weather wasn't cooperating.

When I arrived around 11 a.m., Kirkland stood underneath a tarpaulin tent, sipping coffee and busily talking shop with a few members of the crew. He wore a Yankees cap and a bright yellow slicker dampened by raindrops, which continued to stream off the tarp. Max nodded hello from a distance and asked Penny MacPharland to approach me and explain their next step.

"Sorry it's a rainout today," MacPharland said when I rolled down my car's window. "It's supposed to clear up later this afternoon, but we decided to call it a day and pick it up again tomorrow. Maybe we'll see you later at the Montauk Manor."

A bit dejected, I thanked MacPharland and left. For the next hour or so, I wandered aimlessly along the local roadways until I gravitated towards the Montauk Point Lighthouse. This grand tower and building, sanctioned by George Washington in the 1790s, stood high on a hill as a white-and-red-brick fortress against the sea. "You haven't been to the lighthouse? You really must see it," I remember Vanessa Adams rapturously telling me in bed a few weeks earlier.

My wandering car seemed to follow her command. I parked and watched scores of visitors—the camera-toting tourists emerging from their

SUVs, the joyous schoolchildren and their mindful teachers leaving yellow buses—as they entered the national historic landmark. I paid for an admission ticket and joined them.

Following the crowd, I came to the base of the 111-foot lighthouse and gazed above at its glass-enclosed lantern with the black cast-iron roof. From afar, I stared at the pounding Atlantic Ocean waves against the rocks, a reminder of the earth's eternal pulsing. I thought of the ships and schooners coming from Europe two centuries ago and how the shiny beacon from this lighthouse guided them away from destruction and towards New York City's harbor.

"Are you in line to climb up into the tower?" asked an older woman in a gray national parks uniform.

"No thank you, not this time," I deferred, not mentioning my acrophobia and my unwillingness to put myself in high places.

Instead, I ventured through the landmark's museum and into a room devoted to shipwrecks. The broken ships and nautical disasters reminded me of Max Kirkland's recreated television shipwreck scene as well as something Vanessa Adams told me while driving together. Along with her discourse about Indian spirits roaming the land, she mentioned the ghost of a shipwreck survivor named "Abigail" that supposedly inhabited the Montauk lighthouse. In December 1811, seventeen-year-old Abigail Olsen had washed up alive beneath the lighthouse, the only survivor of a ship lost in the Atlantic, but lingering injuries caused her death on Christmas Day.

"They say Abigail cries out at night in the lighthouse tower and some have felt her presence," Vanessa recalled as we drove together to the recent party at the Kirkland mansion. "I believe spirits can come back to haunt. Don't you, Jack?"

I couldn't restrain my doubt.

"Sorry, I don't believe in ghosts or spirits—holy or otherwise."

The thought of seeing Vanessa again, perhaps reappearing at the Montauk Manor, prompted my early exit from the lighthouse museum. By the time I arrived in my manor room, much of the afternoon had elapsed. I replayed a voicemail left on my cell phone and was startled to hear Max's gruff voice.

"Hey Denton, we have an extra ticket to Tatiana's TV runway show tonight in the city. We thought you might like to join us. If you want to come along, text Penny and be at my place by four thirty. See you then."

Max correctly judged my interest. With less than an hour away from his deadline, I alerted MacPharland and then jumped into the shower, put on fresh clothes and a jacket, and arrived just in time to park my car in Max's huge driveway. A Cadillac Escalade with a driver awaited. Max rushed out of the mansion with Tatiana on his arm and Penny MacPharland by his side.

"Haha, I thought you might like to see all those pretty models, Jack!" Max chuckled. His driver placed us neatly one at a time into the limo. I assumed the ride from Montauk to Manhattan would be nearly three hours or so, but the Escalade soon stopped at a local helicopter pad, where one of Max's leased birds was humming and waiting to fly us into the city.

I said nothing about acrophobia and followed them into the helicopter. Up in the air, my sudden pang of fear, the swirling sense of falling to the ground and being lost in the twilight sky, became quite noticeable across my face.

"You're not afraid of heights, are you?" Penny asked, sensing my discomfort.

"No, not really...." I replied, trying hard not to look down through the windows. "Well, maybe just a little."

Max seemed amused by my tortured response. Tatiana was preoccupied with this big night for her television production firm, the season finale of her popular fashion show. With the loud hum of the helicopter engine, she stared ahead and focused intensely on her cell phone conversation with Diana Trumbull, the fashion editor who was also a regular featured player on her show.

After we landed, Tatiana's entourage quickly made our way to the makeshift studio created at Bryant Park, behind the city's main library. A big white tent had been erected and the television cameras were in place. Still an hour away from the videotaping with an audience, Tatiana and Trumbull went over their last-minute business details. Both were in memorable dresses given to them by friendly clothiers.

Max took a seat in a front row, waiting for the other celebrities and notables to arrive. MacPharland and I found a place in the back row, where Penny explained the intricacies of what I was about to witness.

On the air, Diana Trumbull presided as the show's cheery moderator, encouraging all the designer wannabes. Meanwhile, Tatiana acted as the imperious queen, presiding over a row of judges composed of brand-name clothes makers and often actresses from Max's current or previous films. Penny told me that they planned to feature Kiara Manchester, a star of *The Life Line*, on the judges panel for next season's premier. For a moment, I wondered if Vanessa Adams might appear on this runway, given her chumminess with Max, but didn't ask.

As we watched the crowd trickle in, Penny gave me a detailed explanation. Unlike the other runway shows, *Fashions with Tatiana Kirkland* relied on an algorithm-based computer system in which viewers with an *FWTK* app could easily and quickly order marked-down, mass-market versions of the *haute couture* clothing seen on the show. One click, and throughout America's heartland, there was a delivery the next day at the doorstep. Many winners became top sellers after being promoted in Diana's glossy fashion magazine.

Five years earlier, Tatiana and Trumbull had recruited a hedge-fund investor to become their silent partner in their rapidly expanding fashion business, which they touted as an exquisite blend of commerce and good taste. Max's friend, reality show producer Zach Preston, helped them find a cable network for their show. Like Max, Preston was also an investor in their firm and served as an executive producer along with them.

The show became a hit because of Tatiana's dishing out of curt and awkwardly funny appraisals of the clothing displayed by some contestants on the runway. Her slashing comments could be cruel but satiated the at-home audience's need for blood.

"That ensemble looks like roadkill," she chided one contestant with an overwrought entry, who responded as if she'd been stabbed. Without clueing in her TV audience, Tatiana also played favorites, especially when some of the clothes worn by models and aspiring actresses were from her own company.

While Tatiana's comments were caustic on TV, Diana Trumbull's were muted. She had toiled at Harper's Bazaar but didn't have that cutting edge of Paris couture like other top editors. With her warm smile, she appeared more like a Midwestern BFF, the smart and stylish neighbor next door that women wished for in their dreams. In their show's good-cop, bad-cop routine, Tatiana had become famous for being the infinitely demanding one, saying "*au revoir*" abruptly to losing contestants in their TV competition. To the press, she offered vapid epigrams like after-dinner mints. "Only a woman can define herself," she proclaimed, along with her favorite—"The religion of New York is money, and fashions are its vestments." The press ate them up.

Despite her regal White Russian bearing and distaste for crowds, Tatiana sounded determined to break down America's social strata with her own stylized form of capitalism. "There is no class divide without division" was another of her much-quoted adages. That phrase found its way embroidered onto a chemise in her online collection, which looked to my eyes like a high-priced T-shirt.

"Max realizes Tatiana is a better businessman than he is and he's really proud of her success," MacPharland insisted. "She's made millions."

The symbiotic interconnections of the Kirkland empire were one of many fascinating aspects of the evening.

"Look who's here—isn't that Trump's daughter?" Penny asked, pointing to a young blonde being seated in the front row next to Max. MacPharland hated being unsure. "Isn't that the one married to the creepy guy? Or is that the other one?"

I was no help. Although Trump used his family as props during his early 2016 political rallies, I still couldn't place all the names —Ivanka and Tiffany or is it Melania and Ivana?—with their faces. Given Hollywood's view of Trump, I was surprised his daughter was placed beside Max. But it ensured that she'd be seen in the cutaway audience reaction shots during the show.

"I thought Max didn't like Trump," I inquired.

MacPharland frowned. "Tatiana loves Trump, especially all those Teutonic bad-boy faces he keeps making on the campaign trail," she corrected. "Both Tatiana and Max and Diana Trumbull went to Trump's wedding years ago, so they must like one another."

Then MacPharland laughed to herself, as if she had figured out something. "Max told me to get another extra ticket—now I know who it's for."

Soon the house lights dimmed, the stage lights went up, and the show began with its familiar theme song. Tatiana emerged from behind a curtain to sustained applause. She introduced her panel of judges and then, with great flourish, welcomed the finished creations for this final runway show.

Most of the entrants offered models wearing their best from spring and fall collections. However, one contestant, Charles St. Pierre, a moody but brilliant Jamaican designer (who told Trumbull on camera backstage that he self-identified as pansexual), presented a decidedly warm weather outfit.

His female model, a pale, albino-looking Swede with a flat patch of bleached blonde hair and bright rouge lipstick, wore a cutaway bikini made of black leather, with high matching boots, a studded choker, and a stiff-tassel whip that seemed like a walking stick—a decidedly S&M look in a field of milquetoast also-rans. With such a bold move, St. Pierre sought to win this contest by shocking the crowd and at-home onlookers.

The audience, in a hush, waited for Tatiana's reaction. From the discreet television monitors up on the ceiling, I could see the cameras moving in for a close-up. Tatiana squeezed the moment for all its drama. Like a TV high priestess, she finally signaled her verdict.

"As Coco Chanel once said, 'In order to be irreplaceable, one must always be different,'" she said, pausing some more until she proclaimed, "I *love* it."

The crowd roared its approval. As the show's amiable wash-and-wear moderator, Diana Trumbull smiled into the lens and reacted with delight. She turned to the electronic graphics, projected on a green screen nearby, that gauged the television audience's immediate reaction. The instant call-in orders for this product sealed the win for St. Pierre in the season finale of the show, the *vox populi* of TV fashion. It would surely earn plenty of purchases for the company that Trumbull and the Kirklands owned together.

After the taping, Tatiana and Diana were ebullient, sipping champagne in fluted glasses provided by their assistant producers. Confident of their success, this night would prove to be one of their highest-rated shows ever.

"You must get Kiara to wear that outfit for the cover of your magazine," Max enthused to Trumbull and his wife as they walked over to the emptied front row.

"Oh yes, you must," Tatiana seconded.

"Do you think she'd do it?" Trumbull wondered.

"I'll make sure she does," Max said. "Kiara will do whatever's best for our show. It's in my contract with her."

Both Diana and Tatiana, as business partners, seemed pleased. "I can already see the cover with Kiara in black leather," said Diana. "I'm sure it will be a bestseller on the newsstands, a real winner!"

To my surprise, Max soon indicated he'd be staying for the night in the city. Years ago, he had purchased his own kind of pied-à-terre apartment at Trump Tower on Fifth Avenue with the insider help of Max's friend, Zach Preston, who brokered the deal. As an aside, MacPharland told me she, too, would be spending the night elsewhere in Manhattan. Apparently, both knew models or starlets in the cast to spend the night with.

As an afterthought, MacPharland said a limo would take Tatiana and myself back to the Kirklands' Hamptons mansion. I was a bit relieved, knowing that I wouldn't have to go up in the air in Max's whirlybird and that I'd be returned to where my rental was parked.

After such a triumphant night, it seemed awkward getting into the back of the limo with Tatiana, spending the next two hours by ourselves in a high-speed trek to the East End. Hurtling out of the Midtown Tunnel, with several Long Island Expressway exit signs rushing by, Tatiana gazed broodingly through the side windows. She seemed as much alone in the car as she was with me.

In the shadows, I watched her face move subtly, a beautiful mask still caked in TV makeup. Tatiana claimed she needed to be out in the Hamptons the following morning for a museum meeting, something about an abstract artist retrospective at Guild Hall. But Max's absence was keenly felt.

The Kirklands remained an enigma to me, especially what drew them together as a couple. I began to feel sorry for Tatiana, for reasons I couldn't express. I remained her quiet companion until finally called upon.

"Are you married, Jack?" she asked.

"No, I just got divorced."

"Do you have any children?"

"A girl and a boy. Why do you ask?"

Tatiana expressed apologies for the personal nature of her inquiry. She seemed intent on prying into the existential nature of things.

"What do you think men want from the women in their lives?" she asked.

"You mean, like, their wives?"

"That's right."

I thought of my own situation. "Mostly… loyalty."

"Really? Would you say you were loyal to your wife?"

I didn't want to be reminded of my own behavior. "She left me for an older, richer man—I had no choice."

"So you were a cuckold," she decided, her accent particularly prominent. "Where my family comes from, a man would exact revenge for stealing his wife. Cut the bastard's throat."

"And what about a woman?" I asked.

"Women must learn to look the other way, even when they know for sure. It is not good to dwell on matters where you have no power. That, unfortunately, is the nature of things. I don't want to know where Max is tonight. I don't care. He can take care of himself. He's a big boy, as the Americans say. As long as he doesn't hurt someone, especially me. That I would not forgive."

"Would you forgive Trump?" I asked like a talk show provocateur. The news was full of Trump's alleged infidelities and women who claimed he abused them.

Tatiana wouldn't broach any maligning of her newfound hero.

"Trump knows what America is all about," she said defiantly. "That's why I like him."

She paused to consider my question in the dark as the limo cruised across Long Island.

"Melania knows how to handle herself, how to look the other way—what she dismisses as locker room talk among the boys," Tatiana explained. "But nothing would surprise me about her. She acts like a spy. Very mysterious, gives up nothing. Even her marriage seems what the Russians call *kompromat*. Maybe she's a plant put here by Putin." Uproariously, Tatiana laughed with a snort at her own description.

What began as an idle conversation on the ride home eventually turned into an intense soliloquy for Tatiana, full of contradictions. I gave up talking and just listened. By the time we reached the Hamptons, she had emptied her spleen about the volatile relationship between men and women, the threat to American capitalism for entrepreneurs, and, above all, the need to always watch out for oneself.

"Family is an enterprise, a business long after the love has faded," she explained as we exited the limo at the Kirkland mansion. "I saw that in my own family, especially with my grandparents who came here with nothing in their pockets. The White Russians were very loyal to the czar. They hated the Bolsheviks, and everything that politics stood for. In the end, they realized all they had was themselves."

CHAPTER 11
DEEP HOLLOW

After several days of filming elsewhere, Max Kirkland's traveling company—with long-haul trucks carrying movie equipment and mobile homes carrying the stars of *The Life Line*—landed at a sprawling space in Montauk. The legendary history of this locale easily impressed Kirkland, accustomed to LA's more temporal landmarks like the Hollywood Sign and its sidewalk Walk of Fame.

As Max pointed out, it was home to the Deep Hollow Ranch, the oldest cattle ranch in the USA, first established in 1658 and touted as the "birthplace of the American cowboy." In the late nineteenth century, Teddy Roosevelt's Rough Riders were quarantined here, recovering from malaria and other illnesses after fighting the Spanish in Cuba.

Although Max forgot to mention it, I knew the oldest part of this area contained the Montaukett Village, where the Native American tribe once lived for generations and where many are buried, including the remains of Stephen Pharaoh. Actress Vanessa Adams had mentioned Pharaoh's final resting place when we drove together to the Kirkland party at Lions Head a few weeks earlier. I hoped to see Vanessa again today on this outdoor set.

Upon arriving, I walked towards *The Life Line* encampment alongside the horse ranch. Deep Hollow maintained a Wild West flavor, with its split rail fences, open pastures full of cattle, and ranchers on horseback. Max loved the look of this place, and, for the day, he donned a cowboy hat himself as he steered his camera crew around.

From a distance, I could see Johnny Youngblood, the charismatic young actor in the role of Stephen Pharaoh, as he taught horse riding to Kiara Manchester, the starring actress playing Elizabeth Gardiner. On the ground, Youngblood stood patting a majestically tall Palomino with a white mane and golden coat, while Manchester sat uneasily on the horse's saddle.

This equine exchange looked so real that I wasn't sure if it was a contrivance being filmed for the drama. And because I had been away covering the presidential campaign, I wasn't sure how far Max had progressed in the storytelling. Hoping to catch up, I grabbed a coffee from craft services and sat in one of the wooden directors' chairs next to Penny MacPharland and Sheila Teague.

"Ah, the author has returned," said Teague affectionately. "How is the campaign trail?"

I shrugged and told her briefly about the tribulations of covering Trump. Teague said she worried about those crowds of resentful white people wearing hats inscribed with "Make America Great Again."

"They look to him as some sort of superman," she said in wonderment and disgust, "as if he's ever done anything of substance."

I told her how Trump briefly attended Fordham, several years before I did, and how he evaded the Vietnam War with a medical disability claim.

"Trump complained the bone spurs in his heels were too painful to fight, even though he played on the Fordham tennis and squash teams," I chuckled. I mentioned that another writer friend recently interviewed Trump about his Vietnam deferment and how the would-be commander-in-chief couldn't remember which heel had been injured. It wasn't an opinion, I offered, just a matter of fact.

Teague's face turned suddenly morose. She said her uncle couldn't find any such exemption to that war. He wound up killed in action outside Saigon.

"Trump is just another rich white kid who's gotten away with murder," she concluded.

Overhearing our conversation, MacPharland seemed anxious to change the subject and invited me to the next writers room conference. She admitted Max's claim of gaining extra funding from Comflix for more episodes was "a bit premature." The project now only called for three episodes of two hours each, no more than that. With almost disdain in her voice, MacPharland said *The Life Line* would be best described as a miniseries "rather than anything more grandiose." I made a mental note to alert my agent, but I wasn't going to let anything Penny said spoil my visit.

On the video monitors, we watched the characters of Stephen Pharaoh and Elizabeth Gardiner ride their horses together across the hilly trails of the Deep Hollow Ranch. With an obvious erotic tension, Gardiner expressed her gratitude to Pharaoh again for saving her life from the shipwreck. In the picturesque distance was an oyster pond and, beyond that, the salt waters leading to the Atlantic. Eventually, the two characters, so different in backgrounds and social class, wound up in a big embrace. It was an interracial romance undoubtedly taboo in the 1880s but catnip for today's audience.

After lunch on the set, I heard Max Kirkland direct MacPharland to collect cell phone photos from that morning's filming, especially of his two stars during the picturesque horse scene. Max wanted them slipped to the tabloids, with rumors of an onset romance between Youngblood and Manchester. It was sure to add buzz to his production. The headline, he predicted, wrote itself: "*Johnny & Kiara Together!*"

Turning his head, Max caught me listening. He quickly switched to another topic.

"Sorry, Jack, but you can't come to this afternoon's shoot—it's a nude scene," said Kirkland, protective of this naked encounter between his two stars. "It's a closed set. We can't let you in."

This late-day filming would take place at a white clapboard house nearby rented for the occasion. The old colonial was meant to portray the mansion that Elizabeth Gardiner shared with her husband Edmund. Entertaining Pharaoh inside her home and upstairs bedroom underlined the intensity of their adulterous affair.

Previously in that house, I had watched Kirkland's film crew prepare other interior scenes with clock-like precision. They adjusted camera angles, sound levels, and lighting for repeated takes of the same exchange.

I marveled at the ability of actors like Lester Wolf and Kiara Manchester to recite the same lines over and over with the same intensity of emotion.

But I wasn't disappointed by Max's access denial to the nude scene inside this house. After all, I hadn't requested to be present. It seemed unimaginable to sit around and watch two actors take off their clothes in person. Very apologetic, Max acted as if my dog had just died.

"Maybe next time," he consoled. "You'll have to get your entertainment attorney to include the nude scenes in your next contract." He laughed loudly at his own joke.

MacPharland forced a smile, as if she found Max's comment amusing. Or perhaps Penny was just happy that I'd been thwarted somehow and reminded of my lowly status as the author. Nevertheless, the drama hadn't ended at Deep Hollow.

While still in her nineteenth-century costume, Kiara Manchester came up to Max and started arguing privately with some papers in her hand. Observing this confrontation from several feet away, I first assumed she was upset with the upcoming nude scene for her Gardiner character. As her argument became louder and more pronounced, I heard Kiara's words objecting to another of Max's racy propositions.

"No way! I will not appear in some black leather S&M outfit on the cover of Diana Trumbull's magazine," Manchester protested. "I don't care that your wife made this outfit or we're going to talk about it on her TV show. Do you really think this is a good idea for my career or this project? No way! Tell Diana and Tatiana I'm sorry, but they should find some other sadist. It won't be me."

Manchester, upset and nearly in tears, walked back to her trailer, getting as far away from Max as she could for the rest of the day.

I looked at MacPharland, unsure of what to say to her. Was this an insurmountable rift between Kirkland and his lead actress or simply a passing storm? While I admired Kiara Manchester from other productions, I couldn't help wondering if she would survive this confrontation. In Hollywood 2016, there still seemed no question that a powerful man like Max Kirkland would prevail.

"Do you think Max might replace Kiara over something like this?" I asked.

MacPharland acted noncommittal. "I've seen worse," she said. "It's hard to tell with Max and women... Max and *anybody*." She smirked, pleased with her remark borne of much personal experience.

The cast and crew already had left for lunch or headed to the Gardiner mansion for the upcoming shoot. Would Manchester show up for this filming or would Max have to start looking for someone else? This discussion in my mind made me think of another actress.

"Where's Vanessa Adams? I haven't seen her around," I asked Penny. "She kept saying she wanted to do more in this production. So maybe she can replace Kiara as lead actress? It's still early."

This suggestion was implausible, but I felt compelled to promote Vanessa's career, if only for the best and worst of Hollywood reasons—I had slept with her.

Penny's face remained immobile, but her response was jarring.

"No one has seen Vanessa Adams for weeks," MacPharland said. "She was in the shipwreck scene along the beach and that was it. She hasn't been to work since."

That seemed odd, so unlikely that the ambitious actress would just leave. My last impression of Vanessa was watching her run excitedly into Lions Head, her summer dress fluttering in the breeze, to join the festivities. I had searched for her inside the Kirkland mansion but never found her. I later left the party alone and never saw Vanessa again.

"Any idea where she is?" I inquired. "Maybe she went back to California?"

In reply, Penny acted as if she'd seen many actresses come and go, like soaring objects that lit up the night sky and quickly faded into the Max Kirkland universe. Maybe because I seemed so surprised, MacPharland explained that they'd checked Vanessa's room at the Montauk Manor but everything was gone. They were going to notify the local police, to see if Vanessa qualified as a missing person, until both Max and the streamer's lawyer advised against it, lest this multimillion-dollar production be drawn into some unwanted publicity. She said the cops usually were reluctant to investigate such matters because missing people often wound up somewhere else.

"She was just an extra, a bit player," MacPharland concluded. "She probably got another gig back in California."

Then, as an afterthought, Penny said she remembered Vanessa arriving in my car at the Kirkland party, though she had no recollection of seeing her after that.

"Who knows where she may be," MacPharland said laconically. "I guess the last person to see her, Jack, was you."

CHAPTER 12
PLAYING WITH EXPLOSIVES

The absence of Vanessa Adams on the set didn't seem to bother the cast and crew. Most hadn't enough contact with Adams to even know she was gone.

The role of Adams in the shipwreck scene, the first one filmed for *The Life Line* project, had been a minor, nonspeaking part. On the beach, she stood silently in period costume with the other fill-ins and extras as the camera focused on the life-saving drama between actors Johnny Youngblood and Kiara Manchester in their starring roles.

But the young woman's absence bothered me. I didn't like the casual way that Penny MacPharland—and presumably her boss Max Kirkland—blew off this departure as normal, something routine, like a used tissue. Her disappearance weighed on my mind.

During my stay at the Montauk Manor, I dreamed about Vanessa. With my eyes closed, I recalled little fragmentary moments from our short time together. Her dip into the pool. Her tanned skin and wet bikini. And our car ride to the Kirklands party, with her hair tousled by the wind. All like flashing images from a movie, flickering in my unconscious memory.

The following morning I woke up early, determined to be on the set by dawn. Kirkland planned another extravagant location filming—a simulated explosion at Fort Pond Bay—and I didn't want to miss the fireworks.

"Haha, I *knew* you would be here," Kirkland crowed when I arrived with a coffee and bagel in hand. "Everyone likes a big bang in the morning." He gloated at his over-the-top vulgarity as though it was witty. I smiled sheepishly. While his skeleton film crew appeared half-asleep, Max looked like he'd been up for hours, all ready to go.

The brilliant sun began to rise above the horizon, evaporating the misty morning haze that enveloped Fort Pond Bay. Located at the northerly tip of Montauk, the bay emptied out into the more moderate waters of Long Island Sound. It was shielded from the Atlantic Ocean's pounding waves on the south side of the Montauk peninsula, where the famous lighthouse resided.

For centuries, Fort Pond Bay has been known as a place of deception. The intrigue dated back to the late 1600s when, according to local legend, Captain William Kidd buried some treasure nearby before eventually going to the gallows in London, condemned as a pirate. During the American Revolution, another captain named John Dayton prevented a British raid with a ruse that pretended his militia, marching up and down Montauk's bluffs, was larger than its actual size.

But the biggest deception was Austin Corbin's plan for a deepwater port at Fort Pond Bay connecting with the Long Island Railroad, the centerpiece of his dream of a shorter journey to New York City than by sea. It would require stealing ancestral land from the Montaukett tribe, including Stephen Pharaoh, through false promises.

In my novel, I remained faithful to the historical facts. But in adapting it for a television drama, Kirkland decided to boil down this monumental theft to its essence, even if it meant adding more fiction to the overall story. "We decided to spice it up a little," Max explained when I asked about the changes.

In real life, Corbin relied on a local businessman named Arthur Benson to help him buy up the land from the Montauketts. But in the writers room, Max decided that a fictional town attorney (Edmund Gardiner, a name Max plucked out of thin air from a street sign) would be Corbin's corrupt go-between. For this fictitious role, he chose an old friend, character actor Dempsey Shaw, a thin, pale presence familiar with parts involving deceit.

Also in reality, Corbin lobbied for the US government to use dynamite in carving out a deepwater port at Fort Pond Bay. Eventually, the practical difficulties of igniting explosives in a stone-filled inlet surrounded by million-dollar summer homes prevented Corbin from ever using a stick of TNT. For modern television viewers, however, Max had no such problem. He decided a big explosion on screen would be, in his words, "a surefire audience-grabber."

The more I learned of Max, the more I realized how he relied on such hackneyed showbiz phrases to express himself. Scripts designed to "push the envelope" had to be filled with "showstoppers." Top box office actors were "movers and shakers" while fading stars were "low-hanging fruit." Deals "larger than life" culminated when both sides decided to "open their kimono." And when schmoozing with Comflix or other business types, he never failed to mention his favorite cliche—"synergy."

All of these "Max-isms"—along with his gregarious bear hugs for men and extended kisses for women—were part of "the Kirkland touch," as the press had touted for years. None of these laudatory celebrity profiles and "insider" reports dug very deep into his past.

To reporters, Max offered the familiar, idealized version of himself—the feel-good tale of a young seller of art on the boardwalk, grinding away at his day job in a studio mailroom, before becoming a Hollywood producer. He never mentioned his family's flight as refugees from Eastern Europe before World War II, and, as I later learned, how they changed their name to "Kirkland" to better fit in when they arrived in America.

To finance his earlier productions, Max relied on a lot of shady money. He tapped into alleged Caribbean drug dealers, Russian bankers, and greedy New York real-estate moguls. "It is what it is," he once explained to me about finding patrons for his work. When his past came up in the writers room, Sheila Teague laughed and said Max was "filthy." MacPharland avoided the topic as if it were radioactive.

No wonder Kirkland seized upon my novel about Austin Corbin, a man of action and avarice. In his television portrayal of this nineteenth-century tycoon, Max could find a little bit of himself. I still didn't know much about the ravishing side of Kirkland's nature, his sexual urges and demands on women that had yet to come to light. Like the dark side of the moon, he kept this side shadowed from public view, covered over with his bluster, lame jokes, and industry shibboleth.

Instead, on mornings like this, I witnessed the better side of famous Max Kirkland—an enthusiast for great filmmaking, a bold adventurer with storytelling, willing to break the bank to produce the most lavish and enrapturing production possible. I followed him to the outdoor set, where filming of this key scene soon began.

Through video monitors, I watched the public ceremony at Fort Pond Bay involving the characters Austin Corbin, Elizabeth Gardiner, and Stephen Pharaoh, leading up to the excavation explosion. All three actors playing these roles moved into their assigned positions along the rocky shoreline. A crowd of extras, all dressed in nineteenth-century garb, were part of this scene, portraying curious local citizens waiting to see Corbin's distant dynamite explosion at the site.

One of Max's assistant directors, an exacting British woman staring at her illuminated iPad, made sure every line uttered by the actors followed the script as written. Along with Max and his crew, I put on a headset to listen to the dialogue.

However, as I read the script, I was soon surprised to hear how much of this dialogue, stilted and simplified, varied from my novel. While I was away from the writers room, there had been many changes made by Max without my knowledge or input. Exchanges like this one:

AUSTIN CORBIN

(Blustery and grand gestures, before a big crowd gathered at Fort Pond Bay)

My friends, the day we've been waiting for is finally here. After today's excavation, we will begin our new port, connecting New York and London in a greater way than ever before…

ELIZABETH GARDINER

(On the outskirts of the crowd, Montaukett leader Stephen Pharaoh approaches Elizabeth Gardiner. She is surprised to see Pharaoh. She's wearing a sum-

mertime Victorian gown and a big feathered hat, and holding a parasol.)
What are you doing here?

STEPHEN PHAROAH
(The Montaukett leader, with long, black hair, is dressed in a gray jacket, white shirt, floppy bow tie, and dark overcoat while holding a long walking stick)

(sotto voce)

I must stop this explosion, this *desecration* of our ancestral home. Corbin is like every white man who's tried to push us off our own lands. Only more so.

ELIZABETH GARDINER
(looking around, worriedly)

If Austin sees you, he will be furious.

STEPHEN PHAROAH
(directly into her eyes)

If he knows about us, he'll be even angrier.

As I watched the scene being filmed, the sexual tension between Gardiner and Pharaoh was obvious, established in earlier scenes and heightened by the real-life attraction between actors Manchester and Youngblood. Like the two characters they played, Manchester was a bit older than her lover and significantly more proper in manner and style than Youngblood. Their erotic connection radiated through the video monitors that I watched with Max and his production crew.

"There's a real chemistry between them," MacPharland whispered approvingly to the group in between takes, as if she was Cupid.

Somehow, in the writers room, the nineteenth-century dialogue from my novel had been updated to the twenty-first century's "woke" sensibility, with Corbin condemned as "every white man" and the sexual attraction between Stephen Pharaoh and Elizabeth Gardiner hypersexualized like a nighttime soap opera. The anger swelled in me, upset that the words in my novel had been trampled upon—even worse, cheapened.

Max sensed from my silence that something might be wrong. Like any despot, he had a sixth sense for coups in the making. But I tried not to say anything, following my attorney's advice that authors, like wayward children, are "best seen and not heard from" during the filmmaking process.

"So, Jack, what do you think so far?" Kirkland asked in front of the group, forcing the issue.

My face performed a few contortions as I mulled over an answer. "Well, Max, since you asked..."

But Kirkland left no room for a reply. He really didn't want one. He only wanted to further emphasize why his rewritten dialogue was perfect for the moment. He explained this confrontation scene, found halfway in my novel, was an important "pivot point" in the television drama that needed greater emphasis.

While I digested my coffee and bagel, Kirkland expounded on how this shoot would illuminate the underlying themes from my book. Here was nineteenth-century America, he said, an ambitious land of many appetites, where money, class, and race divided people, where individual character and loyalties were tested constantly, and where force and violence often ruled the day. As if running a masterclass, Kirkland explained that his characters in *The Life Line,* including the manipulative Austin Corbin, were caught up in this maelstrom, this sea of iniquity, like human flotsam in the Montauk waves.

"Is there really any difference from the nation we live in today?" Max asked rhetorically.

I listened to his take, his far more insightful rendition of my work than the potboiler I produced. My anger dissipated with the realization that he was fundamentally right, and I was wrong in many respects. This exchange made me wonder about my own abilities. I had hoped to make the transformation into a scriptwriter, joining a small but select group of journalists who succeeded in Hollywood—from Ben Hecht and Herman

J. Mankiewicz in the old days to the more recent Nora Ephron and David Simon with his cable classic, *The Wire*. I felt sure that my journalism career spent chronicling murders, greed, acts of passion, and insanity could be distilled into must-see TV. Now I realized just how wide this gaping hole of talent was in my resume. I wondered if this revelatory moment with Max was how novelist Mario Puzo felt in reading the script to *The Godfather* or some other pedestrian novel turned into magic before viewers' eyes.

Whatever transgressions I held against Kirkland, whatever doubts I harbored about the disappearance of Vanessa Adams, were kept in abeyance. Instead, I watched Max all morning long put his vision into action, imprinted forever in high-definition video.

With this in mind, I continued to watch the scene unfold, the two characters appearing in close-up across the luminous monitors. After their initial contentious dialogue, Pharaoh walked away from Gardiner, toward the front of the Fort Pond Bay crowd. Defiantly, he faced Corbin and attempted to halt the planned explosion.

STEPHEN PHARAOH
(shouting)

You have no right to take this land, to blow it up for your own purpose!

AUSTIN CORBIN
(his anger brimming, motions to Town Attorney Edmund Gardiner, husband of Elizabeth, who stands quietly beside Corbin).

I bought this land fair and square—just ask the town attorney. This port will be good for everybody.

STEPHEN PHARAOH

No, it's only good for you. Our ancestors are buried here, and their spirits guide us. All you worship is money!

With that angry exchange, according to the script, local police and Corbin's security guards surrounded Pharaoh. They grabbed his arms and walked him away from the crowd, while Pharaoh continued to object loudly.

As they passed Elizabeth Gardiner, Pharaoh halted and beseeched her for help. But Elizabeth stared and said nothing.

Standing next to her, both Gardiner's husband and Corbin took note of Pharaoh's personal plea to Elizabeth. The two powerful older men were jealous of this young Montaukett leader, each in their own way. Both Corbin and the town attorney recognized Pharaoh's danger to them. They would conspire to get rid of him.

Max focused on getting the most visual impact from this confrontation scene. Betrayal, anger, embarrassment, and fear were among the feelings reflected on the actors' faces. The strong emotional bond existing between these two lovers was emphasized by the close-ups that Kirkland's directing style demanded at this point.

As the Pharaoh character was arrested and pulled away by Corbin's thugs, Kirkland arranged for the cameras to pull back their focus and, with a vantage from above, to record the giant explosion in the background. Suddenly, a booming noise from the excavation thundered in the distance. The flash of a fireball quickly appeared along with a rising cloud of smoke. This detonation sounded sufficiently like a gunpowder blast from the nineteenth century, enough so that birds flew out of the trees with its rumble. Gravel and sand pelted the trees like buckshot. Phony giant rocks made of papier-mâché for this purpose went flying into the air, far enough away so none of the actors were endangered.

With the overwhelming blast, separate cameras caught the look of glee on the faces of extras playing townspeople thrilled by the industrial fireworks as well as the stern satisfaction of Corbin, a man incapable of smiling.

Eventually, the filming of this scene finished around lunchtime. Off to the side, Hamptons tourists and curious local onlookers—herded for hours into a roped-off area and told to watch in polite silence—were finally allowed to clap in appreciation for this little piece of Hollywood magic they'd witnessed.

Lester Wolf, the quiet actor who played the bombastic Corbin, retired to his trailer. At the urging of his manager, though, Johnny Youngblood signed autographs for his fans. They remembered Johnny's time as a rocker before he became a thespian on camera. The crowd urged him to return to big stadium spectacles soon.

Meanwhile, Kiara Manchester wandered over to Kirkland and his assistants, all seated in the wooden directors' chairs with their names or *The Life Line* imprinted on the back.

"I thought all this chaos worked out rather nicely, don't you?" Manchester preened, with her cheery British accent. Her mood, I noticed, could change like an on-off switch.

In her brightly colored outfit, Manchester appeared more attractive than ever, the kind of magisterial beauty that other memorable characters of the cinema possessed in period dramas, dating back to Vivian Leigh as Scarlett in *Gone with the Wind*. In securing the rights to my historical novel, Max had gone to great lengths to argue against the corporate suits who insisted such dated material didn't appeal to the young and other desirable demographics.

With Kiara looking so lovely in her costume, Max seemed convinced he'd prove them all wrong. Both the complicated shipwreck scene and now this explosion at Fort Pond Bay had turned out well.

Kirkland looked forward to the next grand scene, when President Chester A. Arthur visited Corbin's mansion on Long Island. The original Tudor-style home of Corbin, built in the 1870s with its own private zoo, had been torn down. But a location scout had found a suitable replica in Sands Point, a mansion built by the founding owner of my old newspaper and now maintained by the county taxpayers.

"I'd like to chat with you about the president's scene—right after Jack and I discuss another matter," Max said to Manchester. "Can you stop by the writers room offices around four this afternoon?"

Kiara wanted to spend time in East Hampton for lunch and perhaps do a little shopping. She said that Max's meeting time fit her schedule perfectly.

"Good," said Kirkland, turning to me. "Jack and I should be finished with our meeting by then."

"What meeting is that, Max?" I inquired, surprised to hear my name invoked. Perhaps Kirkland wanted to talk about an upcoming writing assignment. My contract called for some scriptwriting in this television "special event" to be composed by me—at least a first draft before other professionals cut and "polished" it.

"I want you to meet a relative of the real Stephen Pharaoh," Kirkland explained with an impish grin. "The Montauketts heard about this project and they want to meet us. How about you come by at two?"

Instead of gaining a writing assignment at this meeting, I would be treated as a glad-hander for public relations reasons. Reluctantly, I agreed.

CHAPTER 13
RECORDINGS

Inside the writers room, Penny MacPharland tried to make small talk while we waited. The lights in the conference room were dimmed to a slight pall, providing a sense of cool relief to an otherwise oppressively hot and humid afternoon outside.

Kirkland was still on the phone in his private office. His secretary departed at 2 p.m., waving goodbye as I arrived. Sheila Teague and the show's other staff writers were gone, too. I was left at the conference table with MacPharland and a shiny black speakerphone between us.

"Max's going to be a few minutes," MacPharland explained. A pause followed, what seemed like an eternity, until Kirkland's chief aide and apologist finally blurted out a crude question.

"So how did you find out ... er, you know ... how Austin Corbin screwed the Indians? What got you interested in all of this?"

Penny blunted her awkward inquiry by leaning in, acting earnest. Her eyes widened as she moved up in her seat. The only aspect of MacPharland's personality more annoying than her usual obnoxiousness was Penny's rare efforts to be suddenly ingratiating, as if she was truly interested in what I had to say.

"Gambling and a famous painting," I replied flippantly.

When Penny asked me to explain, I recalled digging through a long-forgotten library archive many years earlier as a newspaper reporter. Inside its files were early Native American artifacts, whaling logs, family bibles, and a Captain Kidd "cloth of gold" gift given after his local stay in 1699. I also discovered something called—"Austin Corbin, Port of Entry"—marked in India ink. It would become my own port of entry into this story.

At the time, my newspaper was writing about local tribes who wanted to establish nationhood and possibly start their own casino. Throughout the United States, Native American tribes had discovered the modern vice of high-stakes gambling and were determined to cash in. In a remote section of Connecticut, another tribe had gained federal recognition as a sovereign nation and opened up a huge resort and gambling facility. It came complete with big-name entertainment, hundreds of slot machines, and dozens of tables for blackjack, craps, roulette, and poker.

The Connecticut tribe's success in the 1990s was so widespread that the revenue streams started to dry up at Donald Trump's Taj Mahal and other casinos in Atlantic City, New Jersey, gaining his eternal wrath. At a Congressional hearing, Trump made clear his opposition to Native Americans getting involved in the gaming industry.

"They don't look like Indians to me," Trump said about another tribe whose descendants were the first to greet the Pilgrims. "I might have more Indian blood than a lot of the so-called Indians that are trying to open up the reservation" to gambling.

In the Hamptons, the Montauketts had little chance of opening a casino, even if they were so inclined. Regardless of the odds, they first would have to gain government recognition as a tribe, a critically important status long denied them. In 1910, a state court declared the Montauk tribe to be extinct, claiming its members had been lost over time to disease, conflict, and intermarriage with whites and Blacks. This great injustice had remained intact for decades, even though descendants of Stephen Pharaoh and many other Montauketts were alive today. They certainly weren't extinct.

At the urging of my editors, I investigated the land documents and business records of Austin Corbin and his associates. These documents revealed how tribal lands were taken through "deceit, lies, and possibly forgery," as I later concluded in my newspaper expose. Evidence suggested Montauketts were hurt and had their homes burned when they protested. It felt like a Long Island version of Wounded Knee. This scandalous story so affected me that, once I saw the Winslow Homer painting of the shipwreck scene, I was inspired to write a historical novel that became *The Life Line.*

"That's quite a story," exclaimed Kirkland, who came out of his office and heard the last part of my recollection. Immediately, he turned the focus towards himself.

"I'm very proud to be turning your book into an even bigger success, Jack," he declared, never burdened by excessive modesty.

Max sat on the other side of the conference table, next to MacPharland, and indicated that the modern-day Montauketts would soon be here for their 2:30 p.m. meeting. I expressed surprise at the late starting time. "I thought you said be here at two," I asked.

Clasping his two hands together, Max looked glancingly at MacPharland and then addressed me. "Well, I wanted to ask you about that bit player who left after the first day of shooting..." he began.

"You mean the missing actress—Vanessa Adams?" I interjected, immediately getting to the heart of the matter.

"The actress who never showed up on the second day, that's right," Max replied. "Penny tells me that she saw you drive Vanessa to the party at my house a few weeks ago, and that you took her home."

I turned to MacPharland, who gave no hint where this interrogation was headed.

"That's only half right," I explained. "We were both staying at the Montauk Manor and she asked me for a ride to your party. That's why Penny saw us arrive together at Lions Head. But Vanessa went into your house when I parked the car and I never saw her again. When I left the party, I looked for her, but she was gone."

A rumbling noise came from the entrance to the writers room, harkening the arrival of the awaited guests. Max dropped the subject of Vanessa Adams's mystery disappearance so he could concentrate on the modern Montauketts and their attorney coming through the door.

Although they had never met before, Max shook each tribe member's hand profusely, especially Skip Lockwood, the chief and a descendant of those wronged by Corbin. On this hot day, Lockwood was joined by three older tribe members, all heavyset men wearing shorts and open-collared shirts, including one inscribed with "Montauketts—Indian Nation" on it.

Kirkland offered drinks and a few bon mots. Everything was always a pitch with Max, an opportunity to win over an audience. His immersion in this story made him feel particularly close to the Montauketts.

"So how can we help you?" Kirkland asked, as the group finally relaxed around the table. "You know, when this project finally comes out, we'd like to invite you to the opening. And maybe your tribe can help promote it, too."

Lockwood, a local plumber by trade, turned stone-faced. He deferred to his lawyer, Chester Lodge Jr., the son of a former prominent New England politician, whose firm had helped the Connecticut tribe gain recognition needed for their casino. Lodge found a new client in the Montauketts and showed his determination to succeed with them as well.

"Mr. Kirkland, you speak to our chief here as if he's a partner in your venture, but what is in this for the Montaukett tribe?" asked Lodge, impervious to Max's glad-handing.

Lodge's blueblood Boston Brahmin origins seemed reflected in his dark navy pin-striped suit, certainly not the kind of stuffy garb to wear on a warm summer's day. "This television extravaganza seems to me to be another example of cultural appropriation—stealing the story of an indigenous people that rightfully belongs to them—all for your own profit."

Max appeared thrown by this response and looked at me. Perceived as an attack on my work, I quickly got on my high horse.

"My book is a novel, a work of fiction that belongs to no one but its author," I protested. "My book is about America. And nothing is more American than the story of Native Americans like the Montauketts." Lodge seemed unimpressed with my grandiose literary claim.

"Mr. Denton, you've said *The Life Line* was based on your previous reporting for the local newspaper after gaining the life stories of my clients—Mr. Lockwood and other members of his tribe—without any compensation to them," said Lodge. "We both know that is grossly unfair."

"Are you kidding?" I objected, my professional pride pricked. "It was my investigation that exposed how Austin Corbin stole the tribe's lands—

and now you're citing my stories in your court papers to get federal recognition, with an eye towards a casino. You should be *thanking* me."

Lodge was unmoved. "My clients don't need to thank you for rightfully gaining what is theirs and whatever they are entitled to by law," he corrected.

We both understood my relative insignificance in this equation. Authors are paid little compared to the flow of millions in revenues to Comflix and their producers, who cook their books so that their profits are hidden. Lodge returned again to Kirkland, his intended target.

"Now, Mr. Kirkland, I have here a copy of your script, and there are several areas of concern in it to my clients, including the use of Stephen Pharaoh's name and how the Montauketts are portrayed," said Lodge, holding a faint photocopy of the script. Before this lawyer could go on, Max jumped out of his padded leather seat.

"How the hell did you get a copy of our script? That's stolen property!" Kirkland screamed, as loudly as he did with a bullhorn the day the shipwreck scene was filmed on the Hamptons beach.

"I can assure you, Mr. Kirkland, this copy was obtained lawfully," Lodge said calmly. "After all, your casting director has sent it all around town—seeking actors and extras to play Native Americans in ways that, frankly, we find offensive."

Lodge adjusted his glasses as he looked at his papers. "Now in the script, I'd like to direct your attention to..." Eventually, he insisted the Montauketts wanted a sizable payment for the "life rights" to their dead ancestors. Otherwise, there would be a loud and nasty protest about unfairness to Native Americans when the show came out.

Kirkland, the auteur, wouldn't have it. "No, absolutely not, what is this—*a shakedown*?" he cried. "Do you think you can threaten me?"

Lodge kept hammering. "Why should the Montauketts be injured by your insensitivity, the slanders and abuse in your script?" he asked rhetorically. "I will complain to your bosses. You work for Comflix, a streamer that is publicly traded, and therefore has to be answerable to the public."

"Max Kirkland works for *himself*," he said in a blaze of glory. "Now, get the fuck out of here!"

Max flung open the door to the writers room. He pointed to the exit, marched his guests through it, and then retreated to his private office, slamming shut the door. Penny MacPharland and I remained at the conference table, listening to our departing guests grumble among themselves as they fled down the stairs.

Manchester, going up the same narrow stairway, watched the angry Montauketts leave in a huff. "Bloody hell, what was *that* all about?" she asked, arriving for her 4 p.m. meeting with Max.

MacPharland fobbed off the question. But I explained that the Montauketts had a copy of the working script and they weren't happy about their portrayal.

"Well, I can't think Elizabeth Gardiner's family is too pleased if they're still around, either," the actress quipped.

Hearing Manchester's voice, Max emerged again from his private office in his usual hurried way. He gave Manchester a perfunctory kiss. "I want to talk to you in a minute," he told the actress, begging her patience.

Turning to MacPharland, Max wondered if the Montauketts and their threats had been recorded.

"Yeah, I got it all on audio," Penny assured him.

"Good, I want to send it to Comflix—they have plenty of lawyers who can handle this," said Kirkland. "I won't be bullied into submission."

Max indicated that I was no longer needed. I made my exit swiftly, getting into my rental outside the writers room building. As I started the engine, I saw Penny MacPharland also depart the building. She raced down the stairway and, seeing my parked car, she headed in an opposite direction.

A sense of dread ensued. I realized that Manchester remained alone in the writers room with Kirkland to plead her case why she shouldn't be dragooned onto the cover of Diana Trumbull's magazine in an embarrassing way. That encounter couldn't turn out well.

As I thought about the conversation with the Montauketts and their lawyer, I realized that Penny probably made her audio recording through the speakerphone on the conference table. And, most likely, she also recorded my earlier words, acknowledging that I drove Vanessa Adams to Max's party and that I was the last known person to see her alive.

CHAPTER 14
HOUR OF DEATH

My late mother's aphorism that "you'll always have your family" proved not to be true in my case. Her prayerful wish, repeated often before she died in a car crash with my father, was grounded in an almost quaint Irish-Catholic belief that marriage was a sacrament, an inviolate union never to be broken. Her belief was as strong as the gold heart-shaped locket necklace, with a small wedding photo inside, that she took to her grave.

As I thought of my own shattered vows, I realized how much of this failure was my fault. Two years ago, at the Nassau County courthouse, my marriage to Tricia came to an end. Now, at this child support hearing, our lawyers argued once again over the financial terms of our divorce settlement, resurrecting painful memories I'd tried to forget.

"Patricia Stanton and Jack Denton," called the court clerk, a dark-haired, attractive woman with good taste in jewelry and a no-nonsense demeanor. She introduced the judge without fanfare.

"I see, Ms. Stanton, you're seeking a modification in child support," said the judge, a black-robed pompous sort sifting through the petition. "And Mr. Denton, what say you?"

I looked briefly past Tricia and her attorney and spotted our two kids, who had entered the courtroom at the last minute. The Denton children, Megan and John Jr., both in middle school, stared anxiously at the judge, as if they were about to hear their entire fractured family story played out in court.

The judge immediately ordered that both kids should wait outside in the public hallway. Once the door closed on their curious faces, the struggle between their parents began anew.

"Your honor, my client is willing to consider an adjustment, but one that is fair," replied my attorney.

As the lawyers conversed with the judge, I appraised the state of my own sorry existence and what it meant to my two children. It was a very humbling assessment.

By the time I divorced Tricia, I had no money. Unlike her, I didn't come from a rich family. Her politician-lawyer father had earned a fortune, which included the Old Westbury mansion. Big Terry enjoyed a wealth of influential friends, including the judge before us. I, on the other hand, was the first in my family to go to college. My father had been a machinist who cut off his fingers twice in his dangerous job. Tricia once joked she didn't mind marrying "a poor boy," a wordsmith who didn't earn much in the dying newspaper industry. In subtle ways, these boundary lines of American class and privilege always defined our relationship.

After the divorce decree, Tricia didn't make the same mistake again in husbands. Instead, she turned to an older but much richer man, Douglas Johnstone Carter, known as "DJ," who owned the real estate firm where she worked. In style and spirit, Carter appeared one of the last WASPs on Long Island, a place where the once-dominant White Anglo-Saxon Protestants of Austin Corbin's era were now just another ethnic group.

This stranger called "DJ" had become the stepfather to my children. During the hearing, he waited outside with the kids, while Tricia and I quarreled over the last remnants of our marriage.

Like a rubber band about to snap, our family finances were always stretched, causing endless tensions. Near the end of our marriage, I insisted on renting a pied-à-terre in Manhattan, an expensive indulgence that fed my worst habits as an investigative reporter. I told Tricia the apartment was necessary for my career, to meet, dine, and drink with sources, especially cops and other law-enforcement authorities who leaked news tips and confidential information. I never wanted to be one of those timid bourgeois journalists who ventured home or to the health club directly after work. My late-night diet at bars usually consisted of Scotch and water, Jack and Coke, and other drinks with self-destructive names like Kamikaze, Rusty Nail, Steam Roller, and Whiskey Smash. Even a few beers after work could go a long way toward getting a source to talk. Afterhours, my apartment became a place to flop and maybe get laid by someone I'd met sitting on a barstool.

In more sober moments inside my tiny Flatiron District apartment, I found enough time to write *The Life Line*. There'd been too many distractions at home on Long Island to get anything accomplished with the manuscript. Eventually, I spent Monday through Thursday in the city and only weekends on Long Island with Tricia and the kids. She ignored obvious signs of infidelity and seemed unaware of my deepening addiction until I nearly killed myself.

Late one Friday night, leaving the city on my way out to Long Island, I crashed headlong into a concrete divider along an elevated highway. My car had been flying along above the speed limit, with the windows open to keep me awake, when it hit a yawning ditch in the cracked pavement. The metal auto frame crunched together like a discarded milk container—"totaled," in the parlance of the cops. Somehow I escaped serious injury, a lucky mug if ever there was one. The police smelled alcohol on my breath, but, with some fast-talking and by flashing a complimentary PBA union card in my wallet, I avoided any criminal charges.

I spent that weekend in a temporary neck brace, while Tricia conferred with Big Terry and her worried mother, all convinced that something must be done about my self-destructive behavior. After first resisting the idea, I agreed to spend a month in an upstate residential treatment center for "substance abuse," the euphemism in my case for drinking too much. I attended many therapy sessions for endless hours, mostly on my own, but a few with Tricia by my side.

"Often there is a genetic predisposition toward alcohol," explained one counselor in a joint session. "Did your parents drink?"

"No," I replied brusquely, not wanting to drag my dead parents into this discussion.

Uncomfortable with my response, Tricia darted her eyes in my direction and shifted her crossed legs, as if she wanted to answer, but deferred to my silence. In the days ahead, Tricia continued to encourage my recovery. But at that moment when I lied to the therapist, Tricia made up her mind privately that she must file for divorce.

The final breakup didn't occur until we attended a Christmas party given by Tricia's boss at a local catering hall, filled with two hundred guests and plenty to drink.

"Are you OK with this?" Tricia asked as we entered Chateau Moreno, the Long Island palace where this workplace affair was held annually.

Tricia had expressed doubts before we left home, before her parents arrived to mind our kids for the evening. I brushed off her concern. I promised there would be no problem, no embarrassment for her as she mingled with her colleagues.

We both knew that the twelve-step protocol, the therapeutic mantra at my expensive residential treatment, forbade any return to alcohol. When I listened to my counselor's strict instructions for staying sober, Tricia sat next to me, acting like a loving spouse. Taking one drink, the counselor warned, would invariably lead to another. I didn't go near the stuff until we arrived at the Christmas Party.

At a corner table alone, I watched Tricia as she got up and chatted with fellow employees throughout the room. Just like her father, the state senator, she'd learned to jovially work a crowd by shaking hands.

When she got to DJ's table, Tricia became more animated, more pleasing. DJ appeared an impeccably coiffed man with gray temples and a porcelain veneer smile, almost like a game show host. He laughed and gave her an extended hug. His bulky gold Rolex stretched out from his navy-blue jacket sleeve as his arm slowly sank towards her waist. Their embrace lasted as long as he could afford, as the company's boss in front of everyone else. But it was telling, even from afar.

Watching her face light up, Tricia appeared captivated by DJ. With a hug in return, she was even more affectionate than this touchy-feely older man demonstrated towards her. Many years had passed since I'd seen that same glow in Tricia's eyes. From a distance, I felt a sharp ache of jealousy run through me, realizing how my neglect had led to this point.

I got up from my seat, and, rather than confront them or make a scene, I walked over to a portable bar and ordered a drink. And then another.

"Are you all right to drive?" Tricia asked, when we finally left the catering hall and the valet delivered our car. She took a sniff. "No you're not—I can smell it on your breath!"

Tricia demanded the keys and drove home. She held her tongue until her babysitting parents left for the night.

"I can't believe you," Tricia burst out when her parents' red car lights faded down the street. "Do you want to ruin *everything* in my life?"

The slight buzz I felt from the drinks had faded but not my capacity to argue with my wife. Without merit, I first contested her claims about being drunk. Then I made vague, crass insinuations about her boss. She could no longer stand for any of it.

"Look, this marriage is over—it has been for a long time," she announced, detailing her unhappiness. "I'm not putting up with any more of your nonsense. I can't expose the kids to this."

I tried to defend myself with dissembling explanations and pleas. Stumbling, I felt like a log roller in a river, trying to stay atop floating timber with rapid steps until he finally falls.

Her arms folded, Tricia gave a withering, unmovable stare.

"I'm afraid that the kids will see you drink and get the wrong example," she stated. "I don't want them to wind up... *like your parents*."

Tricia knew my most painful personal secret and now used it like a dagger. Years ago, she found out the real reason for the car crash that claimed my parents' life. A toxicology report showed my mother, Catherine Quinn Denton, was legally intoxicated when she smashed the family car into a tree. My father, Paul, already way beyond the limit, had been too drunk to get behind the wheel. He died when his body was flung from the passenger seat beside her.

Given their long history with alcohol abuse, I should have deduced the cause immediately. But it didn't occur to me, in the same way science says the mind shields us from the most unbearable realities.

As a college student at the time, I was told by the cops that my parents' Ford Country Squire station wagon had accidentally lost control. Maybe a pothole, they theorized, or some mechanical problem prompted it. If the cops smelled liquor in the car on my parents' bodies, they didn't feel it necessary to tell their only remaining survivor.

For many months, I believed my parents' deaths were caused by some unexplained hand of fate—until it was contradicted by more evidence. While I was dating her, Tricia let me know that she overheard Elaine's parents discussing the crash and their mention of a toxicology report. She said Elaine had been sworn to silence. It didn't take me long to find this report. Tricia remembered how this damning information and its consequences further shattered me. It dredged up all sorts of suppressed childhood nightmares of my parents' drinking. Their boozy quarrels and other car rides equally out of control—with me as a kid in the back seat, worried sick.

Before we wed, Tricia and I agreed to bury this wrenching disclosure about my parents' deaths and never mention it again. But now, in this confrontation, Tricia revisited the great tragedy in my life to help make her point that she wanted out of our marriage. As if she really needed any more reason to say goodbye.

"Why would you mention my parents?" I asked, reeling. "Why bring up such a thing?"

"They say addiction runs in a family—it's genetic," she said without emotion. "The truth is that's why I don't want you around the kids."

We paused for a moment, glaring at each other in the alcove to our front entrance. I was stunned by her judgment, though in no shape to dispute it. And from the unforgiving look on her face, she had no intention of reconsidering.

"Fuck you," I said, bolting from our house, never to return.

Ever since, my family life had been in shambles. My cousin Elaine, who had predicted Tricia and I would always be together, remained sympathetic to me. But privately, she advised our extended family that I was the one to blame.

Seeing my children inside the courthouse, I realized how long it had been since we'd been together on a Little League field, at a dance recital, or to a concert at their school. I always insisted my life, my career, even my bad habits, were more important than anything my wife or family had to offer. My only saving grace, if any, was that I recognized what a shit I'd been.

When the divorce became final, the judge didn't require more money because I had been in rehab and was temporarily unemployed. Tricia didn't worry much because her father always provided a constant flow of cash and gifts to her. A year after our divorce, Big Terry died of a heart attack, leaving Tricia a sizable sum in his estate. Tricia made it clear she didn't want me to attend her father's funeral, and soon she married DJ, the silver-haired realtor.

The publication of *The Life Line* novel—and the impending arrival of Max Kirkland's television adaptation—prompted Tricia to seek an adjustment in my child support payments. Her court papers pointed out that I was currently working for the nation's best-known newspaper and that, with our children only a few years away from college, I could well afford to pay more than a mere pittance. When the judge asked for my response, the best answer was the one about fairness and equity prepared by my attorney in advance.

After the hearing ended, Tricia instructed the children to follow her briskly out of the courthouse. Only one of them, John Jr., stole a glance at me. My attorney gave me some follow-up legal instructions, but I barely listened. I was still caught up in my reverie of doubts and recriminations and wondering what life would have been like if I had done things differently.

A few days after the court proceeding, while working at *The World*, I received an urgent email. I didn't have to open it. Recognizing the sender, Elaine's husband Gary, I accurately anticipated its message: *Come quickly.*

For weeks, Elaine had been in and out of the hospital. After her stay for chemotherapy (when she insisted Gary and I play a round of golf), she went home, wearing a wrap around her bald head. Elaine rallied enough strength to tend to her backyard garden, with its marigolds and zinnias and its plump tomatoes and other overripe vegetables bursting with life. But her voracious cancer came back with force, landing her in the hospital again.

As I entered her room, there were no cheery salutations or false positives. The lights were lowered and Elaine sat upright in the bed, with an oxygen mask and plastic ventilator tubes pulsating with each breath. Her eyes were gently closed, except when another coughing fit began. She looked around the room passively and, then, exhausted, closed her eyelids once more. Her breathing remained so heavy, so pronounced, that it sounded like a moan.

Standing beside Elaine was Gary, his eyes red from weeping. His clothes looked disheveled as if he'd slept in them the night before in the chair beside her. Their two adolescent children, Gary Jr. and Patricia (named for her best friend from college), huddled together in shock at what was happening to their mother. And at the foot of the bed stood Elaine's older brother, Glenn the priest, the same brother I replaced at the restaurant in the singing act with Elaine many years earlier.

With his black Roman collar on, Father Glenn led us in saying the rosary. He held on tightly to his string of white beads and a small cross, as if a life line in this crucible of pain and hardship. Each Hail Mary was punctuated by Elaine's gasps for air, a death rattle that signaled the end was near.

"... pray for us sinners, now and at the hour of our death, Amen," her brother concluded before beginning another verse, each a prayer of hope in our hour of desperation.

In this quietude, I couldn't help thinking of Elaine and how, in earlier times, she mocked death with her sense of humor. I remembered the time as kids when we were commanded by our parents to attend the open-casket funeral wake of an elderly relative in Queens. We crossed ourselves and knelt together in front of dead Aunt Sadie, embalmed for eternity, with smooth, waxen skin and her locks combed as if she'd just come from the hairdresser.

"She looks better than the last time I saw her," Elaine whispered to me, as I fought back laughter.

For Catholics, even for doubters like myself, death was one of the eternal mysteries that called into question faith in God and belief in an afterlife.

Later, as a reporter, I learned to witness death most dispassionately. At a crime scene, for instance, I'd watched a homicide detective put on a latex glove before examining the bloody scalp of a taxicab driver shot in the head over a fare. Or inside a hospital, as a doctor peeled off the facial bandages of a fourteen-year-old swimmer caught in an ocean riptide, and I observed the physician examine his hauntingly white, pupil-less eyes before declaring the boy brain-dead.

The Church was much better with death than sex, another mystery of life that seemed to befuddle the clergy and drag everyone into a morass of corporeal lies. Knowing his brittle nature, I suspected that Father Glenn was far more comfortable dealing with the dying, even his own sister, than counseling pregnant adolescents or rape victims. Yet these prayers for the dead, the embracing words of love expressed by Jesus Christ two millennia ago, and the hope of being reunited someday with friends and family in heaven somehow was an emotional balm for the inexplicable tragedy of watching Elaine die before our eyes.

As the prayers continued, Tricia and our two children walked into Elaine's room, trailed diligently by DJ. They seemed as surprised by my presence as I was with their arrival, though I should have known better.

"Aunt Elaine?" asked fifth-grader Jack Jr., not sure if it was really her. Tricia assured him that the figure behind the oxygen mask was his favorite aunt. The seventh-grader, Megan, had a different reaction. Upon entering, she stopped and just stared in horror at the condition of Elaine. Nearly adult in size but still a youngster unfamiliar with death, Megan burst out crying.

Unnerved by her daughter's tears, Tricia quickly escorted Megan into the nearest lavatory to compose herself. It proved to be the men's room, filled with flustered occupants. Already upset, Megan became terribly embarrassed. She marched towards a hospital waiting room, where she stared through a window until she could compose herself.

Out of some sense of parental obligation, I followed them from Elaine's room, but soon realized I was of no help. Megan kept her head down and ignored me. And Tricia glared with simmering anger at me, once again a family failure.

Gary came into the hallway, leaving his wife Elaine for a moment. He put his hand on my shoulder.

"Jack, why don't you go get a coffee and come back in a few minutes," Gary suggested. "I'm sure things will be better when you come back."

I stared at Gary and concluded he was right. I walked past the nurses' station, down the stairway, and out the door to a coffee shop across the street. After standing in line for a few minutes, I sat down with my drink at an empty table.

Looking at my cell phone, I scrolled through some news headlines, including one showing that 48 percent of American adults approved of candidate Donald Trump's proposal to build a border wall to keep out undocumented immigrants from Latin America. Some Republicans condemned his words, but somehow Trump had divined a darkness in the American character that surprised even his most right-wing competitors. He had become a national obsession, even among those who loathed him.

For a moment, my mind flashed back to my newspaper struggling, like the rest of the media, to keep up with this strange new creature from reality TV. I wondered what my next assignment at *The World* would be. I indulged myself with a few more scrolls about Trump, diverting attention from the true drama in my life.

Then my cell phone beeped. Up popped a text message. It was from Tricia.

"Come back. She's dead."

The funeral mass for Elaine Lubinsky took place at the archdiocese's cathedral with her brother, Reverend Glenn O'Rourke, overseeing every ceremonial detail—from the heart-tugging sermon summarizing her life to the smell of incense pervading the air. In his homily, Father Glenn mentioned St. Thomas Aquinas and *via negativa* and the great unknowns in coming to terms with cancer, especially the inexplicable death of someone as young and alive as Elaine.

Her husband, Gary, had asked me to be one of the pallbearers. But eventually, he opted for the funeral home's staff, made up of husky men in black suits, who mercifully carried Elaine's coffin in and out of the church. Gary sat in the first pew, with his face in his hands, comforted by his children and his Polish immigrant family, including his ninety-year-old mother, Ewa Lubinsky, who emigrated from Tarnow after the war.

Behind them were many of Elaine's friends, including the women who attended college in Connecticut with her. All were now in middle age, most with families of their own. They hugged each other with affection, as if they were still undergraduates living together in a dorm. I recognized some faces next to Tricia who sat beside our two children and her new husband. Enough relatives attended from Elaine's family so that I could blend in on my own in the back until the mass finally ended.

A soft rain began to fall by the time I arrived at Holy Rood, a cemetery not far from the Long Island neighborhood where I once lived with Tricia and the kids. Traveling alone in my rental, I passed familiar streets and was reminded of memories from what seemed a lifetime ago. I was among the last to join the circle of family and friends around Elaine's shiny wooden casket, resting next to a dark open grave and a pile of recently excavated earth.

Father Glenn recited a few prayers and sprayed holy water over his sister's remains. There were barely any sounds except for occasional sobs from the mourners and distant traffic horns beyond the gates. I felt my insides tighten as I watched Tricia, in a somber black dress, and my children lower roses onto her coffin.

When the graveside ritual was over, Tricia and her family approached me dutifully, as though they felt required to do what she considered the right thing. Her new husband shook my hand briskly. Tricia grasped my arm and pecked me on the cheek.

"I'm sorry, Jack; I know what she meant to you," she said, fulfilling her sense of obligation.

Tricia directed the two children to address their father. Megan stepped forward and gave me a perfunctory kiss. Then Jack Jr., still very much a boy, walked towards me with both arms by his side. His face began to tremble.

"Why did you leave us, Dad?" my son cried, unleashing a question that had burdened him for a long time. "I thought we were all happy. I don't understand why this is happening to our family. Mom is married to another man. And now Aunt Elaine is dead. Why did God do this—to punish you? *Why?*"

CHAPTER 15
BRANDING

The next day, I returned to my Manhattan newsroom and sat at my desk without a word to anyone. There was no sense in explaining to Hattie where I'd been or where I was headed. She'd already made up her mind.

"I'm sorry to hear about your cousin," she said dryly. "I know you were close to her."

To someone as hard-driving as Hattie, who viewed this newspaper's mission as a secular religion, my faithless performance so far was unacceptable, as if I needed a doctor's note to prove the reasons for my absence. The disappointment in Hattie's eyes, the slight chill in her modulated voice, revealed her regret in recommending to *The World's* editors that they hire me for this job.

Returning to the newsroom—though maybe not for long—was a relief. Working as a reporter had always been an escape from my own personal realities, whatever family pressures existed at home. Posing questions to strangers about their lives was so much better than asking them of myself.

Within a few minutes of my arrival, political editor Jamal Williams gave me a last-minute assignment to cover a Trump fundraiser in the Hamptons, at the private estate of Zach Preston, the independent producer. Trump had promised to pay for this campaign out of his own pocket. But mega-donors like Preston had been already raising funds for him, anticipating that Trump would gain the Republican nomination for president.

Before I left the newsroom, Jamal made one request: go home, grab a sports jacket, and forget the fedora I was so fond of wearing on the job. "Let Hattie know what you find tonight so she can feed it to the web," he instructed.

I drove out to the east end of Long Island, speeding along concrete highways built by another dynamo very much in the vein of Austin Corbin—twentieth-century power broker Robert Moses. I thought of how both men were fond of mowing down their public opposition to get what they wanted. On the way, I passed the large, glowing billboard that Max Kirkland complained was a traffic clogger, and then relied on my rental's voice-activated GPS to weave through the maze-like residential roads of Southampton.

Darkness had descended by the time I tucked my car along the roadside and approached the Preston mansion. The well-lit house was built to Preston's specifications of what success in America should look like. The huge, two-story sandstone compound, with a winding gravel driveway, featured a dining room the size of a baseball diamond, a two-hundred-seat theater with a gargantuan television screen, two pool houses, and four tennis courts. There were dozens of bedrooms and bathrooms, enough to make one appreciate its enormity and ostentatiousness, even by Hamptons standards.

Once I identified myself as a "guest reporter"—an arrangement made in advance by Hattie—Preston came to greet and show me around his impressive palace.

"We're so excited you're here to cover this great get-together for Donald," said Preston, a rangy man with a deep tan, white capped teeth, a thick Aussie accent, and an all-American zest for salesmanship. He recounted how he first heard of Trump's 1987 book *The Art of the Deal,* which soon became his bible.

"I wondered then if I was ever going to set eyes on the guy who wrote this book," Preston recalled, with the zeal of a convert. "Now I want to help him become president."

Branding was Preston's supreme skill, the ability as an outsider to look into America's voracious psyche and feed whatever it wanted. He made his fortune as a reality-show producer, basing his first hit on the *Lord of the Flies* novel. In this show by Preston, kids selected from around the nation got to live on their own in a jungle while his crews filmed their various hijinks. Notoriously, one teenage boy was sexually abused by the others—supposedly when the supervising producers weren't looking—and he committed suicide before the first episode was to air on a major network.

Part of the Preston legend was the way he spun that catastrophe. His team edited out all video images of the dead teenager from their final product, as if he never existed. Preston assured people at the network that the boy was only an extra and not a major participant in their drama. I was struck by the vague similarity to Vanessa Adams and how her disappearance was so cavalierly dismissed by Kirkland and Penny MacPharland. They planned to wipe her image away from the shipwreck scene, as if she, too, never existed.

"Make yourself at home," Preston told me, pointing to his well-stocked bar. Before I left him, Preston expressed confidence his money-raising soiree would raise more than $500,000 before the night was through. He said many in the Hamptons crowd, like himself, had met Trump before and were impressed by his toughness as a businessman. Trump's self-portrayal on his own long-running television program ("You're fired" was his trademark refrain) convinced Preston of his killer instinct.

Roaming around the Preston mansion, I took note of several well-known businesspeople, including Wall Street investors and media executives like himself. Roger Ailes, the head of Fox News and a Trump whisperer, stood out prominently among one semicircle of acquaintances. Relaxed, with his shirt collar opened and a drink in his hand, Ailes was only a few weeks away from being forced out on sexual harassment charges leveled by twenty women. But on this night, Ailes guffawed at a joke about Hillary Clinton, the *bête noire* among Trump's rogue gallery of supporters. Ailes raised his glass and nodded approvingly as Preston walked by.

Eventually, I bumped into Max and Tatiana and told them I was there as a reporter.

"Geez, Jack, I said you could give up your day job," Kirkland teased me. "Don't I pay you enough?"

Tatiana, dressed in one of her summer creations, afforded him only an apprehensive smile. From the unsettled look on their faces, these two high-powered spouses were clearly wondering how I slipped through their gate in the first place. In circumstances like this, there existed an awkward caste system, an invisible barrier between the moneyed class to which Kirkland and Preston belonged, and the rather "untouchable" state for those in society's lower rungs, including creative types who still worked as journalists.

I asked Max if he was a Trump supporter. "Of course not," he laughed. "I only cut a check to them as a favor to Zach Preston, who I may do business with someday; who knows? I give money to both parties—just like Trump does. But Donald Trump as president? No way."

Gazing around, Max wished me well and then quickly left to mingle with other honchos. Tatiana stayed for a few more moments, perhaps more out of sympathy than interest. We chatted at random about the moonless night and how this area didn't have streetlamps, forcing guests to walk around in the dark before entering the Preston estate with its security guards.

"You're not afraid of a risky neighborhood like this, are you?" I asked in jest.

Tatiana took my question seriously.

"Not at all; I always carry protection," she said, patting her purse.

I looked at the Versace clutch bag, in white calf leather with gold metal chain, and envisioned a pistol inside it among the tissues and makeup.

"Are you a good shot?" I inquired, hiding my surprise.

"The best," she insisted, flashing the pearl-handled weapon inside her purse. "It was my grandmother's gun. My grandfather worked for the czar, and they both taught me how to survive."

With amusement, Tatiana described using a commercial DNA kit to trace her heritage, especially the White Russian roots of her father, Dimitri, the one-time legend in New York's art and fashion world. She noted how Americans, a nation of immigrants, were enthralled by the secrets these chromosome test kits revealed. I told Tatiana that my ex-wife had passed along a similar kit for my son's school assignment, wondering if I might have some Native American blood in me.

"So that's why you wrote a book championing the Montauk Indians?" she asked, with her slight continental accent.

"I'm not sure about *championing*," I replied. "They're threatening a boycott of the show."

Tatiana acted surprised by that news. Apparently, Max hadn't told her (or she didn't care enough for it to register). Looking around, though, she paid great attention to Diana Trumbull, the fashion magazine editor, who was speaking animatedly with Max beyond hearing distance. I assumed that they were talking about something business-wise, like the planned cover photo shoot of Kiara Manchester in black leather S&M garb to publicize the show.

Tatiana and Trumbull were best described as "frenemies" who worked together in business but didn't trust each other personally. When Tatiana realized that I had spotted Diana and Max chatting as well, she turned acrid.

"You know my father Dimitri used to fuck Diana Trumbull—that's how she started in the business, working for him," she blurted out cruelly. "Dimitri had a fondness for the young flowers in the office, as he called them. When I think about my father's behavior, I don't know how my mother could stand it."

I stared without comment at Tatiana, wondering if she had any idea of the rumors and realities of her own husband's philandering. From my own experience, I'd learned that spouses see only what they want to see until it's more than they can withstand and finally something happens. The Kirklands remained a mystery to me.

As Tatiana wandered away, I decided to step outside and call Hattie on my cell with news from this event—the size of the crowd, the notable supporters, and that $500,000 had been raised for Trump, the avowed self-funder.

"I hope you're not wearing your hat at that place," Thompson joked, more warmly than earlier in the day. She sounded like the old Hattie from the former paper where we once worked. I assured her of the straw fedora's retirement.

"Take care, Jack. I hope everything works out for you," Hattie said, ending our call. Hattie was gone before I could ask what exactly she meant.

Coming back into the Preston mansion, I grabbed another drink and maneuvered past waiters carrying trays of hors d'oeuvres. Numerous Trump supporters conversed with Zach Preston, with his open white shirt, blue jacket, and bronzed face. They had no comment for the press. I steered clear of the Kirklands—wanting to avoid anything about the show—until I spotted Kiara Manchester and Sheila Teague conversing in a corner.

As I approached, both women offered a friendly gesture by smiling and clicking their wineglasses with mine.

"What role are *you* playing tonight, Jack—a reporter or TV show producer?" teased Sheila. With her hair up and her tight dress, Sheila appeared more attractive than I'd ever seen her in the writers room.

"I wouldn't play producer—that's Max's job," I replied. "I'll just be a mild-mannered reporter for a great metropolitan newspaper, like Clark Kent."

Both women smiled politely at the joke but avoided my mention of Kirkland's name. They had been talking about Max's private encounter with Kiara in the writers room. From Kiara's reaction, something awful happened. She remained visibly upset at the memory. "I should go over and tell his wife Tatiana what he did to me, what he tried to do," Manchester said.

I demanded to know more. With Manchester listening, Teague summarized Max's unwanted sexual affront upon his female lead, a most accomplished actress, in his latest production. Alone together in his offices, Max demanded that Manchester try on the leather outfit he'd picked out for her magazine cover shoot. When Kiara objected to the whole idea of an S&M theme for the photo—arguing it would be wrong for her career and sending the wrong message about *The Life Line*—Max threw a fit. He grabbed her, pulled down her dress to the floor, and tried to insert himself like a street rapist. Kiara resisted and ran away.

"Oh my God, are you alright?" I asked. "I had a bad feeling about leaving you alone in that office with him. Has he said or done anything to you since then?"

Manchester said she considered filing a police complaint, but, paradoxically, she didn't want the nasty publicity. Since then, Kirkland had been avoiding her on the set. Whatever directing instructions she received during the filming were relayed by Penny MacPharland.

"My parents warned me about Max, about his reputation as an aggressor, as a sexual monster," Manchester admitted. "I thought I could handle this situation. But that clearly isn't possible."

Her eyes welling with tears, Kiara stared at us without further explanation. Then she grabbed her shawl, thanked Zach Preston, and walked into the night.

The hour was getting late, but both Sheila and I shared another drink, becoming some of the last to leave the Preston mansion. Despite my past, I convinced myself if I consumed only one sip or two, it wouldn't matter. Sheila reminded us that we were both expected at the writers room the next morning, followed by a long day of shooting a big scene. Both of us were staying at the Montauk Manor. Sheila said she planned to call an Uber to get herself there. When I offered her a ride in my car instead, she quickly agreed.

While driving, we talked a little about our private lives. Sheila grew up in Los Angeles, graduated from Stanford, and received a scholarship to USC's film school, where so many notable people learned their craft. Sheila said she'd never married, despite some close calls. I mentioned my divorce from Tricia without elaborating. Instead, I asked Sheila why she never became a showrunner in television. From my limited exposure to her work, I knew Sheila was a gifted storyteller, a skilled writer of dialogue. I assumed racism somehow was at fault. By reputation, Hollywood was notoriously a land of mostly male white people, more like a gated community than a common ground. Sheila probably didn't fit their mold.

"No, that's not it—good guess, though," she chuckled. "As a Black woman, I'm not saying there isn't a lot of stereotyping out there. But that's not the case here with this project." Sheila said she had been a showrunner for a short-lived drama a decade ago and then wrote a succession of pilots and spec scripts until she met Max a few years ago.

I wanted to hear more, but my car arrived at the hotel residence. We both got out quickly. As we neared the building, Sheila touched my hand and gave me a kiss.

"How 'bout one last drink?" she said, motioning to her room. Opening the door near midnight, we entered quietly like two undergraduates breaking curfew.

For whatever reason, I'd never considered having an affair with Sheila. Perhaps it was my reluctance stemming from that old adage about not getting involved with the women at work. I could never figure out her relationship to Max, the boss, which made me wary. For some undefined reason, I got the sense that Sheila might be a spy for Max, trying to find out what I suspected about him.

On this night, however, I'd learn much more about Sheila as we downed our last drink and began to undress in her manor suite. Lying naked beneath the sheets, I awaited her return from the bathroom.

When she neared the bed, Sheila turned down the lights. There remained enough illumination so that I could see her magnificent breasts and the shiny glow to her smooth naked skin. But my attention quickly focused on what little she *was* wearing—a leather corset and lacy garter belt. On the night table, she placed cuffs for my wrists and ankles. And in her hand, she held a bondage chain and whip.

"Let's have a little fun," Sheila announced, like some cowgirl about to go bronco-riding at the rodeo. I nearly jumped out of bed reflexively but stayed beneath the sheets.

"Uhmmm, not for me," I exclaimed, obviously squeamish.

"Why not? Men love it," she replied seductively. "Max likes it."

"*Really?*" I asked, astounded. "This is something you do with Max Kirkland—*our* Max, the famous producer?"

Getting frustrated, Sheila placed her hands on her hips.

"Yeah, he loves it—says it makes him more creative," she said, snapping her tassel whip against the night table with a loud crack. "Turns out he's more into S&M than I am. I whip him good, and he says the blood flow goes right to his head!"

Sheila enjoyed her own joke, perhaps the only pleasure shared this night between us. Mentally, my mind was spinning. I began to count how many drinks I'd had during the night.

"We've been doing this for years—ever since I hooked up with Max at a television convention in LA," she confided, resting on the bed. "I came out to be the showrunner for a new show. But Max sweet-talked me into joining this staff. He raved about your book, how he was going to make *The Life Line* into something special. I got a big boost in pay to accept this job. In the end, Max promised it would all be worth it."

We discussed Kiara Manchester's accusations against Max. Certainly his reputation as a sexual marauder wasn't helped by this fondness for hitting women with a leather whip and punishment flogger. But Sheila had less patience for Manchester's claim of abuse than she showed earlier to the lead actress during the party.

"I'm not saying she's wrong, it's just that guys like Max have been acting like this for years—it's part of who they are," Sheila explained. "Pampered girls like Kiara don't know how to handle aggressive men like Max. If he gets out of line with me, I'll whip his ass."

Now tired from words rather than actions, Sheila wriggled across the bed next to me, more in defeat than in triumph. She stared sympathetically at the dullard beside her.

"Yeah, this is part of the connection between Max and me," Sheila confessed. "I told you in the car there were more reasons why I haven't looked for a showrunner job. This is it."

CHAPTER 16
CONNIVING CHARACTER

Lester Wolf, the man who played the brutish Austin Corbin, peered down at the candle-lit cake celebrating his sixtieth birthday and wept with joy. Surrounding him were his fellow cast and crew members in extended applause, appreciative of his distinguished career.

"You're too kind, too generous," said the sweet-tempered actor so adept at portraying evil. "You must remember what the Bard told us."

Wolf paused dramatically, prompting an audible wave of anticipation from his fellow thespians. They were well-acquainted with his mastery of Shakespeare, which he recited during breaks in filming *The Life Line.*

"The play's the thing, wherein I'll catch the conscience of the king," Wolf intoned, his baritone voice like brandy wine—a product he once hawked in a television commercial. "Or at least the conscience of Austin Corbin, if he has one!"

With a big grin, Wolf took a long bow in front of the assembled crowd and blew out the candles. Though in costume as nineteenth-century Corbin, with a grizzled, fake beard glued to his chin, Wolf couldn't help but show his true feelings.

Neither could the organizers of this brief celebration, Kiara Manchester and Johnny Youngblood. They embraced Wolf with their own individual brand of respect.

"You're the bomb, man," Youngblood proclaimed, shaking his hand profusely like he would some rocker on stage.

Manchester, aware of Wolf's sterling reputation back in Great Britain, hugged him. Dressed as Elizabeth Gardiner, she bestowed a stage kiss on Wolf's cheek, mostly for the benefit of onlookers.

"Lester, you're the kind of man I would have an affair with... *in any century*," Manchester said in her best Queen's English. The crew on the set applauded once again, aware of the fateful adultery in their drama between the characters Austin Corbin and Elizabeth Gardiner.

After a few weeks away, I had returned to this set during the final scheduled week of filming and joined the chorus of well-wishes to Lester Wolf. He made reference to my book's adaptation when he shook my hand.

"I'm realizing Austin is quite a conniving character," Wolf chuckled, "even more so than this fellow Trump." Actors always liked a point of reference, a marker on the floor.

Wolf's inspired selection as the rapacious New York railroad tycoon topped off a remarkable late-in-life career as an actor. He'd first played an avuncular warlock in a blockbuster movie made from a beloved children's book. After some forgettable movies, he turned his career around by landing a part in a popular American television family sitcom. In a familiar formula, Wolf played a sagacious suburban dad married to an adoring wife with a bunch of wisecracking kids. But his big breakthrough movie role—as the all-knowing commander of a spaceship lost in the universe—granted him a kind of gravitas with the American public susceptible to autocratic figures on TV.

For this new role, Lester's shaved head, dark eyes, and deep aristocratic sound embodied my idea of what the intimidating Austin Corbin should look like. In real life, Wolf was a gentler soul, different from his early image as a Hollywood leading man. Years later, Wolf acknowledged his own homosexuality in a retrospective "What Are They Doing Now?" feature in *People* magazine. Fame and popularity—as well as a noticeable change in American attitudes about closeted gay men—provided Wolf with a greater sense of freedom late in life.

On the set, after the candles were extinguished, Wolf embraced and kissed his husband, another well-known character actor in his seventies. After years of waiting, they quickly wed when same-sex marriage became legal in June 2015. Wolf and his husband seemed like a contented elderly couple headed towards retirement.

"All right, congratulations to Lester... now everyone back to work!" said Max Kirkland impatiently. He was annoyed that this modest birthday party had taken so long on a busy day of shooting. Kirkland didn't like any activity on the set that he wasn't directing.

Over the past few months, I'd noticed subtle changes between the actors, especially the obvious intensity of the relationship between Manchester and Youngblood. Kiara was married to a tall fellow British actor who came to the States with her in 2010 but had not enjoyed as much success as she did with American audiences. Her husband, never seen around the set, was rumored to be out of the picture altogether.

Now past her fortieth birthday, Manchester flaunted her attraction to Youngblood, a physical specimen in his late twenties, a reversal of the same hormone-driven lust that male matinee idols in old Hollywood displayed in pursuing starlets. After the final take of each scene together, the two squeezed and caressed with passionate improvisation, like lovers who had been apart for years rather than seconds. Kiara initiated this workplace tango with Johnny, and he followed along amiably with this older and better-known actress. Their pecks of affection developed into French kisses and long carnal clings, enough that everyone around averted their eyes.

But these encounters were apparently tame compared to the previously filmed nude scenes between Manchester and Youngblood. These moments of cinematic passion were legendary among those in the crew who'd witnessed them.

Manchester, whose former waif-like body as a model had blossomed into a mature woman's figure, performed masterfully in these love scenes, as if she had studied endless sex manuals. On cue, her proper etiquette and diction could quickly devolve into uncontrollable moans and sighs. And Youngblood, with his rock-hard abs and Fabio-like flowing hair, was a yogi's ideal of flexibility. At the end of each scene, right after Max yelled "Cut!" to the filming, Johnny murmured "Namaste" to Manchester, tantalizing her more.

In Hollywood, nude scenes like these were carefully negotiated in advance. Lawyers, casting agents, personal managers all got involved with their lists of dos and don'ts. Male actors wearing a "sock," a genital pouch on their member, was one common demand. Merkins, pasties, prosthetic genitalia, and flesh-colored undergarments were also discussed. The resulting scripts sought to balance the streaming audiences' taste for flesh with the actors' desire to be taken seriously while cavorting in the buff.

In another case of art imitating life, Manchester and Youngblood proved to be naturals with lovemaking when the cameras started rolling, attested one witness.

"Confidentially, Jack, they were, shall we say, *very intense* together," confided Penny MacPharland. As a producer, Penny had managed to get a front-row seat to these scenes by sitting next to Max. When others weren't looking, Penny showed me the daily rushes on her laptop. Always with public relations in mind for the show, she repeated, "I think they have very good chemistry together, don't you?"

But their alchemy on the set could be explosive. Though known as a cad in the press, Youngblood's growing emotional attachment to Manchester led to pangs of schoolboy jealousy for the first time. When Kiara confided how Kirkland sexually harassed her constantly with his groping and unwanted kisses, Youngblood erupted in rage. Manchester asked Johnny to remain quiet, that she would take care of it herself.

Instead, Youngblood confronted Kirkland on the set. When he spotted Max talking privately with Manchester the next day, he rushed in between them.

"You touch her again and I will kill you, got it?" Youngblood barked.

Kirkland, famous for his own anger management problems, acted unfazed. "Are you threatening me, Johnny?" he said, with his own subtle menace.

Manchester was horrified by the confrontation. She appeared annoyed that Youngblood had broken her confidence.

"Please, stop this," she pleaded, turning to Youngblood. "Johnny, let me handle this, *please.*"

The confrontation ended without further threats, but bad feelings continued for a long time on the set. I heard about this angry faceoff when I returned from my time away covering the Trump campaign. Both Sheila Teague and MacPharland provided varying accounts of the incident, swearing me to secrecy. With a little reporting of my own, I learned more about this backstage drama.

Unafraid of the consequences, Youngblood was determined to call out Kirkland as a sexual harasser. At first, he'd been grateful to Kirkland for taking a chance on casting a rock star who lacked any acting experience. But from Kiara, Johnny learned about Max's reputation for aggression with other women in previous productions. One of Youngblood's friends made a thinly veiled "casting couch" reference to Kirkland's reputation during a televised awards show. The hip audience seemed to catch the joke, but nothing was done about him.

Johnny's outrage grew as his caring for Kiara intensified. He was furious when he learned of Max's demand that Manchester pose scantily in leather S&M clothing on the cover of Diana Trumbull's fashion magazine, ostensibly to promote the show, but actually to hype Tatiana Kirkland's provocative line of fashion.

"How does he get away with this?" Johnny declared when Manchester told him. "He treats actresses like hookers and he's their pimp."

Youngblood decided to take a stand. He consulted his attorney about this "toxic environment" and bravely considered pulling out of *The Life Line* project. His entertainment lawyer advised against it, though, saying Comflix could sue for contract violations. This multimillion-dollar production was not some rock club where Johnny could walk away in a huff.

Manchester was afraid of the consequences even more so. She didn't have a music career to fall back on like Johnny. Despite her considerable accomplishments, Kiara knew Max Kirkland could easily blackball her, even her estranged actor husband. She had heard rumors that powerful people like Max's friend Diana Trumbull could kill a television show with a phone call or, even worse, a letter from their lawyer.

Cowardice was in ample supply in Hollywood, she learned, keeping sexual abuse complaints like hers hidden from the public. Men with reputations as bad or worse than Max could be found throughout the industry, including a reality TV star running for president that year. For the moment, she decided to stay quiet and maintain her distance from Kirkland.

The tension didn't ease until Manchester and Youngblood decided to throw this impromptu birthday party for Lester Wolf with Kirkland's reluctant blessings. Like good actors, they made it appear as though the show's three main stars were all getting along with the showrunner. They even gathered in a publicity photo for Lester's birthday, which Comflix posted on its Instagram account.

After lunch, I watched Kirkland and his production crew prepare to film the next big scene on location. It called for re-creation of the 1882 visit by President Chester A. Arthur at Corbin's sprawling Long Island estate. Before we left the current set, though, Penny MacPharland came up to me with a look of great concern.

"Did you hear from a detective asking about Vanessa Adams?" Penny wondered, unable to conceal her worry. "I think her family hired an attorney to investigate her whereabouts. Max got a call this morning at his office in the writers room and I thought you might have as well."

This news startled me. I told Penny that I hadn't received any such message. Despite my initial suspicions, I'd recently come to believe that Adams had simply left town, beaten down by the vicissitudes of being an actress but not in any physical danger. She would not be the first to give up the dream of acting and go home. But this news about her family's search for her underlined that Vanessa never arrived home or anyplace else.

After Penny left, I dug out my cell phone from a pocket and gazed at the screen for any recent emails. There was one.

"Please call Detective Hutchinson about the Vanessa Adams matter… " it read, with a telephone number attached. Like most pressing questions in my life, I decided to wait before responding.

CHAPTER 17
GREAT MAN THEORIES

President Chester A. Arthur, a nineteenth-century man of more than ample appetites, lowered himself onto the plumped velvet seat inside Austin Corbin's personal railroad car and expressed enjoyment with the ride. Corbin's private car rolled along his Long Island Railroad tracks at a swift speed. It boasted many accoutrements, including mahogany walls, old brass trimmings, and silk window curtains.

"I can see why the press calls this 'a movable mansion,'" said the Arthur imitator, as video cameras captured his every move. "I'm quite impressed, Mr. Corbin."

The actor playing Arthur looked very much like the barrel-chested president with a thick mutton-chops beard. His bombast was a bit louder than usual to overcome squeaks from the train car chugging along.

"With your help, Mr. President, someday we'll travel all the way from Montauk to Manhattan," replied Lester Wolf, portraying Corbin. "And we will greet the ships from Europe arriving in our brand-new port."

Following the script, the Corbin character offered the president a glass of brandy and a big cigar. Arthur quickly downed the drink. Then he lit and slowly puffed on a Cuban Corona.

"I can see why they call you 'The King of Long Island,'" the president said with bemusement.

From a short distance away on his video monitor, Max Kirkland watched this verbal jousting between two characters in *The Life Line* scene. He considered it a prelude to another important turning point in his television spectacle. Out of sight of the cameras, Kirkland let his entourage know he was pleased with the results so far.

"This president looks good—maybe I'll vote for Chester Arthur instead of Trump," Max joked to Penny MacPharland. They both had headsets dangling around their necks. I sat behind them, marveling how well they had reenacted this scene from my novel.

Back in 1882, as the story goes, these two characters were headed to Corbin's huge hotel residence in Babylon, New York, located midway across Long Island's south shore. Though Corbin's estate no longer exists, a restored Gold Coast mansion chosen by Max's location scout looked uncannily like it.

At that time, the purpose of President Arthur's visit was purportedly to make a public statement about improving maritime safety and shoreline life-saving crews. Townspeople would cheer and the press would snap his picture, just like today's White House photo ops.

The real intent, however, was to gain secret approval for Corbin's Montauk building plan, the key to reaping a fortune.

Corbin's flimflam relied on the federal government dredging Fort Pond Bay—deep enough so big sailboats and steamers from Europe could land at his proposed deepwater port next to Montauk's railroad station—and subsidize his private venture at taxpayer expense.

Even worse, Corbin wanted to get rid of the Montaukett tribe entirely in the eyes of the federal government. Insidiously, he pressured the president to nullify all legal claims by the Montauk nation. In court, the tribe was trying to stop Corbin from snatching their ancestral lands for his grand project. Hundreds of indigenous people in the surrounding area claimed their property had been taken unfairly by the railroad tycoon and his business associates.

Corbin needed these Native American lands desperately. They were crucial to building the new tracks for his much touted "mile-a-minute" express trains speeding back and forth between Montauk and Manhattan. These luxury trains would serve American passengers bound for Europe or on their way home. By getting the federal government to enforce its declaration of the Montauk tribe as "extinct"—despite flesh-and-blood evidence to the contrary—Corbin would clear the way for his master plan.

Undoubtedly, there were sizable favors exchanged secretly between President Arthur and Corbin. During this Gilded Age, both were considered great men, living examples of how money and acts of violence defined American life. Corbin accumulated remarkable wealth through chicanery and fraud, while Arthur had gained presidential power when an assassin's bullet led to the end of his predecessor James A. Garfield the year before this visit. Their exchange of favors, both understood, was how business was done among such great men.

On film, Kirkland hoped to capture this underhanded give-and-take from my book. As the president's train slowed down, nearing its destination, the actor playing Corbin moved to seal his private deal.

"So, Mr. President, is it safe to say we have your backing on the Montauk port expansion?" he pressed.

Arthur seemed amused by Corbin's persistent piggishness. "Yes, you have my word," replied the president. "I'll make my views known when we get off the train."

That last line of dialogue was Kirkland's cue to end this scene. The crew readjusted his cameras and prepared for the next scene at Corbin's home. This remote-location shoot would include a life-size luxury locomotive arriving in front of more than a hundred extras wearing nineteenth-century clothing.

"Just how much do I have to pay for a hundred vintage bustles, Victorian dresses, and Edwardian jackets?" Kirkland complained in his director's chair as he signed the receipt for a hefty bill. "At this price, you'd think they came from Gucci!"

Luckily, Max's production supervisor found the fully restored train car from that era at a local museum. Expensive visual effects from digital compositors would recreate the rest of the background magic.

On the second day of shooting, I was joined in the director's circle by Sheila Teague, who settled in the chair next to me. She had been busy in the writers room, recasting scenes and rewriting dialogue. Max's epic vision had been reduced to miniseries size, but it still required lots of last-minute attention from his talented team of wordsmiths like Sheila who made him look good. True to his legend, Kirkland was directing on the fly, making things up as he went along, and asking other people to tie together the loose ends.

As Sheila neared, I didn't know what to say. The last time I was with her, she had described matter-of-factly her kinky S&M relations with Kirkland, the cinematic genius in front of me. Although Sheila and I had shared a moment of intimacy together, I never confided my doubts about Max and the missing actress Vanessa Adams.

"Hi there, stranger," she whispered, a hint of the previous affection between us.

Awkwardly, I said nothing to Sheila, just shared a polite smile.

All eyes in the directors' chairs soon turned to the row of large video monitors and the next act being played out before us. With a boorish gesture, Max insisted everyone be quiet. Kirkland had endured many confrontations during this production. He didn't want any more trouble during these final days of filming.

Once again on the TV screen, Lester Wolf appeared as Corbin, presiding over a large celebration full of spectators in the front of the tycoon's mansion known as The Argyle. Its windows and decks were draped in American flags and red, white, and blue bunting. Next to him was the actor posing as President Arthur, as well as Kiara Manchester as Elizabeth Gardiner, and her husband the East Hampton Town Attorney Edmund Gardiner, played by Dempsey Shaw.

Most notably, Stephen Pharaoh, portrayed by Johnny Youngblood, appeared on the raised dais with them. It was a rare nineteenth-century instance of a Native American being recognized by whites. With his own sense of pride and dignity, Pharaoh dressed in his familiar dark attire—a long-tailed coat, corduroy pants, necktie, and white shirt with a standing collar. He placed his walking cane on the floor.

Despite his loathing of Corbin, Pharaoh had been convinced by Elizabeth to attend the presidential event.

"Your singular presence will make it impossible for Corbin to contend the Montauketts no longer exist," she insisted.

Before climbing the dais, Pharaoh had approached Elizabeth, while her husband and Corbin, from a distance, waved to the crowd along with the president. Pharaoh would only have a moment for this private conversation. The real-life sexual dynamism between Manchester and Youngblood was evident in all the filmed exchanges between these fictional passionate lovers. The cameras inched towards a close-up as they spoke.

"Do you know Corbin is buying the rights to our tribal lands for this railroad project?" Pharaoh whispered to her, angrily. "He's telling people to move from their homes now and live in some shantytown. Promising them they can come back anytime they like. It's a complete lie."

Elizabeth, looking as beautiful as Stephen had ever seen her, with a white, summer-like dress and parasol, tried to calm him. She was more afraid of upsetting the presidential visit than helping to solve this injustice from Corbin's lies.

"Stephen, I'll ask my husband to look into it," she promised. "But, today, here is the president of the United States, and he's going to mention you by name...."

"It's *your husband* who's getting our people to sign away the rights to their land for Corbin," argued Pharaoh, even more furious. "I just learned your husband gave my mother only a few dollars for her home—knowing she can't come back as he claimed."

Elizabeth appeared stunned by her husband's complicity in the Corbin land grab. She stared anxiously at Edmund, standing on the dais beside Corbin, but she said nothing.

"This is the biggest swindle since the white man paid twenty-four dollars in trinkets for Manhattan," Pharoah said disgustedly to her.

Whether Pharoah actually said these words didn't matter to Kirkland, watching from his monitor. Max tweaked it into a modern dialogue for today's audience. As he later explained to a TV news interviewer, Max particularly liked the "Manhattan for twenty-four dollars" line because it expressed "a bigger truth about the historic exploitation of America's indigenous peoples."

With the band music waning, the organizers asked Elizabeth and Stephen to join the others on the dais, including the president.

"I'll talk to my husband as soon as this ceremony is over—I swear," she whispered back to Pharoah, climbing up two steps together. "But please don't ruin this day. I think it's a special honor that you and the others deserve."

Reluctantly, Pharaoh remained silent. He was escorted to his distant designated spot on the makeshift stage, as far away from the president as one could get.

On this day, Pharaoh wasn't recognized as a king of his Montauk tribe but rather for his heroics as a Lifesaver. Months earlier, he'd been part of the volunteer crew that saved the lives of all but two passengers aboard the shipwrecked ship, the SS *Louisiana,* left shattered by waves in front of the Montauk beach.

At this ceremony, representing the survivors were both Corbin, who thanked Pharaoh without mentioning his refusal to accept his rescue help because of Pharaoh's race, and Elizabeth, who praised Pharaoh's actions profusely. Her gratitude to him for saving her life was expressed in the warmest words.

"According to scripture, when the wind and sea came upon them in a boat, the disciples asked Jesus, 'Save us, Lord, we are perishing,'" Elizabeth said, reading from a small piece of paper. Then turning to Pharoah, she added, "I prayed to God that someone would rescue me from the storm—and suddenly, there *you* were."

Grateful for his wife's survival, town attorney Edmund Gardiner unveiled a brand-new painting called *The Life Line* by an artist named Winslow Homer. Living in the Hamptons that summer, Homer heard of the shipwreck's redemption by the Lifesavers. He visited the site himself during a storm and transformed the dramatic moment into a masterpiece. Edmund, with an inherited family fortune, said he'd purchased the painting and planned to donate it to the East Hampton Library's museum.

When Gardiner dropped the curtain that draped the painting, the crowd seemed stunned. For a few moments, they just gazed at the strong male rescuer with the limp young woman in his arms. The two drenched figures were hanging off a rope line, precariously above the ferocious waves, pulling them to safety. In the backdrop was the sinking vessel. No one had to mention the terror still onboard.

Though faces of the male rescuer and his female survivor were silhouetted in the painting, it was obvious to all that they were meant to be Pharaoh and Elizabeth Gardiner. Moved by its sheer beauty, the crowd burst out with applause.

"I'd like to extend my thanks to Stephen Pharaoh, a member of the Montaukett tribe, for saving my wife's life," said Gardiner with his slight, officious voice, "and to Mr. Winslow Homer for capturing this rescue with his marvelous painting."

Then, quite unexpectedly, Elizabeth Gardiner stepped toward Pharaoh and gave her Native American rescuer a kiss, long enough to suggest this might not be the first time. Her husband thought nothing of it, nor did the forgiving crowd, still enchanted by the painting. But Corbin gave him a suspicious glare. Pharaoh accepted the plaudits and kiss without budging.

Delighted by the reception, President Arthur stepped forward, pulled a few papers from his pocket, and began his prepared remarks. Though once the chairman of the New York Republican Party and product of a landlocked upstate political machine, Arthur preferred to tell this downstate crowd how much he loved the sea. Humbly, he said he had started his career as a customs collector for the Port of New York. Next to an unfurled red-white-and-blue banner marked "Montauk to Manhattan," the president praised Corbin's foresight and grand vision—connecting both ends of Long Island by rail—without mentioning any of their underhanded deals. And then, looking at Pharaoh, the nation's commander-in-chief announced that he planned to fund a series of Life-Saving Stations across Long Island's treacherous oceanfront, starting with a new three-story building at Ditch Plains in Montauk.

"The first job of a president is to save American lives, just like Mr. Pharaoh did here, quite commendably," the president declared with vigorous cheers from the crowd. "Each life-saving station house along the coast will be equipped with boats, cannons, and life lines, enough to save victims of shipwrecks still all-too-frequent along the Long Island coastline."

With his public task finished and his private pact with Corbin completed, Arthur began his return to the White House as America's accidental leader. Assassination was still fresh in everyone's memory. Unlike Garfield, this new twenty-first president of the United States made sure to travel with armed bodyguards—men chosen from the Army and police—who appeared ever-mindful of the next assassin.

As he stepped down from the dais, President Arthur was met by a handful of reporters wearing straw summer hats who had travelled there from newspapers based in New York City. They immediately asked him about Corbin's ambitious plans and about the claims by the Montaukett tribe that their lands had been taken away improperly for this purpose. Suddenly, the glow of sunshine and good cheer from the day drained from Arthur's face.

"Our government attorneys have reviewed all the legal documents and concluded the Montauk tribe is extinct," Arthur proclaimed to the men from the press. "They have no legal standing in court. And they will not stand in the way of progress."

As the reporters scribbled down the president's words, Pharaoh could not believe his ears. No longer silent, he burst out in defiance.

"You cannot do that!" he yelled at the president. "You cannot take away the rights to our own lands! You can't let this man Corbin just run over us!"

Arthur stepped away with alarm in his eyes. The president's bodyguards treated Pharaoh more like a violent anarchist than a hero recently recognized. Together, they grabbed this king of the Montauks and pushed him away from the crowd. They made clear that he should leave this ceremony immediately.

Rather than risk arrest and certain imprisonment, Pharaoh righted himself, grabbed his walking stick, and headed east towards his home.

For nearly an hour, the president continued shaking hands and waving to well-wishers before he boarded the rolling mansion back to Manhattan. Corbin waited for his express train to fade from sight and then offered the

Gardiners a ride back to East Hampton in his private horse-drawn carriage. His railroad still didn't reach there.

Dusk was a few hours away, and the rural Long Island roads were winding and mostly undeveloped. Corbin hoped his good deed might earn him the favors of Mrs. Gardiner overnight when he stayed at his nearby summer home in East Hampton. He considered Edmund to be a harmless impotent. And Pharaoh, the most direct challenge for her affections, had been thrown out ingloriously from this presidential ceremony, just as Austin was feeling jealous about her kiss.

Elizabeth became heartsick when she learned what happened to Stephen Pharaoh. She had turned her back for only a moment in conversation when she heard the scuffle and watched the president's men take Pharaoh away. She tried to appeal to Corbin, but he flatly refused.

"I'm grateful that he saved your life, my dear, but these Indians have cost me a fortune in delays," Corbin explained, trying not to upset her further. "The finest New Yorkers can't wait to reach Montauk by rail, and neither can I."

The Gardiners sat in the back of Corbin's big black carriage, with a roof overhead and a large letter "C" painted in red on its two doors. Austin positioned himself near its front window so he could give instructions to the coachman above steering the team of horses.

The ride was bumpy, but the carriage went swiftly along the dry road at a faster pace than expected. After about five miles, the coachman hollered to Corbin that he could see a tall man, a recognizable figure, walking alongside the narrow pike a hundred yards ahead. Stone-and-mortar fences made this section tighter than most.

Austin looked through his window and spotted the distinctive gait of Pharaoh, well-known for his ability to walk long distances. Corbin motioned to his coachman to increase the horses' gallop and sideswipe "this worthless pedestrian" like he would a dog. Finally, he might be rid of this pesky and dangerous interloper.

In the back seat, Edmund Gardiner, his eyes shut, napping from the day's excitement, didn't hear Corbin's order. But Elizabeth did. She stared out her window and saw the horses rapidly approaching Pharaoh. Valiantly, she opened the door of the barouche carriage and stepped out on the running board to stop the husky coachman from crashing into Pharaoh, her secret lover.

When the driver resisted, Elizabeth began hitting him on the head wildly with her parasol until he lost control of the horses in full stride. Angrily, Corbin ordered Elizabeth to get back into the speeding carriage. When she refused, Corbin moved onto the running board to grab her. Instead, the heavyset tycoon slipped and plummeted to the ground, all in one motion. The front right wheel ran over Corbin's body with an awful thumping sound, and then the rear wheel snapped his neck.

The coachman seized the reins, bringing the horses to a halt. He ran back along the road until he reached Corbin's broken, lifeless body trampled in the dirt. Edmund Gardiner emerged from the carriage in horror. He grabbed the hand of his wife, and they rushed toward Corbin.

"Oh my God, what have I done?" Elizabeth cried over Corbin's corpse.

Her lawyerly husband Edmund, as cool and levelheaded as he was in most matters, assured his wife that she was not to blame. He claimed that he had witnessed everything and that she could not be held responsible for Corbin's foolhardy actions outside the safety of his own carriage. The coachman listened and did not dispute this account.

Watching from the side, Pharaoh approached cautiously. He realized Corbin had wanted to turn him into roadkill until Elizabeth intervened and prevented it. He was unsure if the coachman had a gun and whether he would follow his master's final orders to kill him. From hard experience, the Pharaoh family knew white men could not be trusted to treat fairly someone like himself, a Native American, especially under such deadly circumstances. Rather than the intended victim, he could easily wind up an accused murderer.

As Pharaoh neared the fatal scene, however, Elizabeth rushed and wrapped her arms around him. She reached up on her toes to place a kiss on his lips and hugged him with abandon. With her husband and the coachman watching, Elizabeth dropped all pretense of being a married woman. Instead, she showed her gratitude and relief at being able to defend the man she loved. She kept holding Pharaoh's face in her hands and kissing him uncontrollably.

"He wanted to kill me, didn't he?" Pharaoh finally asked Elizabeth. They both knew the answer. Then, with great solemnity, he declared to her, "You saved my life. This time, *you* were a life line to me."

Her debt from the shipwreck had been repaid. No longer scared or horrified, Elizabeth Gardiner cried with joy. "Yes, yes, that's right," she exclaimed in her proper nineteenth-century way. "Now it is *I* who saved you!"

After a long pause over his video monitor, Max yelled cut. The long day of shooting was over, much to his relief. Kirkland had watched the cameras pull in for a close-up of Manchester and Youngblood as their characters embraced in this final scene and then held the shot for at least five seconds so this footage could dissolve into a suitable ending when later put it together in the editing room.

Max felt sure he had a winner. Critics might condemn such a finale as a shopworn cliche or worse. But Max knew that Americans, despite their thirst for violence and mayhem, still had a weakness for romantic Hollywood endings, the dream of an impossible love come true. Even his last film—a science fiction spectacle with space creatures and a median audience age of thirteen—had such a weepy finale.

"Wonderful job, the both of you," Kirkland said to Manchester and Youngblood as they walked by. He was careful not to go any farther. They nodded without a word and headed back to their dressing rooms in nearby Winnebago trailers.

In the cold war between Kirkland and his two stars, this represented a slight detente. Their previous explosive encounters, with shouting and lurid threats, had made Max wary of saying anything on the set more than the most perfunctory compliments.

The passionate relationship between Youngblood and Manchester had deepened during the past few weeks. Initially, it'd been helped along by their onscreen intimacy and Max's screengrab shots of the two, which he'd fed to the publicity department. Eventually, the tabloids picked up on their affair, with printed rumors of a breakup in Manchester's existing marriage.

To evade the gaze of the press, Kiara and Johnny took a ferry to Fire Island Pines where they rented a house for the weekend, away from the rest of the cast and crew staying at the Montauk Manor. A paparazzi living in this traditionally gay summer community sold a photo of a shirtless Youngblood and Manchester in a tiny string bikini to a daily tabloid, which soon spread it around the world. Eventually, Johnny and Kiara gave up their private subterfuge. They came out publicly as Hollywood's newest power couple.

Surprisingly, their off-screen coupling paid off artistically. Under Manchester's influence, Youngblood, the reckless rocker, became a dedicated dramaturg tweaking his script lines. They studied the history of the Montauketts and were appalled how the real-life Corbin stole their lands and how a New York court in 1910 really did declare the tribe extinct. They were surprised to learn that I had written about this historical scandal for the local newspaper and that it was the impetus for my fictional account in *The Life Line.* The two actors bragged that they had read my novel cover to cover, though Max begged me not to quiz them on it.

As a couple in the public eye, Manchester and Youngblood decided to visit the ancient Montauketts cemetery, ensconced on a secluded hill in a neighborhood of modern McMansions. On his Instagram account, Johnny posted a photo of himself next to the gravestone of Stephen Pharaoh. *#FreetheMontauketts,* he wrote, adopting their cause on his webpage. Soon, the couple paid homage to the remaining Montauk tribe members on Long Island. They pledged their support for tribal recognition by the government and reparations if necessary.

"Imagine you've been told you're extinct!" Youngblood explained to celebrity reporters, full of historical frustration and disgust. He insisted lawmakers review the Montauk tribe's plight and repeal the legal sham of their extinction.

Max loved all this pre-opening day publicity. Even if he was barely speaking to his two stars, he knew media hype about his upcoming project served as a good predictor of success. Buzz was the coin of the realm in Hollywood. The suits at Comflix started sending him complimentary notes, promising to increase their promotional budget. Max was thrilled.

As someone once told me, publicity for Kirkland was as vital as blood to Dracula.

Yet despite all the time I had observed Kirkland, including hours sitting in directors' chairs behind him, I still couldn't figure him out. No doubt he possessed the same narcissistic self-regard that defines so many artists and powerful figures. But behind his Hollywood facade, the glad-hander and self-promoter, he seemed hollow, an enigma. Perhaps I couldn't find his core because there simply wasn't one. His true identity seemed covered over in myth, like repeated wallpapering in an empty room. Much of his life's story had been embroidered and fabricated.

With a little checking, I discovered the bogus claims on his IMDb biography—"Max was a poor kid from the Midwest who sold artwork at Venice Beach before he became a Hollywood producer." Max was actually the son of a New Jersey physician and his suburban socialite wife. His real surname of "Kovalenko" harkened back to his immigrant Polish-Catholic grandparents who fled the Nazis.

Everything proved to be transactional with Kirkland. Along with his phony name, Max's union with Tatiana appeared more like a business arrangement than a functioning marriage. A TV star in her own right, Tatiana seemed aware of Max's constellation of starlets and *grandes horizontals*. But her husband's adultery apparently didn't bother her. Throughout the summer in Montauk, I had wondered if she knew of Max's more dangerous side, like his sadomasochistic flings with Sheila Teague and presumably other women in his employ? Did she know of Vanessa Adams and wonder why this young actress, who appeared in the Kirkland mansion for a party, left without explanation and disappeared?

Max fought to control everything in his life. Publicity was one way of exerting this power. For this reason, Max became even more adamant that Kiara Manchester should appear in a black leather S&M outfit on the cover of Diana Trumbull's fashion magazine. He realized it could be the most memorable image from this production.

"And if Kiara doesn't pose?" asked Penny MacPharland, as they walked off the location set together.

Kirkland's eyes turned steely.

"Then I'll make her do it."

CHAPTER 18
FALSE IMPRESSIONS

The remote location where we filmed the carriage ride scene leading to Austin Corbin's death was miles away from the Montauk Manor. Jitney buses, hired for the occasion, would carry many of the cast and crew, myself included, on a long ride back from the nostalgic nineteenth century to today's contentious America.

Climbing aboard, I settled into a velour-covered seat in the luxury bus and gazed through the window, waiting to leave.

Max Kirkland drove by in his cherry-red Tesla Roadster, accompanied by his toadie Penny MacPharland, constantly talking and gesturing to him. Then Kiara Manchester and Johnny Youngblood passed in their chauffeur-driven black Cadillac Escalade limo. No longer hiding on Fire Island, they headed back to what the tabloids called their Manhattan "love nest."

Two rows ahead of me in the bus, Lester Wolf sank into an empty seat, alone and seemingly forlorn. He seemed saddened by the death of his evil character and whether he might have to atone for all his sins.

"Mind if I join you?" Sheila Teague asked, the last to get on the jitney before it took off. She sat close enough in the narrow seats that our elbows touched, and I could smell her perfume. I welcomed her company, for there were many things I wanted to ask.

Cruising along the roadway, we started gossiping about the actors, about Max Kirkland, and how this production might turn out under the corporate streamer Comflix. Nothing was said about what happened between us personally.

Eventually, I asked about the dramatic scene of Corbin's death that Teague had written and all the intricacies of how it was produced. I praised her profusely, perhaps more than I should have as the original author. But a magical alchemy existed between her words, my novel, and what appeared on screen. I wanted to know her secrets.

"This whole experience has me wondering if I should leave journalism and try my hand at screenwriting," I confided. "Covering Trump for the paper these days has really made me think—where is this country going, and what am I doing with my life? Writing screenplays for a living would be a chance to start over. My contract with Max says that I can write future episodes if I want. I'd love to become someone like you."

Sheila turned in her seat and stared hard at me.

"Just like that, huh? No dues paying? No years of learning? No knocking on doors looking for a break, hustling for the next writing job?" Sheila asked incredulously, shaking her head. "Must be great to be a white guy, with the door always open. Just leapfrog over everyone because you can. I see why you're constantly pushing that Great Man theory in your books."

Surprised by her ferocity, justified or not, I struggled for a reply. I remembered our talks about the so-called Great Man theory of history, and why the hero in movies and TV shows like this one always seemed to be Caucasian. Our discussion about sexual fairness and racial equity remained theoretical, and I tended to agree with her points in the abstract. But now, the real prospect of my becoming a television writer seemed to offend Sheila, as if she'd been slapped in the face.

"Listen, I can't rewrite history," I argued back. "I can only do what I think is right for me and my career. Besides, in *The Life Line,* the hero isn't white, he's a Native American—Stephen Pharaoh."

"Yeah, and look who they gave that job to—Johnny Youngblood, another white guy!" she exclaimed.

"I thought Johnny was part Native American?" I asked. "Didn't somebody say that?"

Sheila gave a skeptical laugh. "Penny MacPharland made up that shit for the press and you believed it," she said, mocking my naivete and, no doubt, my racial insensitivity. "Penny only said Johnny was Native

American because Max told him to do so when those Montauketts came to the office looking for a piece of the show. Johnny Youngblood? He's a rocker who went to Skidmore. His daddy is a big hedge fund guy in Connecticut. Supposedly his real name is John Parkhurst or some shit like that. Johnny Youngblood? Nothing true about that name!"

The absurdity of it all made us burst out laughing. In my own desperation to find something new, I had hit a nerve with Sheila. I should have known better. Previously, she'd shared her stories of being bounced around Hollywood as a Black woman, only getting choice writing assignments by chance or when she found dubious patrons like Max Kirkland.

Our loud exchange woke up Lester Wolf, still in costume as Austin Corbin. He'd been napping in the row ahead of us with his head against the window.

"Everything all right between you two?" he said, his white hair and fake whiskers messed from the windowpane.

With a grand gesture, Sheila reached across my shoulders and gave me a hug.

"Couldn't be better, thank you, Mr. Austin Corbin," she replied. Lester beamed with recognition of his role, as if they were one and the same. We both laughed again and then remained silent for much of the ride, gazing out of the windows.

Outside, a street sign finally welcomed us to Montauk as the jitney turned off the highway. We realized our time together would soon come to an end without a satisfactory conclusion. Sheila asked about my plans. I told her how I was going to pack immediately and fly to Florida, where I was supposed to cover another Trump rally.

"If this guy gets elected president, what would that mean for people like me?" Sheila asked, undoubtedly a question entering the minds of many other people of color.

I wondered myself. It seemed America was taking a sharp turn away from the past, away from the noblesse oblige of Yalies like the Bushes and the level-headed equanimity of Barack Obama from Harvard Law, a barrier-breaker as the first African American occupant in the White House. Trump was something very different, selling a brand of coarse, constant lies that he offered to America as the unvarnished truth. And the country seemed to be buying it.

For a moment, I thought of Tea Party organizers I knew from covering politics on Long Island who were now supporting Trump. At first, they might seem friendly and reasonable, especially when approached by a middle-aged white guy like myself. But when they opened their mouth, it became clear that their paranoia, once wrapped in a yellow flag proclaiming "Don't Tread on Me," had given way to red baseball caps embossed with "Make America Great Again." Could these people soon be running the country, and what would it mean for Black people like Teague?

"That's a good question," I told Sheila, looking her straight in the eye. "Honestly, I just don't know."

The heat in Florida dissipated at night, with enough coolness so that I wore a jacket to this Trump rally inside the campus arena in Orlando. At the main gate, I watched hundreds rush to their seats. The Trump campaign, which once seemed like a publicity stunt, had turned into a presidential juggernaut. Trump had already eliminated several Republican rivals for the nomination. His staff said there was little chance of getting an interview with the candidate himself that night, so my editors back in New York decided on a different interview subject for the night. I looked around, but he had yet to arrive.

With an eye on November's general election, my paper wanted me to focus on eighty-seven-year-old Jacob Zellner, once a well-known Jewish figure in New York. Later in life, Zellner migrated to this central Florida community along Route 4, a land of Disney pavilions, alligators, and emerging Trump supporters.

During his time in New York, Zellner had been active in the Democratic Party and the Anti-Defamation League. He survived the Holocaust as a ten-year-old orphan when a Hungarian family sheltered and kept him safe from the onslaught. He lost both parents in the gas chambers of Nazi concentration camps. As a young attorney in Manhattan, Zellner helped put together the ADL's fiftieth anniversary celebration in January 1963, which featured a speech by then-president John F. Kennedy. Zellner idolized JFK who spoke famously of America as "a nation of immigrants" and defender of freedoms against tyranny.

Retiring to Orlando, Zellner had been active in many pro-Israel causes; like many older Jews in Florida, he felt the Democratic Party had become too critical of the Jewish homeland, moved too far to the left from the old days of JFK. My political editor Jamal was pleased when I told him I had contacted Zellner, who'd planned to attend this Trump rally and check out this billionaire Republican New Yorker for himself.

"If folks like Zellner vote for Trump, it could mean Hillary loses Florida and the whole election in November," Williams instructed. I doubted his prognosis but didn't say anything. Like most political reporters, I still couldn't imagine that Clinton—the former secretary of state, the former US senator from New York, the former first lady and lifelong consigliere to her husband, former US president Bill Clinton—could lose to a political newcomer, regardless of his TV popularity.

Eventually, an old man with a full head of white hair, seated in a wheelchair, came rolling up to the accessible portion of the main gate, just as we arranged.

"Are you Mr. Denton?" he asked. Zellner's middle-aged daughter pushed his chair behind him.

Together, the three of us entered the arena. We sat near the front, in a section off to the side reserved for those with wheelchairs. Our closeness to the stage made Trump's face on the jumbo screen appear even bigger when he finally greeted his supporters. At first, his rambling speech seemed run-of-the-mill, perhaps even to Zellner's liking, until Trump suddenly ramped up the crowd's devotion to him.

"Let's do a pledge," Trump began, almost playfully. "Who likes me in this room?"

After the initial wave of applause, Trump led his followers into a vow of obedience to him.

"Raise your right hand," Trump cajoled and recited the pledge he wanted them to take: "I do solemnly swear that I—no matter how I feel, no matter what the conditions, if there's hurricanes or whatever—will vote for Donald J. Trump for president."

Nearly everyone in the area hoisted their right hands in what appeared like a salute. Trump beamed at the throng of raised right hands at his frenzied rally.

"Don't forget, you all raised your hand. You swore," Trump warned the crowd. "Bad things happen if you don't live up to what you just did." Trump immediately acted like he was kidding, but Zellner wasn't laughing. He looked like he'd seen a ghost.

"Get me out of here, now," Zellner instructed his daughter. "I will not stay here another minute." She immediately began rolling her father's wheelchair out to the exit. It happened so suddenly, I hustled with a pen and notebook to catch up to them.

"What's the matter? Why are you leaving?" I asked as we reached the parking lot. I worried this assignment from my new bosses in New York was blowing up in my face.

"Did you see what that looked like? He's asking them to pledge allegiance to him with a 'Heil Hitler' salute," said the old man, his eyes ablaze and voice raised. Zellner had lived through enough history to know what a stiff-armed salute meant. He told his daughter to keep pushing him towards their car while he explained to me why he was so upset with the Trump rally.

"It's a Nazi gesture used by the KKK and white supremacists, the kind we used to fight against at the ADL," he said, his voice nearly out of breath from his anxiety. "Now a candidate for the presidency is asking us to swear allegiance to him? That's something Hitler did at his political rallies."

His daughter assisted Zellner as he got into the car's front seat. She indicated that her father, with his weak heart, had had enough excitement for one day. But the old man persisted.

"He's smart enough to know what he's doing," said Zellner with his seatbelt on, speaking through his rolled down window. "Trump's always saying how smart he is. He knows what all these salutes look like, with their arms and fists in the air, and how this garbage will play on TV and in the press. He knows damn well. I've seen enough of him."

His daughter, now in the driver's seat, pushed a button to roll up her father's passenger window. We watched each other through the tinted glass as the car drove away.

The old man put into perspective what I had witnessed over the past year. I remembered the day that I called into the newsroom with the quotes from GOP regulars more amused by Trump's announcement about running for president than with any real concern he would win. Now Trump was nearing the White House, and Zellner's adopted countrymen were ignoring these obvious warning signals.

I went back to the hotel and quickly filed my story about Zellner's night at the Trump rally. In the vernacular of daily journalists, the story wrote itself. The night editor seemed pleased with my feature describing Zellner, and it soon appeared on the paper's website, shortly after midnight.

I needed to get to sleep, though my adrenalin was still racing. A dirty, emptied plate of food remained on the hotel desk next to my computer. I had ordered my usual room service meal—steak and eggs—to keep me company as I typed up my dispatch. I sipped one last swig from my beer bottle before sliding into bed, exhausted from this busy Saturday on the road. I stared at the white stucco hotel ceiling, like so many other anonymous places before that lulled me to sleep.

Despite the thrill of covering a presidential campaign, I wondered how long I wanted to keep performing this charade. I couldn't get *The Life Line* production out of my head and the possibilities that Hollywood make-believe offered.

Then my cell phone on the night table buzzed with a text from Jamal that read:

> *"Nice job. Come back to the office as soon as you can."*

CHAPTER 19
ON THIN ICE

Coming home from Florida was more sour than sweet. As I entered my apartment in Manhattan's Flatiron District, a small, claustrophobic studio space with brick walls, I flicked on the lights and looked around at this dreary solitude of my existence. A stale, stagnant musk hung in the air, more like the smell of a tomb than a living, breathing quarters.

For two years, since the breakup of my marriage, I'd tried to avoid spending time here. The making of *The Life Line* out in the Hamptons—and chasing the Trump campaign around the country—kept me away frequently.

After my divorce, I threw out the borrowed couch, secondhand chairs, and used kitchen table that came with the apartment. In its place, I bought an expensive sectional sofa with chairs and pillows in a teal-and-gray palette. It was suggested by a girlfriend at that time with a flair for interior design. Another paramour insisted on framed artwork, a Rauschenberg print, and a hanging glass planter with a cactus that needed little care. These furnishings meant nothing to me.

Over time, though, I started placing keepsake photos of my kids on the walls, coffee tables, and atop bookshelves. My eyes often gravitated to these recent portraits and old family snapshots from Long Island, the place I called home for so long (including one with Tricia in the background). Elaine appeared with Gary in another shot, her death still a reminder of all that had been lost. In a black-and-white photo, my parents posed on the day they bought their first house, holding me in their arms and so immersed in their suburban yearning. All these smiling faces, like ghosts from another life, greeted me when I arrived back in the apartment after time away.

In the corner, I noticed a pulsing red light on my message machine, one of the few artifacts from my marriage. The first message contained a familiar female voice.

"Hi Jack, we got back the DNA analysis. You know, for Johnny's family tree project at school," said Tricia briskly. "Give me a call."

DNA? Family tree project? It didn't register for a moment. Then I recalled how I expectorated into a small plastic tube at the beginning of the school year for Jack Jr.'s fifth-grade science project at the middle school. (These days, Tricia referred to our son as Johnny while I still preferred to call him Jack Jr.)

Genetic analysis of my wet and sloppy saliva would help deconstruct the Denton and Stanton family trees going back five generations. I remembered the excitement of Jack Jr., my daughter Megan, and their mother at the idea of spitting into a tube and sending theirs away for analysis along with mine. Who knew where our family's far-flung DNA might have ventured in this world? Jack Jr.'s grade-school experiment had combined Watson & Crick's double helix with the wanderlust of a Marco Polo.

On the night I provided my DNA sample, I returned home to this apartment and took out old videos taken of the kids when they were smaller, only a few years before the big breakup between Tricia and myself. The images were both mesmerizing and haunting, the filmed fragments of my former married life, complete with the squeaky voices of our children. During one trip to Disney, the kids waved with glee aboard the carousel rides, the flying elephants, and Splash Mountain. In an earlier video, Gary and Elaine stood proudly as godparents for Jack Jr. at his baptism. These dusty DVDs contained vestiges of otherwise-forgotten family gatherings at graduations, weddings, and special holidays. They unraveled like dreams without form, like nostalgic, silent home movies spliced together. This vivid soundtrack of familiar voices lingered in my mind. While asleep, I replayed the past, rearranged previous conversations, and imagined different outcomes. Often, I'd wake up with feelings of loss and guilt.

Occasionally in these videos, I caught fleeting glimpses of myself. These self-images were reflected in mirrored walls and glass windows. As I jockeyed around with my little Sony camera, I appeared like a phantom passing by. Watching these videos, I sometimes spotted, on a table or a counter, an open bottle of beer, gin, or whisky. They were all reminders of my "problem" that eventually landed me in an upstate detox clinic.

When the kids wondered about my whereabouts, Tricia said Daddy was "away." Eventually, they grew accustomed to my absences. A marriage ends for a variety of reasons, many unspoken. But the video images of these opened bottles and mixed drinks were evidence of at least one damning reason why.

Instead of returning Tricia's call, I listened to my second recorded message. To my surprise, it was Mark Fresco, a freelance political aide to Trump. I'd known him for years as a good source. Fresco was a thickset man, big enough to have once played tackle on the taxi squad of a professional football team. Now heavier in middle age, he liked to eat and gossip about politics at local diners (a food stain on his tie or white shirt was a constant). In an agitated, winded tone, Fresco asked if I could call him back immediately. When I did, Fresco admitted he'd been let go from the Trump campaign, already notorious for its firings and turnovers. Fresco said he possessed some inside information that he promised would be a front-page story for my new editors.

"I have some documents that I know you'll want to see," Fresco said in a conspiratorial tone. "I know I can trust you. There's not many I can trust."

Like a fisherman with a lure, Fresco dangled a few meaty morsels. He wanted to share them all with me tomorrow. The next day was a Monday, and I was off because of my Florida trip over the weekend. But I agreed to see Fresco anyway. Good reporters don't delay, I'd learned long ago. Fresco told me to meet him for a 9:30 breakfast at a midtown Manhattan restaurant overlooking the skating rink at Rockefeller Center.

When we sat down the next morning, I couldn't resist asking, "So why did you pick this place?"

"That's easy," Fresco laughed. "Who's gonna see us this time of day except some skaters?"

We indeed were alone in a sea of empty tables. We were surrounded by art deco buildings, young skaters on the ice, and the golden statue of Prometheus looking down on us.

"I'm sorry to hear about you leaving the campaign—it must be tough working for a guy like Trump," I began, sympathetically.

On our breakfast table—between the coffee, Danish pastry, and orange juice—Fresco plopped down his package of documents in a large envelope.

"What have you got for me?" I asked.

Fresco grinned, the kind of maddening smile that conspirators and co-conspirators share alike, regardless of the merits of their secrets. It reminded me of another time with him.

Not long after Hattie left our local paper, Fresco gave me incriminating information about a corrupt Long Island politician whom he didn't like. His motivation wasn't an idealistic stance against corruption. Rather, Fresco felt cheated out of his portion of the local political machine's shakedown of neighborhood merchants. This damning tip resulted in another award-winning expose that helped me land a new job at *The New York World* covering Trump. Based on his track record, I felt obliged to consider Fresco's pitch.

"It's crazy, really complicated," Fresco began, "but these papers help explain it." He opened the package and displayed its contents. Each fact was underlined and color coded. Fresco spun an elaborate tale about a Long Island multimillionaire who had become a shadowy benefactor to the Trump campaign through an analytics company with ties to the Russians.

"There's hundreds more on this flash drive—really dynamite stuff," assured Fresco, giving me the black plastic device about the size of a rabbit's foot keychain.

I finished my brunch—slowly picking apart my Western omelet with red and green peppers on a plate with greasy sausages—while listening to Fresco. He expounded on the importance of each thread of information in this labyrinth. Through his thick spectacles, Fresco's dark eyes flared with excitement. His reedy voice became more insistent. He claimed this pilfered material proved that Russian spies were illegally breaking into email accounts, engineering an election year disinformation campaign, and, mostly, that Trump was the beneficiary of this treachery.

"What they're doing here is treason in my book—that's why I left them," Fresco concluded. "They don't know I have this stuff. But I figured you can sort it out and get it into the newspaper."

I stared at Fresco for a moment, ready to reject everything he'd asked me to swallow. America the Paranoid was a land of conspiracies, ever since JFK was shot by Oswald, who was then shot by Ruby. Or probably before Lincoln was shot by John Wilkes Booth. Something in the nation's air and water seemed to breed half-baked plots and outright fabrications. People like Fresco were its denizens, wild-eyed and apocryphal. They seemed impervious to truth, preferring grand intrigue and intoxicating phantasm to sober fact.

I sipped my coffee with an acrid tone. "You left the Trump camp, or they fired you?" I asked.

Fresco responded defensively. Clearly, I had hit a nerve about how he left his job during the last campaign.

"OK, Jack, *they* fired me," he corrected, standing up abruptly. He threw some cash on the table to pay the restaurant bill. "Just let me know if you can do something about this."

CHAPTER 20
HUMAN RESOURCES

The next morning at *The New York World*, I didn't get the chance to do anything with Fresco's tip. I had intended to write a memo about these documents and send it to Jamal. Instead when I arrived, Williams came over and told me to "stand down" with what I was doing and to report right away to the human resources department. He gave no indication of the reason. Nearby, Hattie Thompson was on the phone, deep in conversation with another source.

I wandered through the building with its white eggshell walls until I reached "Human Resources," one of those corporate euphemisms that bore little resemblance to its true task. After I spent nearly an hour in the waiting room, leafing through the only paper edition of the newspaper on the coffee table, Ellen Steplow emerged from her office.

"Sorry to keep you waiting," said Steplow, a bone-thin woman wearing an austere business suit with white pearls. "Let's talk in my office."

To the company's nearly one thousand employees, Steplow acted as the chosen mediator for nearly every work-related crisis, at least the ones that really mattered. As I remembered vividly, her signature was on the letter informing recruits like myself that we'd been hired. To the staff, Steplow sent emails about health care sign-ups, filling out travel and expense reports, and the measly wage hikes negotiated by our dying union. As I soon learned, she also served as judge and jury if an employee was to be fired.

A trained lawyer who had been schooled in psychology and downsizing, Steplow wasted little time beginning her inquisition.

"So Mr. Denton—may I call you Jack?" she asked without waiting for a reply. "Have you read our code of conduct policy, that little green booklet we gave you when you were hired?"

I nodded. "I'm sure I did," I replied, "but I'm afraid I didn't commit it to memory."

My response contained just enough flippancy, a touch of unwanted smart-aleckiness in this grave proceeding, to make her executioner's job easier. Her deep-set eyes of gray, the same neutral dark as her suit, were now affixed on me. Despite years in this role, Steplow still spoke with an upstate twang rather than a Manhattan honk or Brooklyn accent like others in this streetwise newsroom. She executed her task with the swiftness of a hog farmer slicing the neck of an impudent swine.

"I'm glad you did," she said, establishing her predicate. "Do you remember those warnings about sexual harassment and the seriousness with which it is viewed here by this management team?"

Steplow's mental gears seemed in full grind, though I had no idea what she was talking about. Whatever the matter, it was obviously more serious than I'd imagined. My back stiffened on her guest couch, lower to the ground than her executive seat before me.

"Of course I remember, and I also take it seriously," I affirmed, with starch and directness. "It's something I've never engaged in and never would." I glanced around her office to see if this exchange was being recorded.

Steplow gave a sly grin, like a prosecutor seasoned in star-chamber justice. She lifted a sheaf of printouts from her desk.

"I have here a series of text exchanges between you and Anna Melendez...." she said, carefully enunciating Anna's name as if to elicit a response.

"Who?" I cut in. "What are you talking about?"

Steplow methodically repeated Anna Melendez's name and title as a multimedia producer at the paper, careful not to get ahead of herself. By now, I already knew where she was headed with this inquisition.

"Anna told us that you offered to mentor her, but all you wanted to do was talk about her private life," Steplow said. She now glared at me like a homicide detective intent on getting a confession.

I tried to slough it off. "Are you kidding me?" I replied. "Anna came up to me in the newsroom, introduced herself, and asked me about my novel and how they're making it into a television project. I was about to leave and invited her to come along with me to McGee's, that bar around the corner. And when we got there, she started quizzing me on whether I thought director Max Kirkland was exploiting the story of Native Americans in my television show. That's when our conversation ended."

Shaking her head, Steplow reminded me that Melendez was well within bounds. "The paper has often written about the artistic expropriation of life stories among marginalized people," she corrected, nodding to the framed cover of an award-winning project on the subject that the paper had recently published.

Then Steplow put on her reading glasses and handed me a sheet of paper.

"I'm concerned about what Anna gave us—these text messages that you sent to her afterwards. Like this text message...'*Sorry, I wanted to talk more about hanging out than work. Maybe we can get together soon and try it again?*'"

Steplow had cut and pasted my original text, enlarged it, and then printed it out on her office machine. She paused for effect and then demanded, "What did you mean by 'it'? And when you say, 'hanging out,' isn't that same as 'hooking up'?"

Incredulous, I tried to explain my ham-handed text message. "I felt bad that I had cut her off and wanted to see if I could make it up to her by talking again. Outside of work. On our own time. Is there anything wrong with that?"

Raising *The World's* HR booklet in her hand, Steplow suggested that, somehow, I had violated the spirit, if not the letter, of the paper's ethos. In her mind, "it" was something sexual, something coercive.

"Texts like these about 'getting together'—from older men to younger female colleagues—carry an implicit message, Mr. Denton," she said.

"Anna didn't reply to your text on that occasion. There was a reason for that denial. And yet you, again, sent her another text message—*this one.*"

She waved a brand-new text message that I sent to Anna after my breakfast with Fresco at the Rockefeller Center skating rink. At the time, I was feeling relaxed and a bit lonely, so I decided to retext a similar invitation to Anna, hoping she might be free and join me for a drink to watch the skaters pirouetting on the ice. Anna never responded, and I didn't think anything more of it. Now this text, this electronic reaching out for some companionship, had landed in my personnel file.

"I never dreamed I was offending her somehow or running afoul of the paper's rules," I argued, shaking my head insistently. "This is how grown-ups used to meet all the time, remember? In bars and restaurants, all around town. And without anyone's permission."

For a moment, a faint note of human recognition appeared in Steplow's eyes. She had never been a reporter, out there meeting other people in the world. Instead, she'd prospered as a newsroom bureaucrat, always jockeying inside for position and a place on the masthead. But perhaps she, too, remembered a time when she went out for a drink after work with a friend or acquaintance, before she started taking the 5:23 commuter train every evening to the suburbs. I wondered if "human resources" for Steplow might involve compassion and fairness and recognizing the fundamental dignity of another adult. If such a thought existed within her, it didn't last long.

"There's also another matter," she decreed, furthering her relentless assault. "About your TV show and a conflict of interest." She muttered the phrase "TV" with disdain.

I prepared for another incoming rocket headed my way. "You knew in advance about both my book and the TV deal attached to it before you hired me," I objected. "In fact, the success of *The Life Line* was part of the reason why you folks recruited me, and why management asked my friend Hattie Thompson to convey your offer to help her cover this year's presidential campaign."

Steplow knew enough about newsroom politics to take note that I had invoked Hattie's name as a friend. Thompson had a special status based on her remarkable expertise in deciphering Donald Trump's impromptu actions and moods.

"This has nothing to do with Hattie, but it does involve Trump," Steplow explained. "Jamal Williams told me that you covered a Trump fundraiser in the Hamptons—and that this TV producer you're doing business with, Mr. Kirkland, was there and he's a contributor to the Trump campaign."

"Max's not for Trump—he only gave money because he was invited to the party at Zach Preston's mansion," I explained. "It's a TV business thing, not a political thing."

Steplow frowned. "This connection between Kirkland and Trump was something you should have disclosed to your editors as soon as you learned of it. Jamal says you never informed him of it."

"Well, then, how does Jamal know about this?"

"Hattie Thompson told him," Steplow replied. "Apparently you mentioned it to her at some point and she felt required to inform Jamal as her boss. That's why Jamal told you to stand down and report to my office when you arrived back in the office today."

Somehow these rapid-fire accusations from Steplow didn't sting as much as Hattie Thompson's betrayal of my trust. I knew that she'd been disappointed in my performance since arriving, distracted by the glitter of Hollywood and a personal life that seemed chaotic. But how could she blame me for Max Kirkland showing up at a Trump fundraiser? She was too smart, too savvy with politics, not to realize that this embarrassing piece of information could be used as a lethal weapon against me by this functionary from human resources.

"Listen, Jamal and Hattie are only doing their jobs," Steplow explained, as I tried to formulate a response. "As unlikely as it may seem, Trump could wind up becoming president. The world is watching how Trump is being covered by this newspaper—both friends and foes alike—and we cannot afford to have someone with an undisclosed conflict of interest involved in it. The reputation of this paper is beyond any one employee, whatever their individual agenda may be. I'm sure you understand that."

Steplow implied my Hollywood alliance with Kirkland somehow made me out to be a closet Trump supporter, a Manchurian candidate on the paper's politics team. This battery of false charges left me stunned, unable to move on her office couch. It was as if Trump had turned the whole world upside down and his perfidy had infected everyone's judgment and common sense.

Steadily, I grew angry at this effrontery, the distortions and disloyalty, and the smearing of my good name. I stood up and walked halfway towards the door.

"This whole thing is incredible," I declared, my voice raised. "I didn't come to this newspaper to have my reputation sullied and ruined. An innocent social invitation treated as harassment. Are you kidding me? Are you really serious? Is this how you treat people?"

At first, Steplow urged calm and suggested I sit down again. But then, she seemed to conclude that this last angry outburst might make a good ending to her disciplinary report, emotional evidence that she could point to as a sign of my guilt when she forwarded her final recommendations to the paper's top editor.

"I'm sorry you feel that way," Steplow pronounced, "but from this moment on, you're suspended from the paper. I must ask you to leave immediately. The contents of your desk will be shipped to you. I'll let you know when the paper decides on your future status."

There was no use arguing any further. Walking out the door, I avoided the newsroom and headed directly to the exit, still numbed by this turn of events.

For months, I had pondered my future, wondering if streamers, scriptwriting, and filming on location sets held more meaning to me than covering lying politicians and their daily schemes. Was make-believe more of a valued reality than fact, especially to an American public that would consider Donald Trump as its triumphant ruler? Then this morning, abruptly without warning, like a man falling into a sinkhole on the street, my fate was decided for me.

Descending into the subterranean shadows of the subway, I realized my once-shining career in journalism was now over. There would be no going back in my mind. As they say in the cinema: *Finis*.

CHAPTER 21
PIECING THINGS TOGETHER

In front of a camera, Max Kirkland was a natural. He particularly loved talking dramatically about himself and his humble origins in the Hollywood fantasy business. His eyes expanded wide like a camera lens, and his hands moved expressively in recounting his own story.

"Jigsaw puzzles were my passion growing up—putting together *a thousand* little pieces to form one big picture of the Mona Lisa or the Statue of Liberty," he explained to a female network morning news show anchor sitting before him. "It's just like putting together a film or a TV project."

Kirkland made sure his nationwide television interview, taped in advance to promote *The Life Line,* took place along the Hamptons beachfront where the shipwreck scene had been filmed. He performed his well-practiced anecdote brilliantly, aware of the millions of network TV viewers watching at home. Like some coffee-cup raconteur, he relaxed in his tall wooden director's chair pitched in the sand, with the morning sun and Atlantic Ocean behind him as a prop. Fortunately, some warmth still lingered in the air.

There was no finer promoter of his own productions. A true showman in the all-American tradition, Kirkland seemed part of a continuum stretching from modern moviemakers to old-time directors Cecil B. DeMille and Busby Berkeley, even back to nineteenth-century vaudeville, Buffalo Bill's carnival shows, and the Barnum & Bailey circus. In America, each new generation sought out a new form of entertainment, an escape from real life.

Kirkland wanted to be "Mr. Streaming Media," his extravaganzas beamed around the world on internet apps rather than local theaters.

I watched this scene from a distance standing next to Penny MacPharland and Sheila Teague, part of the entourage that included the network's news producer, camera crew, and hair and makeup experts. We were joined by Comflix's publicity agents, security guards, food caterers, and several others whose job descriptions were vaguer than my own.

Everyone clapped when the Kirkland interview finished. The well-known female morning anchor was a longtime friend of Max and his wife Tatiana, summertime neighbors in the Hamptons. Assured that unpleasant questions like Kirkland's "casting couch" reputation wouldn't be broached, the execs at Comflix granted this live, exclusive interview as a teaser for the premiere of *The Life Line* shortly after Election Day 2016.

"I've heard that jigsaw story a million times," Penny moaned in my ear.

With a weary dreadfulness, MacPharland explained how Max liked to please his audience with nostalgic personal stories. Kirkland believed Americans in the hinterlands wanted a glimpse of how it was done in Hollywood—the kind of naïve, flabby folks who bring their kids to places like Disneyland, hoping some of Fantasyland's magic might rub off on them.

I didn't want to admit to Penny that the "jigsaw" anecdote sounded fresh to me. It was an analogy that seemed apt in watching Max piece together his television project.

The making of *The Life Line* called for an endless array of scattered information, random film clips, and sound bites to be assembled just like a puzzle. Each morning, production assistants handed out a "daily call sheet," a yellow paper detailing each assignment, the time that actors would report to work, and even a "shot list" that contained portions of the script to be filmed before the day's end. For five months, through the spring and summer of 2016, Kirkland hurriedly prepared and filmed each major scene as quickly as his team of scriptwriters could compose their pages. Slowly but inexorably, I could see his vision emerging.

My other job, covering the presidential campaign, had kept me away from being a regular participant in the writers room. But one last time, I joined Max's encampment to observe and perhaps offer advice as the final redos were filmed. I realized much of the scriptwriting had been completed without me. Convinced I no longer had a newspaper job in the city, my fortunes were tied more than ever to the success of *The Life Line*.

Lester Wolf, in full regalia as Austin Corbin, stood near the cresting Atlantic waves and waited for direction. Only two hours of sunlight on the beach remained before dusk.

"Move a little further into the water so we can see and hear the slapping of the waves," instructed Kirkland from a safe distance away. Wolf's face tightened, but he complied.

Wolf's pant cuffs were already wet, his shoes submerged by the foaming surf at the water's edge. Over the past few months, he'd endured every one of Max's demands. Wolf had reglued his Corbin beard on and off his chin so many times that he'd developed a rash from spirit gum remover. But Wolf was an actor not to be deterred. He had learned perseverance at the Old Vic, the Young Vic, and generations of other stages and movie sets on both sides of the Atlantic. He realized he was near the finish line on this production.

Ever the perfectionist, Kirkland wanted to reshoot some dialogue, close-ups, and reversals from the original shipwreck scene filmed previously, when the overall shape of *The Life Line* was still in flux in Max's mind. He selected this foggy morning in advance after hearing a ten-day weather forecast that predicted an early September offshore hurricane. It would barrel past Montauk at high tide and raise the swells to the size of what would have swamped an 1880s vessel like the SS *Louisiana*. This little bit of natural verisimilitude was worth the effort, in Max's judgment, the small touches of quality that pay off big-time on the screen. Kirkland asked for a sound test from Lester beforehand.

"I should have you arrested... one-two-three, can you hear me?" Wolf said, riffing off his intended dialogue. His voice was clear and distinct through his wireless lavalier microphone, submerged under his vintage clothing. Listening in with my own headset near Kirkland, I admired Wolf's ability to evoke a Shakespearean tone while in the saltwater foam.

"Now, Kiara and Johnny, get a little closer to Lester so we have you safely in this shot," Kirkland said gently to the two actors playing Elizabeth Gardiner and Stephen Pharaoh. Max received a chilly reception, colder than the ocean water.

Back at Montauk Manor where we all stayed, Sheila Teague had warned me that Manchester and Youngblood were upset about the intense tabloid press interest in their romance. The couple now suspected, quite accurately, that Max had encouraged this gossip in the media because of its publicity value when *The Life Line* finally appeared. Kirkland recalled how another director's film got a box-office boost when its leading man left his wife, America's TV sweetheart, for his voluptuous female co-star. All the chatter from tabloid TV and supermarket tattlers earned the film more than $200 million. No one remembered its lousy reviews.

In Hollywood lore, countless similar examples were told. Max shared the same view as fellow impresario Zach Preston, who, like his huckstering pal Donald Trump, believed that bad news—*any* news—was good publicity if it gained the public's attention. "Without it, you're dead," Kirkland declared.

Eventually, Manchester and Youngblood complied awkwardly with Kirkland's directive. Gossip had caused tension between them as well.

Before beginning again, Max checked with the camerapeople and crew. When finally satisfied, he signaled to Lester Wolf to begin the scene. I followed along with the scene dialogue written out on my daily call sheet.

"I should have you arrested—what is your name?" Wolf yelled at Youngblood's Stephen Pharoah, just as he had done in character on the first day of shooting. The close-up of Wolf's angry face as Austin Corbin seemed worth this extra effort.

Behind Wolf, however, a rogue wave emerged ominously. The powerful force from the distant storm lifted the water swell nearly ten feet, far above the actor's head. Poor Lester didn't see it coming.

The thundering wave knocked over Wolf. It pulled him into the collapsing surf and away into a riptide. For a moment, Wolf sank completely beneath the water, unable to be seen from the shore. Then his limp body, unconscious from the sheer force of the Atlantic's might, floated up to the surface. Only his flooded woolen coat was visible, with his head face down in the water.

This real-life sequence played out like a slow-motion reel, with the horrible realization Wolf might die before our eyes. Sheila Teague, watching on a monitor inside the director's circle, screamed for help. I flipped off my headset and ran to the shoreline. Only a few feet behind was Max, his face in shock, with a frantic Penny MacPharland trailing him.

Quickly, like Lifesavers of old, two cameramen jumped into the surf and yanked Wolf from the oncoming waves. The battered actor coughed up saltwater and gasped for breath. There was an unspoken fear Lester might be having a heart attack from this convulsion. He fainted as he neared the shore and had to be carried in the arms of his rescuers.

"Get back, get back," Max directed everyone who clustered on the beach as Lester passed by, unconscious but still alive.

An ambulance arrived at the parking lot atop the bluff and rushed him to the local hospital several miles away. Max insisted on riding in the back of the ambulance with Lester. Most of the crew, including Sheila and Penny, followed them off the set to the medical center.

Still standing on the beach, Manchester appeared stunned by what happened, a reminder of how quickly the raw power of nature could claim someone. Next to her, Youngblood, in his Lifesaver costume as Pharaoh, found it all inexplicably funny. The rocker in him was accustomed to wild near-death antics while on the road and laughing about it with his band.

"Did you see the look on his face?" Youngblood howled. "Lester had no idea that big wave was coming for him until the last second!"

No one found Johnny's nihilistic humor amusing, least of all Manchester. She was fond of the old actor and his courtly manner towards her. Johnny's words bared the ugliness of his soul, the emptiness behind the ripped abs, Tarzan-like hair, and sculpted physique featured on his Instagram page. He dismissed this near tragedy as mere farce. Johnny revealed himself to be an idiot, just as Kiara always suspected after their moments of passion together, which repulsed her. She gave him a withering stare without comment. Then she walked briskly towards the parking lot without him.

I was near my rented car when I heard Manchester asking others in frustration how she might get to the hospital herself. Did anyone have the number for the limo company assigned to the show?

"I'm going to the hospital to see Lester," I told Manchester. "Do you want to come with me?"

Manchester seemed surprised by my offer. We had barely spoken previously, save for that brief moment in Max's office. I assumed she didn't remember me. Generally, I kept my distance from the actors. When filming began months ago, Penny MacPharland advised it best to "stay away from the talent," lest they get annoyed by intrusions and become troublesome on the set. It sounded like the admonition at the Bronx Zoo not to get near the animals.

Penny's warning came after I took a selfie of myself and Lester Wolf on the set, intending to send it to my kids, who would recognize Wolf not from Shakespeare in the Park but rather his avuncular role as the intrepid spaceship commander in their favorite science fiction show. After MacPharland's scolding, I was too skittish to ask Manchester to pose with me, even though I was the author of *The Life Line*, the IP for the show.

Apparently, over time, Manchester had seen me enough, sitting near Max in the director's circle of chairs, to recognize my face. When I broached the offer of a ride to the hospital, she didn't seem flustered or in doubt.

"Are you sure you're going that way?" she asked with a British accent and distinct politeness. "All this bloody mess with Lester has me in a tizzy. Good God, I pray he's all right." She shook a residue of sand off her costume.

"I'd be happy to give you a lift," I said, extending my hand to shake. "I'm Jack Denton, the author."

"Yes, yes, of course I know," Manchester insisted. "I remember Sheila Teague introduced us. I've spotted you a number of times around the set but would never want to bother an important person like you."

I smiled, not sure if she was serious or in jest. We both climbed into my rental and drove out of the parking lot together. In my rearview mirror, I could see Johnny coming up from the beach and looking around the parking lot, presumably for Kiara.

On the ride to the hospital, we chatted about our shared mutual respect for Lester and our hopes that he'd be all right. Sitting beside me, I got a better look at Manchester's costume as Elizabeth Gardiner, wearing the bustle, bodice, and pleated skirt of the 1880s with its lavish decorations. Though I'd watched her face many times on the video monitors, her beauty was never more apparent to me.

When we arrived at the Hamptons Medical Center, I searched for a place to park. A big crowd already stood outside its door. Paparazzi, listening to the police radio, had shown up immediately when they heard a television actor was being rushed to the hospital. TV news crews in trucks hoisted their large microwave antennas up into the sky, like white masts on a fully rigged ship.

The media onrush caused Manchester to rethink her desire to lend comfort at Lester's bedside. From a hidden pocket in her costume, she pulled out her private cell phone and managed to reach Penny MacPharland inside the emergency room with Max. When she got off the phone, Manchester relayed their instructions.

"Penny says dear Lester will be fine and that they're just keeping him for observation—thank heavens," Manchester said. "Penny insists it's best that we not go into the hospital. Instead, she suggests we go back to the Montauk Manor—especially with the sun going down—and that she and Max will follow soon."

I realized Manchester, dressed as Elizabeth Gardiner, didn't want to fend her way through the phalanx of photographers and TV reporters and have her picture taken in her soggy costume and disheveled hair. So I made a U-turn and headed east towards Montauk.

Dusk enveloped the narrow highway, rendering the road ahead harder to see. I squinted at the shining headlights of cars passing by. Manchester gazed out the window at the little shops and restaurants along the way. The traffic paused in front of Nick and Toni's, a popular eatery, but it was too crowded for us to stop.

"Let's find a place to eat if you'd like—I'm famished," Manchester said. "I'm afraid saltwater—and the prospect of losing Lester—has taken its toll on me."

Like a good chauffeur, I rerouted the car towards a quiet, out-of-the-way restaurant. This red brick place, tucked behind a storefront in East Hampton, had been a personal favorite for years. I remembered finding it a decade ago when Tricia and I double-dated with Gary and Elaine and drove to Guild Hall on a winter's night to hear a well-known local actor host a classic movie. Afterward, we ate at this informal restaurant with its wooden decor and rowdy clientele.

Walking inside, Manchester immediately approved. Though she was still in period costume, no one seemed to notice.

"It's just like a British pub," she said with delight. "I'll order the finger food."

Over fish and chips, we talked about Manchester's career. There was no reciprocity on this evening's menu. In the past, I found actors have little interest in writers or how the words they uttered on screen came to be. I listened as Manchester ("Call me Kiara," she allowed) recounted at length how Max Kirkland recruited her for *The Life Line*. She had long admired Kirkland's impressive, high-quality feature films, always on the hunt for Oscars and Emmys. As an artist, she said, she particularly valued how Kirkland used his powerful position in Hollywood to avoid the usual mendacity when a studio's bureaucrats started meddling.

Gradually, with increasing candor, her tone changed as she dissected the relationship with her showrunner that emerged during production. She said her theatrical parents had warned about Max's long-time reputation as a "masher"—their quaint term for a sexual aggressor—and how this prepared her to avoid becoming trapped when Max made an unwanted advance inside her private on-location trailer.

Without details, Kiara intimated that Max had "crossed the line" in somehow affecting her relationship with Johnny Youngblood.

"Johnny wanted to rip Max's head off when I told him how he came on to me in my Winnebago," she recalled, abruptly lowering her voice. "Do you know Johnny carries a gun? He says it's licensed, but I wonder if he'd ever use it. What is it about America and guns?"

I shrugged without an answer, so she went on about Kirkland.

During the filming, Manchester recalled, she felt that Max's cameras lingered too long on the nude scenes between Youngblood and herself and that he treated her affair with Johnny as fodder for the gossip columns. She said she's complained repeatedly to her agent about Max's behavior. As a result, they vowed never to work with Kirkland again once this production was over.

Kiara remained most bitter about the sadomasochistic photo shoot she recently performed for Diana Trumbull's fashion magazine at Max's demand. Despite her objections, she said she had no choice but to do it under the "promotional terms" of her contract. On the sly, she'd received thumbnails of this photo layout and was appalled. With her hair tied back, Manchester wore virtually nothing except a black leather thong and bra designed by Max's fashion designer wife Tatiana, praised lavishly in the photo credits.

"I look like a bloody whore in those pictures," she fumed, her high-brow accent suddenly a bit more Cockney. "He's willing to ruin my career as a serious actress—all to promote his fuckin' project." She seemed ready to cry.

"I should tell his wife, Tatiana, what he's up to—all the women whose lives he's ruined, all the women who say he groped them," Kiara added. "I suspect she knows already."

We left the restaurant and drove in silence for several minutes in the darkness towards Montauk. A few illuminated signs warned of deer crossing the roadway and how many innocent beasts had been killed by man-made vehicles in the past year. Kiara's mind still seemed obsessed with Max when she finally spoke again.

"Have you heard of the detective who's been trolling around about this actress named Vanessa Adams?" Manchester asked.

I denied knowing about it. I kept staring ahead at the roadway, careful not to look over at her.

"The detective interviewed me the other day, but I told him I know nothing about this poor girl," Manchester continued. "He showed me a photo—one of those glossy casting-call types. He said her parents are worried sick about her."

I commiserated with Vanessa's plight but was careful not to reveal how much I knew, especially about driving her to the Kirkland's party many weeks ago. The cold fact remained that I was clueless about Vanessa Adams's whereabouts, just like the detective knocking on Manchester's door.

As we swung into the Montauk Manor driveway, I noticed many cars already parked for the night in its lot, including Max's cherry-red Tesla sports car. Kiara thanked me for the ride and dinner. My dashboard said ten o'clock. As she opened the door, she appeared to have an epiphany.

"I bet Max's involved," she said somberly. "I bet Max knows what happened to that girl."

She stared at me until we finally made eye contact. Then she exited alone into the lobby of the Tudor-style manor and to her rented duplex while I diverted myself to its bar for a nightcap.

Sitting alone in a cushioned chair inside the lobby, with its elegant furnishings and high Spanish ceilings, I thought about this crazy, eventful day and how much of it revolved around the enigmatic figure of Max Kirkland. There was much I had learned about him, but so much more I still didn't know. I took a few sips and then headed towards my own room.

As I neared its entrance, I heard faint voices in the distance. The walls of the hallway curved around so that I could not see immediately who was talking. The whispers sounded familiar. The padded carpet kept my steps from being heard. Coming a little closer, but still several doors away, I spotted Kirkland, in a shadow, embracing a woman. They were kissing passionately as he fumbled with his key card. Max finally opened his door and the two stepped into the room. I stood entranced: the woman with Max was Sheila Teague.

Rather than risk a surprise confrontation, I quickly entered my own room. Lying alone in my own bed for another hour or so, I thought of what I'd witnessed and what it meant. Earlier in the summer, as I remembered, Sheila confided that she and Max had been lovers and that his tastes tended towards S&M and the rougher side of sexuality. Sheila didn't seem alarmed or particularly bothered. She readily shared this information about her patron while we were in bed together. She portrayed it as something from the distant past, and all that was left was their working relationship.

But the affair between Sheila and Max remained very much alive. Their encounters occurred whenever the opportunity presented itself. As I thought of all the drinks I once shared with Sheila, and how easily I found myself in her bed, perhaps I was right to think of her as a spy for Max, someone who fed him compromising information about others in his world, just as Penny MacPharland did in other ways. I would not view Sheila again in the same unguarded way.

The next morning, in an act of counterespionage, I inquired discreetly about who was registered in the room down the hallway. I assumed Sheila was staying there. I was wrong. It was a duplex that Max had kept at the manor ever since *The Life Line* production started many months ago. At that moment, I realized it was next to the guest room where Vanessa Adams once stayed.

CHAPTER 22
ART IMITATES LIFE

The idea of borrowing *The Life Line*—the actual oil painting by Winslow Homer—first occurred to Max Kirkland in one of the earliest writers room discussions, when Max was spitballing notions with his staff and suddenly posed a pointed question to me.

"This is a great painting—where'd you get it?" Kirkland asked, as if suddenly seeing the cover of my novel for the first time. We had been talking about his show's opening shipwreck scene when a copy of my book, on the big table next to a bag of bagels and morning coffees, caught his eye.

"It's in a museum in Philadelphia, part of a collection of paintings by Winslow Homer," I replied.

"Homer Winslow, yeah—the guy who painted it, I remember," said Kirkland, who always seemed more confident when he was in error.

"No, it's *Winslow* Homer," Penny MacPharland interrupted. "Homer is his *last* name."

No matter for Kirkland, the great impresario, who recognized a golden marketing opportunity. He didn't acknowledge Penny's correction. Instead, he kept his gaze on me.

"Do you think we can get our hands on that painting for our premiere in the fall?" Kirkland wondered. His eyes lit up as he now addressed the whole group of writers around the table. "That would be a pretty classy touch, right? Have that painting on special display when the press and Comflix brass arrive to see the show." Accustomed to Max's sudden bursts of self-proclaimed genius, a low grunt of approval emerged from his staff.

Max again turned to me. "I want you to contact the museum in Philly and arrange to borrow that painting for our opening," he ordered. "Most film premieres give out goody bags with all that tchotchke type of stuff. Sure, we can hand out the T-shirts and the mugs with *The Life Line* printed on them. But we will have the real thing at our opening—the actual painting of the shipwreck scene. Jack, I want you to get that painting for us, OK?"

I shook my head dubiously, so Penny jumped right in.

"Don't worry, Max," she said, "we'll make this happen, right, Jack?"

I remained mum.

Several weeks of negotiations with the Philadelphia museum followed without results. Max became exasperated and sarcastic with my ineptitude. I overheard him telling Penny on the set that "the only real task I gave him wound up in failure." Surely these complaints were about me.

Eventually, Constance Skilling, one of the founding family members of the Comflix corporation, fixed the problem. As a Comflix exec, "Connie" Skilling was known for her heavy hidden hand in company decision-making. In the City of Brotherly Love, however, Skilling carried far more clout as a cultural patron. She ironed out a compromise with the Philadelphia museum, where she happened to be a board member. Skilling let Max know that the original Winslow Homer painting could be borrowed for his Manhattan premiere under one condition: that I give a lecture in Philadelphia about Homer's painting and *The Life Line* story about the Montaukett tribe portrayed in my novel. It was a request easy enough to fulfill. I arrived in Philadelphia two weeks before the television show's debut.

Next to Homer's masterpiece, about two by four feet in dimension, my novel poised on the speaker's podium appeared small and inconsequential, especially in terms of artistic achievement. It was easy to see why the painting caused such a sensation in its day. The power of the massive waves, the semiconscious young woman hanging over the deadly water, and the heroic strength of her Lifesaver was even more captivating than the image replicated on my book cover.

To begin the lecture, Skilling, a refined woman in her late sixties, spoke with the gravitas of inherited wealth rather than any artwork expertise.

"We are all waiting to see Mr. Denton's novel come to life as an upcoming television event by the famous director Max Kirkland," Skilling concluded, with my book in hand. "At Comflix, we are proud to be producing *The Life Line,* inspired by this magnificent painting by Winslow Homer."

Polite applause trickled through the museum's auditorium.

"Hopefully it's art imitating art," I whispered to Skilling as she sat in the chair next to mine.

Moving to the lectern, I spoke briefly about Homer, a reclusive artist whose life took many unexpected turns, and how his body of work—oil paintings and watercolors, many of them along the Atlantic shoreline—reflected a time of change in America. Although Homer came of age during the Civil War, he was nearly fifty in 1884 when he finished *The Life Line.*

Both romantic and horrifying, the painting played upon the public's nightmare of drowning at sea, a common fear in a nation of immigrants and ocean travelers. I mentioned Homer's wood engraving of the SS *Atlantic* shipwreck a decade earlier, when 562 people died on their way to New York. The loss of this ship remained America's biggest maritime disaster until the 1912 *Titanic* sinking. It carried a memorable shock equivalent to the 9/11 terror attack of the twenty-first century. During Homer's time, views about God, nature, and science were in conflict, much like our own. In the painting, a simple device like the breeches buoy—then a newly invented device seen saving the would-be drowning woman—captured the nation's can-do spirit, a triumph of human ingenuity over the elements.

From there, I explained how my novel sprang from previous reporting about the Montauk Indian tribe and New York's famous nineteenth-century railroad baron Austin Corbin. In my enthusiasm, I gave away some spoilers from the still-unseen TV show. I particularly dwelled on Corbin's shady deals in stealing away the indigenous people's lands to make way for his railroad. The more I described Corbin's greed, avarice, and petty obsessions, the more the crowd responded to this figure from yesterday with the familiarity of today. Some Americans were still swayed by the bullying of a rich man.

"This fellow Austin Corbin sounds just like Trump," exclaimed a white-haired man with whiskers during the question-and-answer period. "I would have voted for him, too!"

Nervous laughter from the crowd soon ended the evening.

On the way home, driving along the New Jersey Turnpike, I could see Manhattan's twinkling lights towards the east, an empyreal vision with its towers and spires in the distance. New York's jagged skyline pointed to the heavens, its silhouette shimmering off the Hudson. Amid the mass of cars and trucks switching from lane to lane, I thought about the old man's comments and about where America was headed.

Since the summer, Trump had gained the presidential nomination of his party, and now, in the fall, his improbable campaign seemed increasingly a likely bet in the general election, impervious to enemy attacks and self-inflicted disasters. On a recent television news show, I watched Hattie Thompson and a group of journalists condemn Trump for groping women—even boasting about it on a videotape—and getting away with sexual harassment. Yet the enthusiasm for Trump by this old Philly man with whiskers—as well at the MAGA rally in Pennsylvania I attended earlier in the year—reminded me that something else was brewing in places they called "the heartland," where they viewed Trump as a savior rather than a sinner.

The prospect of *The Apprentice* television star in the White House sounded like an absurd joke, an upside-down version of reality, as if the Great Chain of Being was about to be broken by the ascendancy of this wayward king. Vice now seemed like a virtue. For years, men like Max Kirkland had abused all sorts of women—particularly actresses, models, and coworkers. Just like Trump, Max believed the rumors and allegations against him would all go away so long as his new venture was successful, that he made a bundle of money for his partners, and that he proved himself a winner.

Before reaching the highway entrance into Manhattan, I noticed two voicemails on my cell phone. Pulling into a gas station, I played the first message, recognizing the number as Tricia's. I'd forgotten to return her call more than two weeks ago. Add that to my list of marital crimes and misdemeanors. I listened intently to her voice as I slowly descended the winding corkscrew approach to the Lincoln Tunnel:

> *"Jack, this is Tricia. I just wanted to tell you about the results for Johnny's family tree project. He got an A. I thought you might want to know what the DNA found. It says you're a little French and German, half Irish, and get this—two percent Native American! I wonder if it's the Montauk tribe? This DNA gives me a clue of who you are, I guess. Damn if I could ever figure it out. Bye."*

Tricia laughed two or three times during her message. Her voice sounded almost whimsical, as if she'd been freed of an awful burden. None of the old harsh resentment in her tone, of being saddled with a lousy husband. She now possessed a new man who adored her, who paid for more things than I ever could as a journalist. Our dead marriage was swiftly fading in memory. Thanks to my own carelessness and obsessions, the children's lives were in her total control. Tricia set the financial terms and the limits of visitation and shared information about them on a need-to-know basis. Given my long absence, I figured my two kids stopped wondering if they'd ever see me again. Probably gave up caring, too.

However, Tricia's message did contain one trenchant insight, a cutting remark hitting close to the bone. Undeniably, it was true when she said my DNA might offer "a clue of who you are," more than I ever provided to her about myself during our many years together. Her cruel wisecrack stung, but she was right. I still seemed a stranger to her. Like an invisible man, I had made no lasting imprint on the lives of Tricia and our children.

Too often I had been an observer rather than a participant. Lies were the currency of my personal existence, despite a professional insistence on truth from others. When Tricia accused me of adultery, I remember how I acted hurt rather than denying it directly. We both knew I was lying, a bravura performance of betrayal and twisting of the facts. For years at home, I'd pretended to be a make-believe husband, until one day Tricia finally went out and found a real one.

But this DNA analysis revealed only a fragment of the falsehoods surrounding my life. For years, I repeated family claims that my father, reared in an orphanage, had a significant Native American lineage, a possibility that appealed to me. Perhaps I was born of Montaukett heritage, or, more fantastically, I was somehow a descent of Geronimo or Crazy Horse? Now this forensic gene test proved me wrong, revealing only 2 percent, well within the margin of error. Tricia had gained enough distance that she could make a joke of it on a voicemail. Everything about me seemed phony.

As I neared my downtown Manhattan apartment, I pulled the car into an underground garage around the block. The time was now past midnight. With the streetlights dim, I walked gingerly along the pavement. I didn't slow until my cell phone chirped again. I stepped inside the open lobby of the Flatiron Building, the triangular, steel-framed home of my book publisher. Virtually no one was inside this landmark building near my apartment. Leaning against the Flatiron's glazed terracotta walls, I listened to the second voicemail on my phone. It was an urgent cryptic message from my Hollywood entertainment attorney, Frank Worthington.

"Jack, call me as soon as you get this," Worthington instructed without further explanation. "Don't talk to anybody and *don't* go home."

I'd never heard Worthington's voice quite like that. For years I heeded his advice as an entertainment attorney, which he offered in witty internet correspondences and an occasional catch-up telephone call. In a world of Hollywood sharks, Frank acted as a watchful lifeguard, always looking out for his writer clients who had no idea how things got made. After a Hollywood producer once butchered an earlier book of mine, Worthington warned me, "Whatever you do, don't show him *The Life Line*." To my everlasting gratitude, Worthington put together the lucrative deal with Comflix and Max Kirkland that would make us all rich when this television streamer extravaganza finally appeared.

Perhaps Worthington's call was about some new perk or "goodie" in *The Life Line* deal, like getting a bonus or at least a few extra tickets for the premiere. When I called back to his office, Worthington answered immediately.

"What rathole are you calling from?" he demanded. "I tried every number I have for you, including Tricia's cell phone. No one knew where you're hiding out."

"Philadelphia. Finally got to see *The Life Line* painting in person."

As always, Worthington immediately turned to business. No chitchat here.

"Vanessa Adams—do you know anything about her?" he asked.

My heart sank when I heard her name. Deep in the recesses of my mind, I worried about the request by her family's detective to talk with me. Like many other matters in my life, I believed that if I ignored this inquiry, trouble would simply go away.

"Well, she's a young actress who appeared in the first scene filmed out in Montauk—the shipwreck disaster in the pilot episode—and then she disappeared and didn't come back," I explained, still far from full disclosure.

Worthington coughed into the phone, allergic to my evasive answer. He paused and then moved the conversation several steps ahead.

"The police called me today and they want to interview you. They think you may have had something to do with her disappearance, Jack. The family's detective told the cops that Vanessa attended a summer party at Max Kirkland's house and that you brought her there in your car. There's some kind of tape recording of you admitting that."

These stark incriminations swept over me like a cold wave, with the kind of pain and light-headedness that deep-sea divers must suffer from the bends as they struggle to the surface. I took a breath and collected my thoughts. Evidently, the family detective had interviewed Kirkland—and probably Penny MacPharland, too—who passed along this information to the police. As I suspected, these two producers had taped my comments in the writers room. When the cops asked about Vanessa, they provided a secret recording of my casual admission about driving her to the party. If something criminal happened to this missing actress, they were prepared to blame me.

I figured there was no sense holding anything back from Worthington. "That's right, she was staying at the Montauk Manor with me and the rest of the cast and crew. She asked for a ride to Max's mansion that night.

Because the party was so crowded, I dropped her off and parked the car down the street. I later wandered around the party but never found her. It was strange, like she had vanished. But they say actresses in bit parts drop out all the time...."

"Who told you that?"

"Max Kirkland and his top assistant Penny. They even edited Vanessa out of the big shipwreck scene. I've seen the footage. How was I to know any better?"

Worthington sounded exasperated. Before he became an entertainment attorney, he had worked as a cop, getting his law degree at night, and then as a state prosecutor. He could smell bullshit instantly, especially from a longtime client and friend like myself.

"Tell me something, Jack. You stayed at the same place as she did. Were you fucking her?"

There was no place to hide from his question and the fornication it implied.

"We met at the pool and she asked about *The Life Line*, how the book became the show, and she told me about herself. She even talked about the Montauk tribe. She claimed to have seen the ghost of one of them..."

"... and then you fucked her," Worthington interjected.

"We went for a swim together and she invited me to her room. I was depressed from my divorce and feeling alone. She looked fantastic in a bathing suit. So that's right, I did. *We did it.* Right before we went to the party. But so what?"

I noticed my voice had become louder and more desperate—echoing in the hollow Flatiron lobby with its high, cathedral-like ceiling. I lowered my tone in offering a defense.

"Look, I feel sorry for her family, searching all around for their missing daughter and having to pay a detective to find her. But I have no idea where she is. Haven't seen her since I dropped her off at Max's party. Honestly. If anyone knows where she is, I suspect it is Max Kirkland."

"What makes you say that—besides, of course, Max's reputation as a major league groper here in Hollywood?" asked Worthington. He always kept his ear to the ground for "Tinseltown gossip," as he called it. These dirty rumors never stopped Worthington, though, or any others in town from negotiating a lucrative deal with Kirkland, a top producer adulated by the industry.

"Just the way he acted around Vanessa, the jealousy and control," I explained. "He had his arm around Vanessa on location at the beach and acted kind of funny when I talked to her. Max's got to touch and feel and kiss every woman in this production. He has Kiara Manchester in tears with the way he's manipulated her. And he's apparently big into S&M, according to a woman on his writing staff who I've gotten to know. If something happened to Vanessa, I think Max is behind it."

"Whew, that sounds like its own soap opera, a show within a show," Worthington said, perhaps believing me. Then, with years of investigating past homicides himself, he raised a good line of inquiry.

"What about this guy Johnny Youngblood?" Worthington asked. "He certainly doesn't have a very good reputation with the ladies out here in Los Angeles. Looks like a creep to me. What's the possibility he may have something to do with Vanessa?"

I confessed such a twist never occurred to me. As I contemplated it, though, certainly Youngblood, a former lead guitarist with a hair-trigger temper, could have accosted Vanessa. With his salacious manner, Johnny was accustomed to having his way with groupies. And I knew he carried a gun. If Vanessa resisted, he might very well have abused such a young actress who turned to him for advice, the same way she approached me.

"Maybe you have something there," I conceded. "I never thought of Johnny before as a killer."

Worthington's tone no longer sounded vexing. "Listen, the police consider this a missing person case, at least for now, and they want to interview you. I told them I want to be there as your attorney and that I will be flying into New York next week for the show's premiere. I told them we could meet the next day, before I fly back to LA, and they agreed."

"What am I supposed to tell them?" I asked, frustrated and a bit annoyed at this agreement, which I didn't know about in advance.

"The truth. Do you think you can manage that, Jack?"

I chuckled, as if a joke among old friends, though we both understood the seriousness at hand. Worthington confided that he might consult a Long Island criminal lawyer for help. He advised me to be careful and not to discuss anything with anyone, especially Max, if it could be avoided.

"In the meantime, I want you to stay away from your apartment, stay away from any snooping police detectives knocking at your door—anything that might bring more trouble," Worthington warned. "Go stay at a friend's house. But keep out of sight until I get there for the premiere next week, and we can figure this all out together."

Worthington abruptly ended the call. Though still annoyed, I felt grateful to have him as a lawyer and perhaps my only friend.

Wind and rain were now swirling around the Flatiron Building. A security guard passing by appeared to wonder what I was still doing in the lobby. Clasping together my jacket, I exited the building and headed back down to the parking garage to retrieve my rental. Then I headed away from the city, in all its midnight magnificence, not sure in what direction I would be headed. My only certainty was a promise I made to myself. Despite the advice Worthington gave, I wasn't going to avoid Max Kirkland, the director of my project and perhaps my fate. Whatever he did with that young woman, I was going to find out.

CHAPTER 23
THE UPFRONTS

"A *world of wonder at Comflix!"*

On the big stage at Radio City Music Hall, Comflix presented a sneak peek of its new television shows, including *The Life Line*. Singers and dancers gyrated to the company's familiar theme music, while a sizzle reel above flashed the faces of its stars on a megascreen.

Inside this cavernous auditorium, the biggest movie theater in America, the TV industry gathered for an event known as "The Upfronts." Each year, top advertisers received an advance look at the offerings of Comflix and other Hollywood competitors, like a kid peering into Santa's gift bag before Christmas. Any pretense at art here quickly gave way to the needs of commerce.

Comflix CEO Steve Loomis, at an illuminated podium stage left, acted as master of ceremonies for his company's presentation. His publicly traded company had a wide and diverse array of executives, but at these events, Loomis preferred to be the only recognizable face of his organization.

"... and we also have *The Life Line*, a miniseries which will certainly appeal to the thirty-five-to-fifty-five female demo and has tested very well in our focus groups," announced Loomis, acting more like a movie star than a media exec. Attractive demo numbers now appeared on the screen above him in place of the sizzle reel.

"We're very excited to say the showrunner, making his first bid into this new arena, is Max Kirkland, the famous director whose films we've all enjoyed for years," said Loomis. He was fond of speaking in the corporate third person, using the imperial "we" and "family" to describe Comflix. "Max, stand up and take a bow, will you?"

Next to me, Kirkland rose and saluted the crowd. On his opposite side, Max's friend, reality TV producer Zach Preston, clapped while waiting for one of his own shows to be promoted.

Kirkland had invited me to this event as a goodwill gesture. He acted like I was his long-lost friend. After a few days of being hard to find, I was glad to attend, though I couldn't yet figure out Max's ulterior motive. This promotional celebration was a reminder that my long-awaited project was ready to appear. And so was I, despite my attorney warning me to stay out of sight during the pending Vanessa Adams investigation.

The stylish art deco facade over the Radio City stage was designed to look like a sunrise with its succession of orange-colored curves. But to my eyes, it appeared more like an old gramophone, a symbol of how quickly technology in American media can become outdated overnight. Indeed, the television industry was changing radically.

Much of the buzz at this conference concerned the aggressive moves of new streamers like Comflix and other corporate barbarians and how their over-the-top offerings were overwhelming the old cable and network powerhouses. A whole new generation of cord-cutters were redefining television. *The Life Line* would be part of that assault. Yet Kirkland's mind seemed elsewhere.

"Isn't this great?" Kirkland exclaimed to Preston and myself. "I *love* Radio City." He appeared jubilant from all the applause. "I remember coming here every year as a kid and seeing the Rockettes. They really know how to put on a show here."

Preston smiled, amused by Max's love of showmanship. This nostalgia for the old days didn't strike Preston as odd. But to me, it didn't make sense. How could Max visit Radio City as a kid annually if, as he claimed, he grew up in the Midwest, more than a thousand miles away? Perhaps Preston didn't pick up on this inconsistency in Max's life story or just didn't care. But I did after learning Kirkland grew up in New Jersey. I wondered how Max could lie so matter-of-factly, like some sociopath who

could beat a polygraph machine without a sweat. Dissembling was second nature to him.

As the morning Upfront session ended, Max corralled Preston and me, and then gave a hands-up wave to a figure on the stage. It was Loomis.

"Let's all go to eat to celebrate this great presentation," Max announced. "Steve Loomis will be joining us." Max's corporate clout was enough to compel the CEO of Comflix to attend this private lunch.

In the huge Radio City lobby, Loomis embraced Kirkland and Preston like old amigos. He gave me a polite handshake, not certain if we had met before. We followed Max into a company-leased limo, which took us slowly through the crowded Manhattan streets to a nearby restaurant.

"Where are we going, Max?" asked Loomis.

"I first thought about The Four Seasons," Kirkland said, loud enough to be heard above the traffic noise. "But since we have my friend Jack Denton, the author of *The Life Line*, joining us, I made a reservation at the Algonquin."

Loomis and I smiled, recognizing the literary allusion to the famed midtown restaurant. Throughout the twentieth century, many well-known New York writers gathered at the legendary Roundtable at the Algonquin Hotel to trade jokes, barbs, and other bon mots.

Preston had never heard of the place, casting doubt on its selection.

"It's your choice, Max, but does it have good food?" Preston asked, in a jousting way. "All these dead writers, who cares? They say print is dead too, right Jack?"

I felt the obligation to defend all writers everywhere but stumbled a bit, tongue-tied and out of place. Max came to my rescue. He explained the Algonquin's history and why he picked it as the place for our lunch.

"Zach, your idea of reading is checking Trump's tweets on Twitter—or the bonus clause in your contract," Kirkland jibed, laughing the loudest at his own joke.

Just in time, before this verbal battle could continue, we arrived at The Algonquin. We sat unobtrusively at a secluded table for four. The restaurant's dark paneled walls and tall potted palms provided an upper-crust ambience. It appealed to Preston's surprising level of snobbery, particularly for one whose shows competed weekly against the Kardashians and the Housewives shows.

Our relaxed conversation wandered from highlights of the Upfront convention to Preston's recent trip with his wife to Hawaii, to favorite golf courses in the Hamptons, and, finally, to a few matters of pressing business about *The Life Line*. Throughout lunch, Max appeared relaxed and loquacious, more than happy to discuss his production. Occasionally, he allowed the rest of our party to get a word in edgewise. I was the only one who said nothing.

As he finished his lunchtime salad, Loomis mentioned another matter.

"Is Tatiana going to be at the Morgan Library for *The Life Line*'s premiere?" asked Loomis.

"Of course, she's my wife," Kirkland replied. "Why do you ask?"

Loomis squirmed in his seat. He explained Comflix's dilemma. Its board of directors had redirected increasing barrels of company cash towards its streaming app efforts. Surveys showed cable subscriptions were fading, just like free TV from rabbit-ears antennas did a generation earlier. Faced with this giant ground shift, Comflix wanted to make sure it was ready for the digital divide. *The Life Line* was, fortunately, part of that vital effort. But the rest of the company's offerings on cable were being re-examined. Because of its sagging numbers, Tatiana's show was on the cutting block, he explained.

"We think *Fashions by Tatiana* is getting a little long in the tooth," Loomis said. "It's had a great run. With *The Life Line* coming out, I figured now would be the time to mention our plans for the other show by your production company."

Max's mood turned from festive to combative.

"That's not my show, it's my wife's show," Kirkland said. "Why the fuck don't you tell her?"

Preston jumped in. "Max, don't get upset, Steve is just trying to give you a heads-up."

"That's right, I didn't want to spoil your premiere with bad news," Loomis said. "I just wanted to tell you Comflix's thinking. It's not etched in stone. Not yet. But I just wanted to tell you as a courtesy. After all, it was you who brought that show to us, not Tatiana."

Kirkland was unappeased. "Doesn't matter, it's Tatiana's show. She brought in Diana Trumbull and the whole fashion community. Next season, they're planning to have Kiara Manchester on as a guest to help promote *The Life Line*. And Diana plans to have Manchester on the cover of her magazine."

Loomis nodded his shiny, bald head dismissively. "We all appreciate what Tatiana has done in the past, but there's nothing I can do now," he claimed. Max continued to argue with him.

"I think we better get back for the afternoon session," Zach Preston advised Loomis. "We present the teaser for my show at two-thirty."

Preston arose from his chair, with Loomis following along. Together, they left the lunch table and headed back to Radio City.

For the longest moment, Max just stared at me across the table, fuming at what had happened.

"That fuckin' Loomis, he's afraid to tell Tatiana himself," Kirkland finally mumbled. "What am I supposed to say to her?"

Max seemed to want my advice. It was the first time we'd been alone together in a one-on-one conversation since my project began. I expressed sympathy for his predicament and offered a curative.

"I guess you can tell her the truth," I said.

Max slowly smiled, a conspiratorial grin. "That would be a first," he said. "How do you think we've stayed married for so long?"

I pursued this chance to find out more about Max.

"What brought you two together?" I asked, trying to move away from the Loomis confrontation. "She's from this Eastern European family that fled from the Nazis, and your biography says you're from the Midwest."

At first, Max seemed amused by my attempts to play both reporter and psychoanalyst. He let his guard down slightly.

"Tatiana is a remarkable woman," he explained. "I can't think of any woman who would have allowed me as much freedom as she does. Just the sheer amount of hours that making a movie or a show like *The Life Line* entails. But she never complained or was jealous. She has her own life. I'm very proud of her for that."

"So you didn't meet her in the Midwest?"

Max gave a quizzical stare. "You've been doing your homework on me?" he asked.

"I don't know of any kid from the Midwest who went to see the Rockettes every year at Radio City. Sounds more like Dr. Kovalenko's kid from New Jersey."

Kirkland realized that I had been checking into the truth of his background, perhaps into other mysteries as well.

"That's right, I grew up in Freehold, New Jersey," he admitted, with a laugh. "Saying you're from the Midwest sounds more all-American out in Hollywood. What are you going to do with all that information, Jack?"

For once, Kirkland, the great and powerful showrunner, took me seriously, almost as a threat.

"Information can be very powerful, a dangerous thing if it's misused," I warned. We now stared intently at one another, like two growling dogs. "Listen, I've heard detectives have been asking around about Vanessa Adams, checking me out. I don't know anything about what happened to her. And you know that."

"I do?" he asked, coyly. "Seems like you know more than I do, Jack. And the cops think so too."

With this stark assessment, Kirkland proved he could be far more calculating than myself. Frank Worthington's instructions to keep my mouth shut, not show any cards as this detective mystery played out, had been ignored. My brave intention to grill Kirkland about Vanessa's whereabouts gave way instead to cowardly self-interest. With a multimillion-dollar project on the line, there was no sense in antagonizing him any further.

Max stared intently at me, wondering what my next move might be.

"Let's hope all this foul stuff about a missing girl goes away and doesn't ruin our party at the Morgan Library," he finally offered. "Right, Jack?"

Silence made clear my acquiescence. Without further word, we left the famous writers room and went our separate ways.

CHAPTER 24
THE MORGAN PREMIERE

Outside the doors to the Morgan Library, an anxious group of publicity agents, photographers, and Comflix company execs milled about, waiting for *The Life Line* premiere to begin.

Obsessively, they looked at their watches, stared at their cell phones, and checked for names of celebrities on the invitation list. Behind this quiet, nervous activity, there was a distinct "calm before the storm" feeling.

Hanging above the Morgan entranceway, a long, unscrolled banner featured images of *The Life Line* painting and close-ups of the show's three stars, Kiara Manchester, Johnny Youngblood, and Lester Wolf. Top billing belonged to "*Max Kirkland Presents…*" No mention of my name as author appeared on this pennant.

In the lobby, a tall runway screen imprinted with "Comflix" and the show's shipwreck logo stood ready as background for the celebrity photo sessions. Each famous invitee would prim and smile, maybe say a few words to the press, before being ushered into the museum's festivities by their handlers.

"You're kind of early, aren't you?" Penny MacPharland said, coming up to me as I strolled up the long entrance stairs still devoid of guests. She wore a tuxedo dress designed by Tatiana and tightly clutched a clipboard with the list. "Where have you been lately? People have been asking about you."

"I've been waiting for my entourage to arrive," I teased. Penny gave her usual quizzical stare and then scampered away without waiting for further explanation.

A handful of five complimentary tickets for this event were just enough to cover the immediate needs of my "entourage." I felt the obligation to invite my two middle-school children—even though they were probably too young to appreciate or even remember this event—and therefore, because of the juvenile chain of custody, I had to include my former wife Tricia and her new husband, DJ the Realtor.

On the surface, Tricia's hubby appeared an amiable enough fellow who she could count on to shake my hand and congratulate me for the new show. But with his self-satisfied grin, DJ seemed mindful that, in matters that really count, he had won, if not bested me. He had taken command of another man's wife and kids—what once had been my whole life, the family I ignored until it was too late. In my lesser moments, I viewed this glad-handing man, with his Grecian Formula hair dye and perfect teeth, as an interloper. I certainly didn't look forward to greeting him with my ex-wife and kids.

Rather than wait in the Morgan lobby, I decided to go for a short walk around this Manhattan neighborhood and give myself a pep talk. I wanted to find myself in the right frame of mind when I returned. This event would mark one of the biggest days of my life, certainly my professional career, despite plenty of trouble prior to this point.

After weeks of suspension, I'd been permanently let go from *The New York World* for "unprofessional conduct." A new Scarlet Letter for "unwanted advances" and "conflicts of interest" sullied my name. I considered asking my attorney Frank Worthington to intervene during the paper's star-chamber human resources proceedings. But Worthington didn't think he could get involved unless I sued the paper, which would only bring more attention to this wrongful decision. He advised focusing on my new career in television instead.

"You were going to leave anyway, so let's just keep this personnel matter to ourselves," Worthington advised. "I don't think it will hurt you in Hollywood. Just look at what they say about Max Kirkland—all those bad rumors about women, and he's doing great."

These were hardly comforting words. Since my Flatiron phone call with Worthington, I had avoided any questions about the Vanessa Adams investigation, circling about the metropolitan area as if I were on the lam. That first night, I drove around aimlessly until I called and convinced Gary, Elaine's widowed husband, to let me stay as an uninvited guest for a few days at his Long Island house. Like a loyal family member, he never asked why.

"Are you alright?" Gary finally inquired one night as we watched the Jets football game in the living room like old times, when we were both married. "Is there something you want to tell me?"

I shook my head and sipped my beer without describing my predicament. Gary probably thought I was upset about Tricia or my job, never dreaming it involved a missing young woman.

Eventually, I wandered out to the Hamptons. In the crisp autumnal off-season, there were far fewer people than in the warm weather, when much of *The Life Line* filming took place. I drove past the white brick building that housed the writers room and other offices used to produce the show. I stopped when I saw lights on through the windows.

Inside, the only person still working was Oscar Sanchez, a visual effects supervisor. He stared intensely at an array of television screens, adjusting ever so slightly the color and tint in the opening shipwreck scene. He turned around when he heard my footsteps.

"Oh hey, how are you?" he said, pausing to recognize my face. A talented video wizard who immigrated from Barcelona, Spain, Sanchez had worked for years with Max Kirkland. "So, what did you think of that Liverpool win over Real Madrid?" he asked teasingly, immediately remembering our soccer conversations months earlier during the filming on set.

Sanchez said he'd spent this afternoon tweaking some scenes, the last touches before handing in the entire series to Comflix the following morning in advance of the premiere. He seemed awestruck by the final product.

"This whole thing really worked out well," Sanchez said. "I think it is undoubtedly Max's best, and that's saying something. He really is a genius."

Once again, Sanchez hit the play button from the very beginning. This time, we both fell into a trance watching the two-hour-long opening episode. Sanchez gave a running narration of the editing decisions made with key scenes. I had never seen the completed pilot, finished in all its glory with music, credits, and a smooth flow that I only imagined when I watched the show being filmed. I remembered certain sequences being photographed on location and now looked with fascination at the various angles that were cut and spliced together by computer with Sanchez's skill.

When the showing finished, my face lit up with joy, delighted that *The Life Line* had come to fruition in the way I had long ago intended. Sanchez hit another button, automatically returning us to the opening shipwreck scene, where the key credits came up in tiny titles. Sanchez pressed the pause button at the point he thought I'd like most.

"See, there it is—'Based on the book by Jack Denton,'" he read aloud. "Congratulations to the author!" He laughed heartily in a good-natured way.

The sound of anonymous footsteps climbing up to the writers room interrupted our merriment. At the top of the stairs arrived a stylishly dressed figure whom I immediately recognized as Tatiana Kirkland. She said she was looking for her husband. I still remembered my first conversation with Tatiana at the Kirkland mansion months earlier, the same night I drove Vanessa Adams to that party. Tatiana gave us a glowing smile when she saw the color images on the video monitors.

"Are you fellows watching the shipwreck scene? I remember watching that day from the sidelines, up on the bluff," she said. "I don't like to get in Max's way when he's working."

Sanchez pressed the play button and Tatiana watched the shipwreck scene with us once more, with all the sound and trembling fury displayed at full volume. This time around, I appreciated Max's quick close-up of the red cloth that covered Johnny Youngblood's face while carrying Kiara Manchester in the breeches buoy, a sort of an homage to Winslow Homer's *The Life Line* painting. Magically, the editing process wiped away the long delays, setups, and reverse angles of the same scene that I remember enduring during the original filming. Sanchez had created a new reality on the main editing monitor, the work of art that Max envisioned.

But Tatiana spotted something else. "Where is that girl in this scene—that Vanessa Adams, the one who is missing?" she asked in an evenhanded but curious tone. "I know she was standing along the beach with some other extras in this scene. I was there that day. But I don't see her in this scene."

Halting the tape, Sanchez gave a matter-of-fact explanation, just like our earlier conversation about the pilot.

"Max told me to cut her out, that she wasn't coming back," Sanchez said. "It wasn't easy, because he originally said to focus on her, that he liked her and planned to expand her role. But when she didn't show up again, he said to remove her from the scene—to hell with her!"

I watched Tatiana's face tighten as Sanchez turned to me for support. "We had another actress who pulled that stunt on us a few years ago in Canada while on location," Sanchez explained, sympathetic to his boss. "She never showed up again and we cut her out of a scene, too. It's not easy to reconfigure an editing sequence like that."

Tatiana turned very chilly. She asked if Sanchez knew where her husband might be. He said Max mentioned hours earlier about going back to the Montauk Manor to fetch something. I agreed that I'd not seen Max that afternoon. With her mood suddenly changed, Tatiana turned on her high-fashion heels and left without a goodbye.

For the next few days leading up to the Morgan Library premiere, I wondered if Tatiana harbored the same doubts about Max and the Adams disappearance as I did. I wondered if she ever learned about his private suite at the Montauk Manor and who may have entered the room with him.

The stroll around the Morgan Library's neighborhood failed to ease my mind. It wasn't enough to stop worrying and properly prepare myself for this museum celebration, which Penny MacPharland estimated would cost Comflix more than $100,000 in expenses.

On this November evening, the streets of New York seemed to throb with nervous anticipation, as if on the precipice of something dramatic. The sirens wailed louder, more urgently. People rushed even faster across busy intersections, over gaping potholes and simmering cracks in the surface. As I passed by, the illuminated Empire State Building appeared like a fiery sword sticking into the titian sky, just as the Greek gods would have it.

Unfairly or not, I attributed these atmospherics to the overwhelming uneasiness caused by Donald Trump's election victory. In the immediate days afterward, Manhattan's streets overflowed with protestors and police in riot gear. They marched in midtown near Trump Tower, angry that a fast-talking grifter—a former city Democrat turned GOP standard-bearer—had somehow conned a nation. "Not our president!" they shouted, carrying "Dump Trump" signs.

On the other side of the Hudson, the rest of the country did not seem as alarmed. I remembered those Trump rallies in "the heartland" and realized that his rancor had metastasized rather than been cured. From the long view of history, America seemed ready to be plundered, a house stripped to the studs of its democratic framework and taken over by kleptocrats hungry for their piece of the loot. I remembered how J. Pierpont Morgan, owner of the brownstone home that was now part of the modern museum, had been a business associate of Austin Corbin. It was an amusing coincidence that I had no intention of sharing with anyone at tonight's party.

As I turned the corner, the only demonstration in town appeared to be the protest in front of the Morgan Library. Dozens of people who claimed to be from the Montauk tribe marched outside, complaining about Max Kirkland's new television project. The once-serene setting outside the Morgan had turned chaotic. Strangely, I didn't recognize any of these faces, none of the familiar Montaukett leaders I had known in writing about their plight. Nevertheless, the TV news crews were now filming these unexpected protestors along with the usual paparazzi and celebrity PR photos at a premiere. In the distance, I spotted prominent tribal attorney Chester Lodge Jr., who had met with us before in private. I still remembered Max's bullying and how he accused Lodge of being a shakedown artist trying to get a payment from him.

Coming closer, I studied each placard, a habit I'd acquired as a reporter covering many such gatherings. "Comflix: Treat Us Fairly" read one rather bland sign, along with "Montaukett Nation Deserves Respect." Some were a bit more showbiz savvy, like "Max Kirkland's *Life Line* Steals Our Life Stories" and, my personal favorite for its historical allusion, "Stop, Thief! Austin Corbin Took Our Lands!"

Nearing the entrance, I felt sad that the Montaukett people still did not have the government recognition that they deserved, a century-old legal battle with Uncle Sam and the often-indifferent whites who populated their homeland. I had hoped that my novel would help the Montauk tribe in their quest for justice. Certainly, this big-time television production adapted by Kirkland would highlight their cause. Yet I also felt a sense of dread as I walked through the roped-off line for guests. Lodge, the media-savvy lawyer, spotted me and started calling out my name.

"There's the author, Jack Denton—*he's* to blame," Lodge yelled accusingly so the TV camera operators would pan and capture my image, the same way they do with criminals during a perp walk. I ignored Lodge and rushed through the crowd like a man avoiding a pelting rain.

Inside the museum lobby, calmer air offered a temporary reprieve. Unlike the deafening cries outside, there was little noise here—only the clinking sound of wineglasses being filled by waiters and polite conversation among guests whose invitations were vetted by security guards before being allowed in. I marveled at all around me. Celebrities were having their photos taken. I could see Max, smiling and waving to others in his hefty-sized tuxedo, holding court over in the corner.

Penny MacPharland checked to see how I'd survived after running through this gauntlet of bad publicity.

"Quite an angry crowd out there," I said, smoothing out the wrinkles in my jacket. "I saw Chester Lodge calling us out for cultural theft. I guess he didn't like Max accusing him of extorting money from us."

MacPharland, fond of correcting those in error, made sure I knew of Max's prior arrangement with the tribe's attorney.

"After that nasty meeting with Mr. Lodge, Max convinced Comflix to give a very generous payment for the 'life rights' of the Montauks. He called it a 'donation' rather than a payoff. The company didn't want to do it at first, but Max prevailed. He did insist, however, on one condition—that Lodge's group protest outside tonight's premiere," Penny said, very pleased. She stared through the museum's large bay windows at the crowd of people screaming outside.

"Look at all those TV news cameras out there," Penny marveled. "We couldn't pay enough for that kind of publicity! Around the world tonight, people will learn about *The Life Line* and be sure they watch it. Isn't Max a genius?"

Kirkland's publicity scheme was too duplicitous for words, so I said nothing. Instead, I delved further into the Morgan Library with its rich tapestries and antique furnishings—impressive booty from the Gilded Age of robber barons—until I reached the large concert hall downstairs where tonight's television treat would be served.

The event organizers directed me to my seat in the second row. It was part of the large front section reserved with place cards for the cast, crew, and other VIPs. I watched the spacious auditorium quickly fill up. Far in the back, many rows behind me, I spotted Tricia and my two kids sitting down with DJ the Realtor in the section assigned by Comflix for friends and relatives. I gave a big, friendly wave but didn't move towards them. I decided I would thank them for coming later on, after the show ended.

In my jacket, I felt a buzz coming from my cell phone, flashing a text sent two hours earlier from my attorney, Frank Worthington. At this Morgan Library event, I had saved a seat for Worthington as my longtime career consigliere. His text started with an apology: "*Sorry the plane from LA is just leaving now. I'll catch up with you at the afterparty. Good luck and knock 'em dead! Frank.*"

Seating arrangements are always revealing. Out of curiosity, I looked at the place card on the seat to the other side of mine and read the name: *Tatiana Kirkland*. I remembered Penny telling me that Max wanted to sit in the first row with his stars, Kiara, Johnny, and Lester, and next to the executives from Comflix. Max's wife was relegated to the second row beside me. On Tatiana's opposite side was fashion editor Diana Trumbull in a glittering dress, and further along the second row were members of Max's staff, all in formal wear, including writer Sheila Teague, video virtuoso Oscar Sanchez, and aide-de-camp Penny MacPharland.

Eventually, Max came bounding down the center aisle, leading the parade of headliners and supporting actors. He worked the crowd like a Tammany Hall pol, schmoozing and kibitzing and almost dancing on air as a supreme entertainer. He eventually worked his way toward Tatiana, who let him kiss her cheek once but no more. In any marriage, there are public and private moments, and decisions on how to regard each other in these different settings. But Max wasn't picking up his wife's signals. He was too hot, almost vibrating with self-regard, to notice her coolness.

Max took note of me standing in the wing, waiting to shake his hand dutifully. I thought he might be guarded, a residue of our fractious luncheon at the Algonquin. To my surprise, Max's face lit up with explosive energy.

"Jack, did you see that review in the *Times*? They loved it!" he rejoiced. "And *The New Yorker*, the same! They called your book 'lively' too! Not bad, eh?"

My wan smile couldn't conceal a new reality about *The Life Line*—the television show was better than the book. I realized that fact when Sanchez showed me the finished product a few days earlier in the writers room out in the Hamptons. For all of eternity, at least in my competitive judgment, people would say they preferred Max Kirkland's version of this story rather than mine.

Perhaps my eyes revealed this vanquished thinking, for Max suddenly hugged me, magnanimously and genuinely, and not in the grand overwrought gesture for which he was known in the Hollywood community.

"Thanks again, Jack. Without you, none of this would be possible," he whispered so only I would hear it.

I was stunned, wondering if I had heard these words correctly. Suddenly, I found myself second-guessing so many foul judgments of him. Could this be the same man who had groped and harassed women and whom I suspected of causing Vanessa Adams's disappearance? After all his bully-boy words and actions on the set, had the notorious Max Kirkland revealed himself as a thoughtful and caring artist, capable of sharing this moment of triumph with someone else?

This moral equivalence in my mind was short-lived. Max grabbed my right hand, held it aloft with his, forming a "V" for victory, and offered an uproarious laugh to the auditorium crowd.

He was back in character as the famous Max Kirkland, the one and only.

CHAPTER 25
AFTERPARTY

Up on a wide television screen two stories high, our long-awaited show, *The Life Line,* appeared like a moving cinematic tapestry, visually expressing big ideas about America that my novel could only describe in small print.

From my second-row seat in the Morgan Library concert hall, I stared ahead, motionless and in awe, at familiar scenes filmed earlier on location in the summer heat. Like an old master, Max Kirkland had transformed these images from yesteryear into a parable for our time.

Most memorable was the shipwreck scene, as rescuers on the beach bravely extended a life line rope for passengers otherwise doomed in the Atlantic. The ghostly hulk of the SS *Louisiana,* battered in the waves, appeared on screen as large as Moby Dick, an allusion Max no doubt intended. This vivid depiction of gothic horror at sea contained all the terror and desperation Winslow Homer envisioned with his painting.

Never had the power of television been so apparent to me, how video in our society had replaced words. My attempt to tell this story, in some vague facsimile of a great American novel, now seemed feeble and antiquated, like something itself out of the nineteenth century rather than the twenty-first. Years from now, my children would remember *The Life Line* not as their father's creation found in some dusty library but rather as a richly detailed television event available in the cloud for a global streamer.

When the final credits ended, three hundred guests stood up and cheered for Kirkland's achievement. They, too, were mesmerized until its finish. Their glorious reaction reminded me of the old Hollywood maxim Max often repeated about judging a show's worth: "If my fanny doesn't squirm, it's good." The Comflix execs appeared pleased and a bit relieved.

Max's entourage shared hugs, high-fives, and fist bumps with him as they exited the hall. The celebrated showrunner glanced over at Tatiana, chatting with Diana Trumbull. He motioned to his wife, sitting next to me in the boondocks of the second row, to follow him to the reception upstairs in the library's museum. Tatiana nodded but did not move right away.

"Congratulations, Tatiana, the show was wonderful," I offered, holding out my hand to shake hers. I assumed spouses were somehow responsible for the grand achievements in their marriages. She didn't return the compliment. Instead, Tatiana seemed concerned with a different drama going on in her head.

Down the side aisle, an elderly couple—a gray-haired man and his wife dressed respectfully in their Sunday best, not in the glittering formal wear of the evening—addressed me in a hushed voice.

"Are you Jack Denton?"

Though the older woman did all the talking, her husband seemed to have urged this confrontation. I figured they wanted to meet the author of the novel but had no idea what he looked like.

"Yes, I'm Denton, the author—did you like the show?" I asked with a flip insincerity, anxious to depart. I was met by dead earnestness.

"We are the parents of Vanessa Adams, the actress," said the woman. "She wasn't here tonight, not even on screen." Her flat Midwestern tone possessed a sobering honesty. "Our daughter is missing. And the detective we've hired says you might know where she is. But you won't talk to him. What we want to know is—why?"

The couple's presence blocked the second row, enough so that neither Tatiana nor I could slip away. Further down the second row, I noticed Diana Trumbull, Sheila Teague, and others exiting in the opposite direction.

"That's not true," I blurted out. "I'm going to speak with the police tomorrow along with my attorney. I'm very concerned about Vanessa. And I can tell you, I have no idea where she may be."

Vanessa's mother persisted. "We know *you* took her to a party at the Kirkland mansion...."

"I drove her there but never saw Vanessa again the rest of the night," I insisted. "I have no idea what happened to her. I'm very sorry and wish I could help. "

Unsatisfied with my answers, Vanessa's slightly built father became agitated, cupping his hands into angry fists. The mother seemed ready to raise her voice and make a scene.

But Penny MacPharland swooped into this tense exchange like a Secret Service agent on high alert, appalled by this security breach. With a threatening tone in her voice, Penny instructed the couple to leave the concert hall immediately or she would have them arrested.

Vanessa's parents, frustrated and upset, stared at me and then at each other. They retreated up the aisle's stairway, away from view.

Penny was indignant that such an uninvited inquisition, by people who clearly eluded security, could threaten to upset this big celebration.

"How are we supposed to know where their daughter might be?" MacPharland complained, her voice dripping with disgust. "She showed up for work one day as an extra in the shipwreck scene and then she was gone. They've been trying to ask Max the same questions for weeks, but we wouldn't let them."

I let my misgivings show. "Well, I can't blame them," I admitted. "I've wondered the same thing regarding Vanessa's whereabouts." This time I looked at Tatiana rather than Penny. From the apprehension in her eyes, it seemed she shared my doubts.

"C'mon Tatiana, Max is waiting for us," Penny said, ushering her past me. "We don't want to spoil Max's big night, do we?"

The corporate reception following the two-hour pilot screening was brief and perfunctory, as most midweek social affairs in Manhattan tend to be.

After the show, Comflix executives hastily excused themselves so they could get home before their 11 p.m. witching hour. The press photographers had already taken all their photos and departed. After shaking my hand, Tricia left with our two kids and her husband, promising to call later in the week.

However, *The Life Line* celebration continued for Max, his top stars, various cast and crew members, and about fifty select guests. They all headed to an afterparty organized at a posh downtown hotel not far from the Morgan. I was invited as a courtesy due to my listed credits as a producer and the author.

The night in Manhattan was unseasonably warm. I decided to walk rather than take a limo, taxi, or Uber like the rest of the party guests. I appreciated being alone for a few moments with the street sounds. It allowed me to savor the moment.

In my mind, I now felt confident *The Life Line* would be a public success, affirmed by the Morgan audience's reaction. The lingering doubts of many months seemed over. My escalating debts from divorce and child payments, along with the loss of the newspaper's biweekly paychecks, had left me bereft of any means. I needed this television project to bail out my sinking fortunes.

Eventually, I reached my hotel destination in the West Village. Waiting to get in, I recognized several celebrated guests entering this afterparty at The Whitman—a boutique establishment reconverted from an old bohemian place where the poet Walt Whitman once stayed. As I neared the door, my cell phone beeped with another text message, again from Frank Worthington, to call immediately. I assumed he had landed at JFK and was now headed into Manhattan. I decided to return his call once inside the landmark hotel.

"Are you here for the afterparty?" asked the doorman, eyeing me suspiciously. Once satisfied I belonged, he directed me upstairs to the *Leaves of Grass* rooftop bar and terrace atop this Georgian-style building.

To enter such a private affair, Penny told me in advance, I would need to say the password—"Life Line"—to get past the security guard. It sounded a bit silly, like Ali Baba saying "open sesame" to a forbidden cave full of treasures.

After I uttered this magical phrase, the bulky watchman put a plastic band with the show's logo on my wrist. He said it entitled me to two drinks at the bar.

"So, all I had to say was 'Life Line' to get in, huh?" I teased the watchman. He wasn't amused.

Nearly everyone invited was already in attendance at The Whitman. I looked around to gain my bearings and find a place to return Frank's call. Relaxing on a studded, red-leather couch, Penny chatted animatedly with Sheila Teague, Lester Wolf, and Lester's husband. Other actors and assistant producers milled around with drinks in their hand, laughing aloud, like the triumphant vibe of a winning team's locker room.

I wandered past the spacious barroom, with an antique chandelier hanging above, and walked out onto an open-air garden terrace surrounded by the city's skylights. On this rooftop, there were wicker patio chairs and couches, swaying potted palms, and metal gas heaters all aglow. And in the middle was a surprisingly large, blue-lit pool, with water warm enough to form a foggy mist above its surface, adding to the mystical aura.

Off to the side, next to a teakwood deck railing overlooking the Hudson River, I tried to return Worthington's call. In this forgotten corner of the terrace, I hoped for good reception and some limited privacy while I gazed around at the other guests. The phone had difficulty connecting.

In the distance, I could see Max Kirkland, still holding court like a king. He was deep in conversation with the reality television tycoon Zach Preston. With their backs to the crowd, Max and this Trump ally seemed oblivious to all around them, including the precarious edge of the pool. Undoubtedly, Preston was talking about the recent upset victory of his pal, the new president-elect, and how they might capitalize on it.

In another direction, closer to the bar, I was surprised to see Kiara Manchester talking animatedly with Tatiana Kirkland and Diana Trumbull. At first, I couldn't decipher the exact substance of this exchange. There seemed a Kabuki nature to their dance of recriminations. On a night that should have been victorious, Manchester appeared overcome with dejection. No doubt the reason had to do with Kirkland. I assumed Kiara had confronted them about the sordid S&M photo shoot. Or perhaps Kiara revealed how Max sexually harassed her throughout the production, just as she confided in me at the Hamptons restaurant recently.

As I heard more of their words, I realized this confrontation was about another disturbing piece of information from Kiara that startled Kirkland's wife—Tatiana's long-running TV fashion show had been cancelled. At the Morgan Library, Kiara learned this bad news unofficially from a Comflix executive and felt compelled to tell her. With a certain wrathfulness, she blamed Max for not backing his own wife's production. At first, Tatiana refused to believe her ouster was true and then seemed stunned by its reality.

"Look, Tatiana, I'm sorry Comflix killed your show, but I'm sure your husband could have done something to stop it if he really wanted," insisted Manchester, apparently the first to break this news to her. "Maybe Max should have spoken up for your program instead of his own. Seriously, Tatiana, do you really think Max cares about anybody but himself?"

Manchester's outlandish accusations offended Diana Trumbull, who began to object. But the stinging words left Max's wife speechless. From the shocked look on her face, Tatiana clearly didn't know Comflix had axed her TV program, the pride and joy that made her internationally famous. Max never warned her that the show was in danger, never shared what he heard at the Algonquin. In their marriage of accommodation, Max's business disloyalty was worse than his infidelity, more devastating to her perception of herself. It was deeply humiliating.

Without response, Tatiana just stood and glowered, like a woman not sure what steps to take next.

At that moment, my cell phone call finally connected. I heard Worthington in a panic.

"Jack, listen to me, where are you?"

"At the afterparty. Where are *you*?" I repeated, not recognizing the graveness in his voice. I expected Worthington would have arrived at the hotel celebration by now.

"Shut up, *listen*—they found the girl's body, Vanessa Adams," he shouted over me. "Somewhere out in the Hamptons, not far from Max Kirkland's mansion. She was *murdered*."

His burst of words stunned me, like the oncoming headlights of a truck headed in my direction. I struggled to keep my wits and find out more.

"Murder?" I whispered into the receiver, letting all the implications seep into my consciousness. "Are they sure?"

As a former prosecutor, Worthington kept his composure, as I began to lose mine. "She was strangled in some kinky S&M sex thing," he explained hurriedly. "Asphyxiated with some fabric they found around her neck. I just got a call from my detective friend on Long Island who says the cops are on their way to arrest you. This Kirkland fucker told them he thinks *you* did it."

Fear and fury, and a cascade of other emotions, flooded my mind. I thought of Vanessa's beautiful, expressive face and remembered how we spent an afternoon last summer at the Montauk Manor after a swim. I also felt shame as I pictured her desperate parents asking for my help at the Morgan Library earlier in the evening, and how I fobbed them off until Penny MacPharland finally had them ejected.

"That poor woman" was all I could say about Vanessa. I didn't think in terms of defending myself until my attorney snapped me back to attention.

"Jack, listen, you've got to get out of there *now*—before the cops arrive, before it's all over the news," Worthington instructed. "I'm here on the street, in front of the hotel. Come down right away and don't say anything. I want to be with you when the police start asking questions about this. Now go!"

It was too late. Clicking off the phone, I looked around and sensed the awful news of Vanessa's death spreading across the party like wildfire. It was evident in the shocked expressions of the cast and crew as they read the news on their cell phones, beeping all at once. I looked at my screen, which blared: "*Life Line* Actress Found Dead." I now realized Kiara Manchester, sobbing uncontrollably, had learned about the young actress's death as she confronted Tatiana and Diana Trumbull.

From this moment on, an air of unreality pervaded everything, as if I was watching my own life through a video monitor. A sequence of unlikely events, mostly violent, came at me in a blur. Like a bad dream played out in slow-motion. Like some unscripted television show gone off the rails, more than any chaos I could have imagined.

In this mayhem, the parents of Vanessa Adams managed to slip through security once again, gaining entrance by overhearing the secret "Life Line" password. They maneuvered through the crowd until they found me. Vanessa's father demanded an answer.

"They found her—she's dead," he declared, with a stupefied gaze in his eyes. "How could you do this to our girl?"

The old man slowly reached inside his jacket's breast pocket for a pistol to fire in vengeance. But Vanessa's mother grabbed her husband's hand to prevent it. She had spotted a group of detectives in the distance, who'd arrived at the party intending to arrest me.

"Here comes the police. Let them handle this," Vanessa's mother pleaded to him soothingly, desperately. "They'll know what to do." From her condemning glare, she already appeared convinced of my guilt.

The detectives made their way through the party crowd but were still a distance from the open terrace with the pool. I realized I was about to be charged with murder. A tremendous dizzying pressure swirled inside, as if the whole universe was now coming down on my head.

"No, no, you have it all wrong," I insisted, convinced this was my last, best chance to explain myself to Vanessa's parents. "I didn't kill your daughter—but I know who did."

I turned and glared at Max Kirkland, the sex-crazed Hollywood potentate, who surely thought he'd get away with murder. Kirkland seemed annoyed by this commotion sweeping through his big celebration. He stopped conversing with his buddy Zach Preston, turned around, and faced the crowd. Penny MacPharland ran up to him and whispered in his ear. I could see the word "dead" register in Max's eyes.

Kirkland spotted me in the corner of the terrace walking angrily towards him. My fury over Vanessa's death countermanded my attorney's warnings about constraint. Max had ruined everything, including this young woman's life, with the belief that somehow homicide for pleasure was part of his entitlement.

In my madness, I thought of punching Kirkland viciously about the head, maybe even throwing him over the balcony guardrail into the street below. Instead, Max made the first move, a preemptive strike.

"You killed her, Jack," Kirkland growled, loud enough to be heard by those standing in the garden terrace. "You were the last to see her. We have it on tape. *You're* the one who murdered Vanessa Adams."

Max's self-assured cockiness—his lifelong ability to tell lies, grab women, and commit an array of crimes and misdeeds during his rise to Hollywood power—seemed convincing enough to this audience of witnesses. They waited for me to respond, to declare my innocence.

I didn't know what to do. Preston stepped away from this confrontation. But Penny MacPharland compounded her boss's outrageous claim with one of her own.

"We kept you around because the police said you were a suspect and didn't want you to flee," MacPharland said, piling on the accusations. "Seriously, Jack, you don't think we *really* wanted you to write scripts, do you? Nobody wanted you."

The monstrousness of their words halted my forward motion. A detective grabbed my arm and told me not to move as he began to handcuff me. I stood frozen as the room full of guests stared at me like a heinous criminal.

Then from the other side of the pool, through its hazy mist above the crystalline waters, the sharp crack of a gun silenced everyone. Even the police stopped in their tracks. I could tell from Max's reaction that the bullet pierced through his tuxedo and into his chest, perhaps his heart. But he seemed most wounded by the identity of his attacker.

"You lousy bastard—it wasn't *him,*" Tatiana cried out without tears, pointing my way. "It was *you,* Max, who killed her. Like she was your little plaything. Just like you let them kill my show. I'm not going to look the other way. Not this time."

Tatiana held tightly onto the smoking pistol, pulled from her clutch and used to strike her husband. It was the same pearl-handled weapon once owned by her grandmother, the lethal double-agent spy in Paris during the war. The same hidden gun she proudly showed me once before when Vanessa Adams was still missing.

Though bleeding profusely, Max moved along the pool's edge and toward his wife so he could take away her pistol. Red stains seeped through his white pintuck shirt and black cummerbund. Maybe he felt he could talk himself out of this final verdict. But Tatiana remained intent on retribution and revenge, no matter what the cost.

"You've never shown any loyalty. Not to me, not to our marriage—to nothing but yourself," Tatiana continued. "Did you think I would forget what you did? Did you think I would just *take it*?"

Before the police could stop her, she fired another shot. With an executioner's precision, the second bullet struck Max in the forehead, bursting into a much gorier mess than anything he ever produced on screen. Fatally wounded, Max spun around and collapsed into the pool. He fell face down, so I could not see his final ending. I later wondered what type of expression a man wears when, in a moment of triumph, he is called to account for his sins.

Trapped by circumstance, the onlookers screamed in horror and fright. "Get down!" some yelled, ducking for cover beneath the outdoor furniture lest the gunfire be aimed at them. Instead, Tatiana let the deadly weapon drop to the floor.

Without remorse, I watched the cops jump into the pool as MacPharland and others pleaded for help. Eventually, Max's arms and legs stopped flailing. A few last breaths left his body and bubbled to the surface. I realized this torturer was dead.

Within moments, the police fished Max Kirkland's beefy, whale-like corpse from the murky pool, its pure warm waters now tainted by crimson streams of his cold blood. All attempts failed to resuscitate this giant of the entertainment industry, as the press later lionized him in their obituaries.

Tatiana, her face drained, was placed in police custody. Her pistol was retrieved from under a chintz couch near the pool. She shook visibly, chilled by the night air. She was only now realizing the enormity of this action against her husband.

By now, though, it became clear that Max Kirkland's crimes against women were legion. In a sense, Tatiana had been one of his victims, almost as much as Vanessa Adams and others in the past whom he abused, groped, molested, raped, and left for dead in countless other hushed-up situations.

As Kiara Manchester gently put a blanket around her, Tatiana gazed at me with sad and tired eyes. A police officer clasped handcuffs over her bejeweled wrists.

"I'm so sorry, Jack. He ruined everything," Tatiana said in her slight Eastern European accent. "I couldn't let him go on any longer. . . ."

Her voice ebbed away, as if there was just too much to tell.

By now, Worthington had rushed into the embattled hotel at the sound of gunfire and appeared on the terrace like some intrepid rescuer. He made sure I didn't answer any police questions until he fully understood what happened with Tatiana and talked to a junior prosecutor sent by the District Attorney's office. Worthington argued that the night's tragedy shouldn't be compounded by false charges against me, an innocent man.

From now on, the infamous afterparty for *The Life Line* premiere would resemble its own shipwreck. In its wake, Max Kirkland's cast and various well-wishers fled the hotel—including Zach Preston, Diana Trumbull, and the PR people from Comflix. They hoped not to be photographed scampering out to the street or to appear publicly on social media at the scene of the crime. Among themselves, though, they declared the whole evening a disaster of epic proportions.

CHAPTER 26
SALVAGING THE WRECKAGE

Over the coming days and weeks, the reverberations from Max Kirkland's *The Life Line* were felt far and wide, like a modern-day Fatty Arbuckle scandal, with tales of murder plots, kinky sex, and a long list of women who now claimed to be victims of one of the most notorious casting couches in Hollywood.

A steady stream of sordid headlines emerged, from flashes and snippets on TMZ and *The Today Show* to long, detailed exposes in *The Hollywood Reporter* and the august pages of my former newspaper. Without much of a stretch, this morality tale became a metaphor for the incoming Trump era, especially when Max's contributions to the campaign became known. The newly elected president expressed sympathy for Kirkland's "passing" on his @realDonaldTrump Twitter account.

The police were first to sift through this wreckage, seeking a semblance of the truth. After intense questioning by detectives, with Worthington by my side, I was ruled out as a suspect in the Adams murder. I had feared that somehow Max, like the villain in some bad noir movie, had set me up as the fall guy for Vanessa's bizarre death. I wondered if traces of my semen, from my encounter with Vanessa before the party, might be found by the forensic experts.

But Tatiana's confession cleared my name, as Worthington later explained to me. She told detectives that her husband's shooting was the boiling point of many indignities. In her tearful account, Tatiana admitted seeing Max leave with Vanessa from their summer party, part of a long-simmering jealousy that her husband preferred younger women to their static marriage. When she learned the actress was missing, Tatiana's suspicions deepened—especially after Max erased Vanessa's image from the shipwreck scene, as if wiping away all evidence.

Meeting Vanessa's parents that night at the Morgan haunted Tatiana. The police discovery of the body in Montauk's underbrush confirmed her worst fears, compelling a violent response. If not, she felt certain her husband would escape culpability once again.

"Max's plan to deflect attention—acting as if you, Jack, had killed the actress—left her with no other choice but to stop him," Worthington explained, based on what he gleaned from the homicide cops. "She knew her husband was an extraordinary manipulator of human emotion. With friends in high places, he had a good chance of avoiding any blame."

Tatiana's ultimate rationale for killing her husband was something cryptic, a French phrase she mentioned to detectives without further explanation. It remained a mystery to police, who relayed it to Worthington, hoping his exonerated client might have a clue.

"Tatiana said her family learned long ago how to deal with evil," Worthington explained to me. "The cops have no idea what the hell she meant by that. But it got you off the hook, Jack."

Worthington laughed aloud at the absurdity of how close I came to being named as a suspect in Vanessa's murder. But unlike the man who is shot at without result, I wasn't exhilarated or amused. Instead, I wondered about the motivations for Tatiana's criminal behavior, including the cancellation of her show.

Police also questioned the cast and crew from *The Life Line.* From Sheila Teague, they learned of Max's penchant for leather-strapped sex and using his powerful role as a showrunner to extract sexual favors from women, including herself.

From Penny MacPharland, detectives learned Max kept a special suite at the Montauk Manor to carry out his affairs, just as he did on other location shoots during other big-budget productions. They vowed to investigate any unexplained disappearances linked to Kirkland's past productions. Police nearly charged MacPharland with criminal conspiracy—for agreeing to help her boss implicate me in Adams's murder—but concluded they couldn't make the charges stick.

In the wake of its bullet-ridden premiere party, Comflix immediately cancelled the debut of *The Life Line,* scheduled for worldwide distribution that weekend. The following morning, corporation executives huddled together in a mournful teleconference call to discuss the fallout from their suddenly radioactive project. At Max's urging, they had spent millions around the country for TV ads, billboards, and promotional signs, a marketing steamroller for the big event. Some now felt foolish for believing Kirkland's hype and letting the budget get out of control, the way greed and stock options can blind good judgement. Most board members truly believed *The Life Line* would be Max Kirkland's great epic, the work of art he promised would transform streaming television, just as introduction to the talkies did a century earlier in Hollywood. Now they would never know. The board of directors agreed they had no other option than to kill it.

In a press release, Comflix confirmed the show's cancellation "out of respect" for the deaths of "supporting actress" Vanessa Adams (giving her the promotion in death that she'd hoped for in life on the set) and the project's "creator" Max Kirkland (a puffed-up title beyond "showrunner" that reflected his outsized, God-like power over the production). That morning, Comflix's stock plummeted 17 percent and rumors began of a takeover by a giant search engine firm or other competitor looking to capitalize on its misfortune.

The following morning, Worthington called to say my contract had been suspended by Comflix and there would be no payments until the company's lawyers reviewed the whole mess. What little money I had coming in for daily expenses was now gone. I would have to find a new job quickly, but probably not in Hollywood as I'd intended. Already, *The Life Line* was becoming a laughingstock in the industry. Insiders recounted this calamity amid crocodile tears and occasional sympathy for the shockingly violent way it ended. Most assumed the finished product wasn't very good or Comflix would never have cancelled ("A disaster somewhere between *John Carter* and *Heaven's Gate,*" hooted one critic who never saw it).

Over time, however, the fate of *The Life Line* underwent a reappraisal in the public mind. There remained a sordid fascination with what really happened behind the scenes leading up to the two murders. Moreover, there arose a curiosity about whether Kirkland's TV saga was as truly great as claimed by guests who cheered that night at the Morgan. Some wondered whether this "lost treasure" would ever be shown.

One of the few unscathed figures from this disaster, Kiara Manchester, eventually spoke about her sexual harassment from Kirkland. By then, the #MeToo movement had gained national attention. Manchester joined a chorus of other women now willing to say how they'd been sexually victimized by powerful men in Hollywood and elsewhere. In a widely publicized television interview, the British actress broke down in tears on camera as she described Max's various groping attempts on the set, in her trailer, and at his Montauk Manor suite. Kiara sat beside her co-star, Johnny Youngblood, her former lover whom she'd accompanied reluctantly to the Morgan Library premiere at Max's insistence.

With more emotion than he ever displayed on screen, Youngblood attested to Manchester's claims of abuse. He revealed how Kirkland exploited their onscreen romance in exchange for tabloid gossip about his upcoming show.

"There were times I wanted to kill Max myself," Youngblood admitted, clearly going off script.

In the most viral moment from the interview, both actors grieved for the loss of Vanessa Adams, whom they said paid the ultimate price for Hollywood's culture of misogyny and assault. Then Kiara lifted her fist and showed the world a rubberized wristband and what was written on it: *#IAmVanessa*. The memorial gesture was quickly adopted by Manchester's fans, who began wearing the same band in various colors. Eventually, thousands of protestors with signs of "I Am Vanessa" marched outside Comflix headquarters, calling for reforms so a monster like Max Kirkland would never emerge from its gates again.

The public animus for Max eventually turned into sympathy for his imprisoned wife, Tatiana. Her former friends and associates, like fashion editor Diana Trumbull, had steered clear of her for months after the shooting. As a possible witness, Diana didn't want to be drawn into the legal crucible as Tatiana's murder trial neared. But sensing a shift in the public mood, Trumbull decided to feature "The Confessions of Tatiana" on the cover of her magazine. She sent a legendary photographer to capture evocative portraits of Tatiana behind bars, looking out beyond barbed wire fences. The cover story's writer, well-known within the women's movement, convinced Tatiana to be completely candid and turned her into Everywoman ever wronged by a callous and brutal husband. In an editor's note, Diana championed Tatiana's cause. She described the shooting as a matter of psychological self-defense, another sinister by-product of the Trump era, with a photo of Trumbull wearing the #IAmVanessa wristband in solidarity.

Public pressure eventually led to a plea bargain deal for Tatiana. She spent a year in jail without enduring a trial and the possibility of much greater punishment. By the time of her release, the widespread publicity surrounding *The Life Line* had become overwhelming, far greater than Max ever hoped for on the night he was killed. Comflix reappraised their earlier decision and announced they would show it to their massive streamer audience, just as Max had intended. Vanessa Adams's name would now be listed in the credits.

The Life Line became Comflix's biggest hit. Even Kirkland's toughest critics hailed his final work as a masterpiece, the template for a six-hour movie in a bingeable world, keeping Americans on their couch instead of a theater. Within the company, Max's vilified name was now spoken with a kind of financial reverence for the numbers he brought in. They said he still retained that "Kirkland magic" even in death. His postmortem success prompted an anthology reality TV series about today's Native American tribes and their battle for survival, an extravaganza Max outlined shortly before his demise. Sheila Teague took over that project and was eventually promoted to the top job at Comflix's studio in California, the first woman of color in that position. She left word that she'd hire me as a scriptwriter if I wanted to move to the West Coast.

The wave of international publicity from *The Life Line*—a "special television event," as Comflix advertised it incessantly—boosted sales of my novel onto the bestseller list. After a long drought, both emotionally and financially, I had a few bucks in my pocket. Eventually, I possessed enough to move on with my life after a standstill for so long. Maybe even enough to send my estranged kids, still living with Tricia and DJ the Realtor, to college as I'd promised.

By then, in summer 2019, I had taken a job as an adjunct professor of journalism at a state university. For a meager salary, I taught the craft of fact-finding and truth-telling to eager students. They were undaunted by dim prospects in a diminished field derided by their president as "fake news." Perhaps their commitment to journalism's ideals was more clear-eyed, less preening than the previous older generation who romanticized the post-Watergate years. I found teaching young, inquisitive minds to be refreshing, my life saver after being fired from *The World* and blackballed in the business. (Worthington eventually worked out a settlement so any claim of harassment was expunged from my employment record.)

For a while, I didn't have any future in Hollywood after being badmouthed by the now-prominent producer Penelope MacPharland. She claimed that I was to blame for all the trouble on *The Life Line* set. She kept perpetuating Max's lies, hoping they would be believed and would deflect any culpability on her part.

"This guy [Jack Denton] hung around the set for weeks, like some drifter we couldn't get rid of," MacPharland complained to *Variety* in its one-year anniversary retrospective on the Kirkland killing. "He kept bugging poor Max, wondering why he wasn't being 'consulted' as a producer, which he was—in name only. Like we were going to let him write a script or something! It was so sad and pathetic, and probably contributed to the tragic ending."

Instead of suing MacPharland for her slander, I decided to push on with my writing in New York. Better to keep my main relationship with the blank sheet of paper, I concluded, rather than try in vain to become a Hollywood dream-maker, just like F. Scott Fitzgerald discovered in another tumultuous Twenties. Searching for a purpose, I even thought of somehow returning to my old job as a reporter, with a hard-won appreciation for its nobility in a time of doubt.

The American Dream was now changing before my eyes. I struggled to keep pace with the tectonic shifts in our society, with ancient passions and prejudices erupting all over the land. Truth seemed to be changing its definition, beyond the old-school lessons in the classroom and more like the mendacity every night on the cable television screen. With Wall Street fortunes booming and no signs of calamity on the horizon, Donald Trump appeared primed for reelection in 2020.

"Zach Preston told me there's no way his friend Donald can lose—now or maybe ever," Max emphatically told me shortly before his death. After the Kirkland killing, Preston convinced his pal in the White House to give him a small European ambassadorship, even though he was ignorant of foreign policy and fluent only in reality TV.

As a way of trying to make sense of it all, I decided to write a new book, a thinly disguised version of what really happened with Max Kirkland and the making of his now-classic *The Life Line*, rather than another historical novel. The publication of this new book garnered polite reviews and invitations to various authors luncheons and book fairs, including one held under a large white tent in the Hamptons as a library fundraiser by the local glitterati.

Sometime later, like summers before, I rented a car and drove out from the city, where I still maintained a tiny, crowded apartment in the Flatiron District. At the book fair, I sat at a long lineup of tables, each with several authors and their literary offerings. Curious onlookers stopped to consider the new book, but, invariably, they stared intently at my first novel and whispered about its notoriety before asking for an inscription. It was a reminder that *The Life Line* would be with me forever.

Afterwards on this nostalgic journey, I planned to stay the night again at the Montauk Manor and maybe dream about Native American ghosts before their lands were stolen or perhaps a heavenly Vanessa Adams still alive in her yellow bikini and waiting by the poolside.

On the ride to Long Island's farthest end, with the sunlight fading, I decided to stop by the beachfront park, where the opening shipwreck scene was filmed by Kirkland, and get one last glance. There remained a handful of families and day-trippers around as I got out of the car and walked across the rocky sand and empty shells.

Looking out at the Atlantic, with its windswept waves and dangerous tides, I remembered the many hours sitting here, watching my literary dream come to life on Kirkland's video monitors. I once again thought of nature's beauty and savagery in Winslow Homer's dramatic painting and its suggestion that fate, the hand of God, played such an important role in our lives. Overhead, I watched a red-tailed hawk swoop by, seeking its prey, just like the one I saw on the first day of shooting *The Life Line*. Somehow it was another reminder of Max.

Near the water's edge, I saw a lonely figure wrapped in a dark shawl and jacket, what seemed to be an older woman with her head down, deep in thought. In a slow but steady pace, she walked along the narrow, smooth pathway between the seaweed and the sea. She kept her balance until she looked up and saw that I recognized her. Her ankle bracelet, worn by convicted murderers on parole, was the dead giveaway.

"Tatiana..."

Her face flinched and her body recoiled as if I had wounded her. She didn't want to be noticed, and she certainly didn't want any reminders of the past, even if what happened was still playing out in her mind. I moved closer, hoping for a conversation.

"No, *please* don't...." she said painfully, waving her arms. "Just *don't*."

Without another word, she walked past me into the twilight horizon along the beach. This frail, thin woman, not yet forty—who had once starred in her own television show, taken endless paparazzi photos with her Hollywood producer-director husband—was now virtually unrecognizable, a ghostly presence. Only her expressive eyes, hidden beneath the shawl, appeared the same.

I ran after her in the sand, desperate for answers.

"But *why*?" I asked, out of breath when I finally caught up. "Why did you have to *kill* him?"

Tatiana sensed my desperation but offered only the slightest clue. She recalled our conversation in the limousine ride from the city, when she'd asked me the most important thing in a marriage, and I'd said loyalty.

"Maybe you were right, Jack," she replied, her voice barely above a whisper. "I remember a Paris designer once told me, '*Sans loyauté, il n'y a rien*.'"

My high school French skills were poor. It was the same cryptic phrase she'd mentioned to the homicide detectives interrogating her about motive. Only later did I figure out its translation: *Without loyalty, there is nothing.*

At that moment, though, I had no patience for word games and obfuscation.

"What does that mean?" I demanded.

She stared soulfully into my eyes.

"Everything."

On that emphatic note, Tatiana raised her hand like a crossing guard, as if silently warning me not to breach her emotional barrier any further. She wouldn't allow it. Perhaps she recognized my need for more explanation, to come to some resolve. But she couldn't bear any more inquisition.

She walked away alone.

Weeks after this strange interlude, I appeared on a podcast with a well-known radio host about *The Life Line* and its bloody aftermath. After warning her nationwide audience about possible spoiler alerts, the host asked a question for which I still didn't have an answer.

"I'm really curious why Tatiana Kirkland killed her husband," the host wondered. "Do you think Max's cheating was at the heart of her reaction?"

Particularly after *The Life Line* won several national Primetime Emmy awards—including one for Max, posthumously—journalists haunted me with insider questions about the now-legendary Kirkland project. Every interview, even the longest and most probing, obsessed on the bizarre crimes behind this Hollywood production.

None of the media seemed interested in how the Montauk lands were stolen from the Native Americans, the nineteenth-century, life-saving scene depicted in Winslow Homer's painting, or my historical novel that started it all. Inevitably, I was quizzed about the Vanessa Adams murder, its #MeToo implications, and what made Tatiana snap at the afterparty and shoot her husband.

"Do you think Max's involvement in this young actress's death—and the other charges of sexual harassment leveled by Kiara Manchester—compelled Tatiana to act?" the host inquired. "Or was she upset that Max never tried to save her cancelled TV show and that she was in a rage for believing his lies and deceptions for so long?"

My cautious response, prepared by Frank Worthington, avoided legal liability but also any kind of self-reflection.

"Surely her husband didn't deserve to die," I replied, "but sometimes justice has a way of stopping those who squeeze the breath out of others."

"Did you ever think you were going to jail?" the host pressed.

Of course I did; I remembered how the detective grabbed my arm before Tatiana's gun went off. But in my answers to millions of listeners, I needed to remain careful.

"Without Tatiana's intervention, violent as it was, I still don't know what would have become of me."

It was the most honest response I could provide. Privately, I had an overwhelming desire somehow to right all the wrongs Max had inflicted. I struggled to adapt to this new world of avarice and strife created by Kirkland's pals like Zach Preston and their new ally in the White House. Never was I so unsure of America's future or my own.

Following this interview, and every conversation like it, I returned to the memory of Tatiana on the beach, wondering what more I might have said to her. Before she faded into the night, I had wanted to thank Tatiana for saving my life, for standing up for the truth of what really happened, and for not letting her husband cover it up with more lies. She'd made me think about loyalty and how little there was of it in my own existence.

I had become like one of those survivors on that ancient ship in my novel, battered by fate and facing my own mortality. Watching my own life collapse, I was drowning in the wreckage, and Tatiana had thrown me a life line. For when I needed it most, she had given me that rarest of gifts, another chance at redemption.

Stephen Pharaoh

Austin Corbin

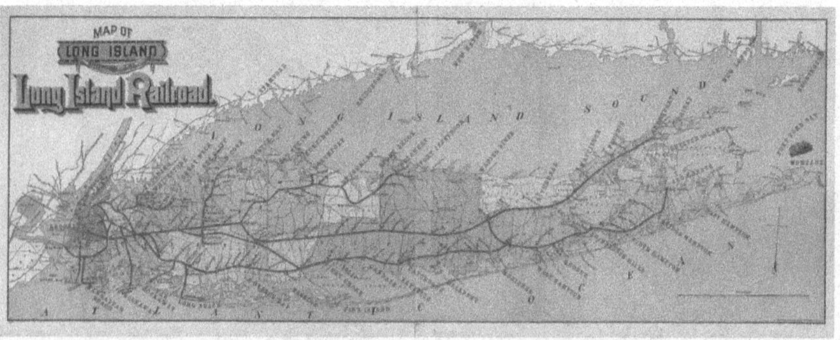

Corbin's Proposed Montauk to Manhattan Route: Long Island Railroad Map circa 1895, with Montauk still not connected to the main line leading to Manhattan. Austin Corbin schemed to steal Montauk Native American lands to make this Montauk to Manhattan route complete. This map reflects his plan to have ships and steamers coming from Europe and elsewhere land at Fort Pond Bay near his intended railroad station (see little ship insignia at upper right).

Treacherous Waters: Montauk, the Hamptons, and Long Island's south shore were the scene of many ships wrecked on their way to New York City's harbor in the 1800s.

Inspired by a Painting: In the 1800s, Winslow Homer's painting *The Life-Saver* captured the horror of shipwrecks and the heroics of those who saved passengers from drowning. More than a century later, it became the inspiration for an award-winning television drama by the late director Max Kirkland based on a novel by Jack Denton.

ACKNOWLEDGMENTS

I owe a debt of thanks to several people in putting together *Montauk to Manhattan: An American Novel.* First is my family for their love, support, and abiding sense of humor. My longtime entertainment attorney Scott E. Schwimer has been a constant source of wisdom and guidance for the past thirty years, and I owe much of my career success to him. Several Newsday colleagues offered their advice along the way, including Mark Harrington, Lawrence C. Levy, Rita Ciolli, Sandra Peddie, Ellis Henican, Joe Calderone, and the late Jim Dwyer. I'm grateful to Post Hill Press Publisher Anthony Ziccardi for bringing this story to the world, and to my literary agent Joe Veltre of The Gersh Agency. Special thanks to editor Madeline Sturgeon and her talented Post Hill Press colleagues for producing this handsome book with such care and precision. After forty years as a Newsday investigative reporter, editorial board member, and columnist, as well as the nonfiction author of seven books, I have finally written my first novel at age sixty-eight. Hopefully there are many more to come.

—Thomas Maier, July 2024